CASTLE OF WATER

ALSO BY DANE HUCKELBRIDGE

Bourbon: A History of the American Spirit

*The United States of Beer: A Freewheeling
History of the All-American Drink*

DANE
HUCKELBRIDGE

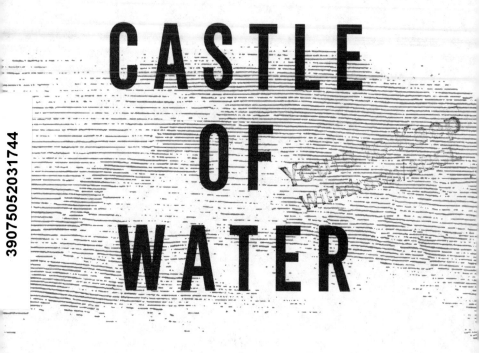

CASTLE
OF
WATER

THOMAS DUNNE BOOKS
ST. MARTIN'S PRESS
NEW YORK

THOMAS DUNNE BOOKS.
An imprint of St. Martin's Press.

CASTLE OF WATER. Copyright © 2017 by Dane Huckelbridge. All rights
reserved. Printed in the United States of America. For information,
address St. Martin's Press, 175 Fifth Avenue, New York, N.Y. 10010.

www.thomasdunnebooks.com
www.stmartins.com

Designed by Jonathan Bennett

The Library of Congress Cataloging-in-Publication Data
is available upon request.

ISBN 978-1-250-09822-1 (hardcover)
ISBN 978-1-250-09823-8 (e-book)

Our books may be purchased in bulk for promotional,
educational, or business use. Please contact your local bookseller
or the Macmillan Corporate and Premium Sales Department
at 1-800-221-7945, extension 5442, or by e-mail at
MacmillanSpecialMarkets@macmillan.com.

First Edition: April 2017

10 9 8 7 6 5 4 3 2 1

To you, my love, my Piment d'Espelette.

Thank you.

The cyclone ends. The sun returns; the lofty coconut trees lift up their plumes again; man does likewise. The great anguish is over; joy has returned; the sea smiles like a child.

—PAUL GAUGUIN

*Moi je t'offrirai des perles de pluie
Venues de pays où il ne pleut pas.
Je creuserai la terre jusqu'après ma mort
Pour couvrir ton corps d'or et de lumière.*

—JACQUES BREL

PART ONE

1

The flat is in the tenth arrondissement of Paris, on a derelict street called Château d'Eau. To find it is simple: Just take a right at the arch, go down rue Saint-Denis, steer clear of the dog shit, and you cannot miss it. To find beauty in it, however, is a bit more daunting. The charms of the alley *do* exist, if one squints past the worn-out *tabacs* and disheveled *filles de joie* that ply their trades along its curbs. Fortunately, the man who lives there is accustomed to squinting and proud to call the place his home.

He wakes earlier than usual on this particular morning. He does not rise immediately but lies awake for a moment, savoring the stillness of the chill blue hour. Then, at last, he decides to get up. A splash of water on the face, a quick brushing of teeth, a puckering spit, and a satisfied gargle. He smiles at his scarred and bearded reflection—grayer, it seems, with each passing day.

Ablutions complete, it's time to get dressed. First he slips on an old moth-hounded sweater, followed by corduroy trousers flecked with white paint. A Harris Tweed jacket is pulled

from the closet, the elbows of which are worn down to fuzz. Oh, and shoes—can't forget those. The man puts on argyle socks and scuffed leather brogans and tiptoes out of his bedroom door. He considers briefly leaving a note in the kitchen but doubts he'll be gone long enough to even be missed. He does, however, pause at the end of the hallway, to press his ear to another door and give it a listen. Satisfied with the silence, he leaves the flat, padding delicately down the winding stairs, past the dim halos of hall lights conferred upon wallpaper, only to realize halfway down that he's forgotten yet again to put in his contacts. *Damnit.* He trundles back up and plops them in without so much as a glimpse in the mirror. *Then* he leaves.

The man decides to have breakfast at a café in the neighborhood, and he sits outside despite the chill. Huddled in his chair, fingers laced around his coffee, he watches the city yawn back to life. The rising sun scrubs the indigo out of the air; the streets for once smell washed and clean. Shopkeepers are slowly raising their shutters, starch-crisp waiters are unstacking their chairs. Even the *femmes de la nuit* have called it a night. It's all part of a timeless ritual, one of which he never tires.

The man finishes only one of his two *tartines,* perhaps because he is not very hungry, possibly because of something more. The untouched piece of toast is wrapped in a napkin and pocketed away for general safekeeping. He pays the waiter, slurps back the last of his coffee, and heads next door to a Turkish grocer. The door chimes and he vanishes inside, only to reemerge seconds later with a paper bag tucked under his arm. With his free hand he hails a taxi and asks to be taken to Père Lachaise.

The driver is a friendly West African named Noël. The melodies of his homeland pulse quietly through the radio. The man likes the music and asks the driver where it is from. Senegal, the driver says. The man settles back into his seat, ab-

sorbing the rhythms and enjoying the ride. He gazes out at the fountains etched in verdigris, and the monuments steeped in history, and the streets lined with cracked cobblestones. He clutches his paper bag both tightly and tenderly, as if it is a precious thing that someone might take. He closes his eyes and lets the light bleed through his eyelids, as marimbas hint at warmer climes.

The sun is still low but fully risen when the man arrives at the gates of Père Lachaise—which are, incidentally, in the process of being opened by a jumpsuited groundskeeper lame in one leg. *Bonjour, Claude,* the man says to the groundskeeper. *Bonjour, monsieur,* the groundskeeper replies. Also waiting beside the entrance is a quartet of American art students, smoking cigarettes and laughing to themselves. Unlike the man with the paper bag, they are young and have been up all night. In a burst of drunken enthusiasm, they decided to pay the famous cemetery a visit.

One of the Americans thinks he recognizes the man with the paper bag—he looks very familiar. The boy's eyes bulge, the beard and the scars. Holy shit, he whispers, his unlit Lucky Strike tumbling from his lips. Is that who I think it is? His friends cast glances over their hunched shoulders. *It is.* To think, they came to see a dead rock star and instead happened upon a living legend. They titter among themselves, giddy just to be standing so close. They know he lives in Paris. And they've certainly heard all the stories. Should they follow him in? The groundskeeper stands aside and the man with the paper bag enters. They should, and they do.

The man with the paper bag does not notice them, however. His mind is on other things. He walks with serene intent through the inordinate quietude and beauty of the place, a monument to France itself. The fading names above the crypts are soft as feathers when uttered upon the lips—which he does,

without a breath, with hardly a sound, the downy purr of double r's, the agile sweep of *accents aigus.*

His path takes him beneath a wicker of frosted elm trees, down a brief and chestnut-scattered embankment, to a cluster of old family plots on the cemetery's edge. He goes delicately but with purpose—he knows the way, he is intimate with these surroundings. The American students trail behind by a respectful distance. They are curious but have no wish to disturb him. Wait until we tell our friends back home, they say, the insatiable lot of them murmuring as one.

The man stops at last in front of a grave, newer and less faded than the rest. The moss has yet to even stake its claim. The students hold back; they suddenly feel guilty, unintentionally intrusive. But they know they can't turn away. They look on as the object of their curiosity kneels before the grave. His head is bowed, and his hands are resting upon the headstone. He seems to be speaking—but what is he saying? They can't make out a single word. Whatever it is, it goes on for some time, until at last, his vigil concluded, the man wipes his eyes and rises to his feet. He takes something from the paper bag, something thick and clustered—what, they're not certain—and sets it down upon the grave. Then he turns and walks away.

The students wait until he is well out of sight before they dare approach. They are flabbergasted by what they have seen. Whose grave is this, anyway? they wonder aloud. And, like, what kind of flowers *were* those, exactly? They gather about the headstone in the cold morning light, the four of them shivering and gooseffleshed and dying to know.

The marble is inscribed with a name they don't recognize— it sounds French, but they've never seen it before. And as if that weren't enough, the flowers the man left behind are not flowers at all. Instead, resting atop the grass and loam and dried husks

of chestnuts is something bizarre, something out of place, something that they can neither understand nor believe.

A single bunch of green bananas.

The American students shake their heads and relight their cigarettes. They purse their lips and exhale in wonder. What exactly just happened? one of them asks, a girl in blue jeans and artfully trimmed bangs. I mean, like, do you think the stories are true? I have no idea, another answers, scuffing the cobblestones with his canvas sneaker. But it beats the hell out of Jim Morrison any day. And I'm, like, totally starving. Anybody want to go get breakfast?

They all do. And they count the crumpled remainder of the night's euros to make sure they have enough, and they leave the bananas behind for the departed to keep.

2

At the first sputter of the engine and hint of a downward pitch, Barry Bleecker had uttered a prayer. He had prayed for a miracle. And a miracle was precisely what he received, although perhaps not one as helpful as he had hoped. For despite his entreaties to God, Buddha, Allah, and Vishnu, the engine did *not* kick back to life, the little Cessna 208 Caravan did *not* cease its dive, and no, he was *not* spared the soul-wrenching impact. The screams, the weeping, the bracing for death—all of that went on as fate had planned. But Barry, still semiconscious amid the floating debris and flaming oil, was spared his contact lenses and a single bottle of saline solution—neither of which seemed particularly miraculous, drifting by in a sealed Ziploc baggy at that dark and desperate moment. He almost forgot to gather them up, preoccupied as he was with staying afloat and expelling the salt water from his lungs. But gather them he did, perhaps compelled by the hint of buoyancy that the baggy provided. He tucked it up under his shirt, moaned once more toward the god(s) he assumed had forsaken him, and pushed off from the smoking hunk of fuselage to which

he had been clinging barnacle tight . . . from the blue haze of the horizon, a fringe of palm beckoned.

The promise of firm ground proved more elusive than Barry had thought. The swim felt interminable, and in the dips between swells, when he lost sight of his destination, he nearly gave up hope. But the pure, reptilian desire to prevail goaded him on. His leaden arms kept paddling, his wooden legs never ceased to kick. When his body was finally washed up, dragged back, and then washed up again onto the sand, he wept like a baby, rolling onto his back, roaring with grief, although for what he did not know. Once that wellspring of emotion ran itself dry, he sat up, blinked, and looked at his surroundings. Or at least attempted to look—what met his eyes was a myopic blur. At some point—possibly in the crash, but more likely during his ordeal in the water—Barry Bleecker had lost both of his contact lenses. A loss of vision that could easily lead to a loss of life for a horribly nearsighted man stranded on a desert island 2,359 miles from Hawaii, 4,622 miles from Chile, and 533 miles from the nearest living soul. And at that moment, on the palm-lined rim of an uninhabited South Pacific atoll, Barry Bleecker was just such a fellow. Or almost such a fellow. For no sooner had he realized his predicament than he remembered the Ziploc baggy, which by then had tumbled from beneath his sopping Charles Tyrwhitt dress shirt and settled atop the soggy crotch of his Brooks Brothers slacks. At which point Mr. Bleecker, nerves and clothing equally frayed, laughed hysterically. A miracle, after all.

Barry dragged himself a few yards to drier ground, whisked the sand from his fingers, and peeled open the precious plastic bag. The foil top of the first contact lens package (there were six packages, which meant three pairs) was stubborn but gave. He set one on the tip of his index finger and examined it like the precious jewel that it was. Then, after a quick and cleansing

splash with the saline solution, he plunked it into his eye. Hallelujah! What had been an inscrutable haze transformed with a blink into a vivid seascape. With a pirate's one-eyed squint, Barry took stock of the foam-wreathed shoreline, the waltzing fronds, and the dappling of cirrus clouds that crawled across an otherwise impeccably blue sky (the storm that downed them having by that point passed). It was midday, and the sun was high. Quickly, he inserted the other contact as well and took to absorbing his new environs in their full three-dimensional splendor. On rubbery legs he executed his first tottering steps, calling out for help as he explored the beach. He walked for some time, shouting through cupped hands and listening through cupped ears, with waves and rustling the only response. And then his heart leapt—up ahead, a set of footprints in the sand. A tart joy overtook Barry as he raced forward, nearly tripping over the tattered cuffs of his slacks. Footprints! It could only mean . . . And then he stopped in his tracks. Literally his tracks. The footprints were his own. He had circled the entire island, and he was suddenly horrified by both his loneliness and its tininess. Circumnavigating the thing had taken less than ten minutes. And Barry wept, not for the first time on that diminutive island and certainly not for the last.

The arrival of night brought Barry little solace. The screams of tree frogs and the pitched chatter of insects, yes, but no solace. Crouched and shivering in a crude bower of palm fronds, surrounded by darkness, he reached instinctively to his pocket for a cigarette, only to dump out their mashed remains. In doing so, however, he remembered the plastic Bic that was tucked in the cellophane. And that, unlike his Parliament Lights, was still serviceable—he flicked at the flint and summoned a flame. And an idea came to him: a signal fire. Surely rescue planes would be out combing the waves. They would likely even pass over the island in their search for survivors. Barry

struggled to his feet, again tripping over his tattered cuffs, and began gathering the driest palm fronds he could. After several trips to the beachhead, he had a rather impressive pile and, after a few dabs of his lighter, a convincing flame. He stood beside it, watching and waiting, certain the spotlights of some chopper or seaplane would come blazing from the murk. When they didn't, and the fire burned down to embers, he scurried for more fronds to resuscitate it—an exercise that proved less than fruitful. Halfway into his second armful, it began to rain. Not a demure tropical sprinkle, but an honest-to-goodness downpour. Barry hurried back to his palm bower and huddled beneath its meager shelter. At some point, exhausted, he curled up to sleep, but on the cusp of obtaining it, he realized he had forgotten to take out his contacts. *Crap.* With exquisite tenderness, he removed each from its respective eye and deposited it carefully into its respective holder. He placed the plastic case in his pocket, beside the suddenly priceless Bic, and finally, blanketed by chill rains, lulled by the high whine of midges, he fell headfirst into a cavernous slumber.

3

Barry awoke to a parched throat, sore muscles, a mild sunburn, and the sickening realization of the predicament he was in. But first things first. Water, and then food. He had swallowed a considerable amount of ocean the previous day, and his last meal had been a granola bar consumed at the airport in Tahiti. Slowly, achingly, he crawled from beneath his little teepee of palm fronds and rose to his feet. He cracked his neck and squinted into the sunlight; it was overcast, but still bright. The waves rolled in, steadily, incessantly. The air tasted faintly of brine.

After a quick and unsettling bathroom break (the darkness of his urine was a disturbing reminder of his dehydration), he put in his contact lenses and turned for the first time away from the sea, toward the little island's bosky heart. And bosky it was. Columns of trunks propped up an ever-shifting ceiling of frond leaves, through which fugitive slats of sunlight escaped. He stepped gingerly over the prickly undergrowth, as he had lost both his loafers the day before. The terrain became increasingly rocky the farther in he ventured, until he came to

the base of a mountain or, perhaps more accurately, very steep hill. Boulders, bedded with some form of ferny moss, rose to a peak some five or six stories overhead. And nested snugly in their crevices were birds: gulls or terns or cormorants. Barry didn't know, but they were living creatures sharing in his fate. And even more important, he found water. Two separate rock pools, both about the size of Jacuzzis, were coolly waiting, filled to the brim with the previous night's rain. Barry inspected the pools first before consuming their contents. They both looked clean enough—one had a few odd squigglies jetting about its edge, some larvae, perhaps, but nothing that screamed befoulment. Barry chose the slightly more pristine of the two and brought several handfuls of the water to his lips. Its flavor was fresh and deliciously minerally, not unlike a white wine he had once tasted while touring Napa Valley with his girlfriend—fine, ex-girlfriend—Ashley. Well, perhaps that was a slight exaggeration, but after all he'd been through, a gulp of clean, cold water was nothing to sneeze at.

Once his thirst was slaked, all that remained was for his appetite to be sated, and that came courtesy of the island's banana trees. Somehow he had missed the bunches of green, starchy fruit, dangling just above head level. But upon noticing their presence, he also became aware of their prevalence. Good, thought Barry, chewing on his sixth banana and fully prepared to eat six more. Water and bananas. I shall want for neither hydration nor potassium. And he laughed at his little joke, which, anyone with experience in survival situations can tell you, is a promising sign. Attitude is everything, and those that turn negative can be just as ruinous as diseased streams and toxic berries.

With his most basic of needs addressed for the immediate present, Barry returned to his post on the shore, ripping off the lower half of his slacks as he did so. They were shreds anyway,

and cutoffs seemed more appropriate to the conundrums of a castaway. His sleeves he rolled up past his elbows, then muttered, "What the hell," and took his shirt off entirely, wrapping it around his head in a sort of improvised French Foreign Legion hat. He breached the tree line and scanned the horizon, having transformed in a few short minutes from a high-yield-bond salesman at Lehman Brothers into a passable Robinson Crusoe. "Shit," he muttered to himself. "Goddamn." And goddamn was right—no rescue boats sat poised on the horizon, and no choppers hovered above the unfurling waves. He kicked sand at the remnants of his signal fire and considered his options. If only his cigarettes weren't mush—he was dying for a smoke. After some deliberation, he vetoed a signal fire for being too labor-intensive and decided instead to write a message in the sand. After some scouring (he was surprised at how little loose wood there was, but then again palm trees didn't exactly have branches), he settled on a rock with a jagged edge. Using it, he carved out SOS as large as he could. He then repeated this in several other locations, doing another lap of the island. He considered again starting a fire, but the palms he found were too damp, and he ultimately gave up on the idea altogether. A school of ominous storm clouds was quietly gathering, squirting its dark squid ink deep into the horizon; finding shelter took precedence over everything else.

Barry thought for a few minutes, studying the tree line and hoping for an idea. After considerable grumbling, head-scratching, and additional sand kicking, he came to one palm that hung especially low, jutting out over the beach at a shallow angle. Yes, it was just close enough to the ground to do the trick and was sheltered quite well by the surrounding trees. Newly inspired, Barry set to work, harvesting the larger fronds he could find and leaning them in thick layers against both sides of its trunk. Within an hour, he had something resembling

a tent. When the rains came later that evening—and boy, did they come—he was even able to stay relatively dry. It was a definite improvement over the leaf pile of his first night, which offered some relief to Barry, although not much. He was still stuck alone on an island not much bigger than Madison Square Park. Still uncertain if anyone was searching for him. Still at the mercy of a negligent sea and a vastly indifferent sky. And then of course there was the pilot and the other two passengers. *Christ.* Barry hadn't even thought about them in that flaming mess of twisted steel and surging water. Had he seen them, he would have certainly tried to help, but he had not. Chances were, they hadn't survived the crash. No, the Filipino pilot with the Hawaiian shirt was probably at the bottom of the sea, the young French honeymooners were likely food for fishes—a thought that alarmed and saddened Barry, but comforted him in a strange way, too. It alarmed him because they had all seemed like nice people, in no way deserving of their fate. But it also served as a reminder of the fact that there were far worse places he could be at that moment. Like the ocean floor, for example. He stifled a shudder and listened to the rain, damp, weary, very afraid, but also very much alive, and in that fact alone he found vast reassurance. "Crap," he said out loud, once again on the edge of sleep. He'd forgotten yet again to take out his contacts.

4

Had Barry not plucked out his contacts, had he taken a midnight stroll instead around the island's sandy perimeter before hitting the hay—or palm fronds, as it were—he would have come to discover just how mistaken he was about the other passengers. Or at the very least, one of them, anyway. For on the shore directly opposite his, a Day-Glo orange raft was slowly deflating. And curled fetally inside its rubbery womb was Sophie Ducel, exactly one-half of the French honeymoon duo that Barry had assumed to be joined for eternity underwater. Her eventual destination proved identical to Barry's, but the manner of her arrival was markedly different.

Unlike Barry, she had stayed at the site of the crash as long as she could, hidden inside a floating portion of the cockpit, trying with determination to keep her dying husband afloat. The pilot was nowhere to be seen (Barry had been right on that count; his seat was dislodged by the force of the impact, dragging him down to the ocean's bottom), but a brightly colored emergency package of some sort could clearly be seen strapped to the floor where his seat had been. Keeping the bleeding

form of her Étienne from sinking required Sophie's full strength and attention, however, giving her no opportunity to unbuckle the box. She sensed its importance, its absolute necessity to her survival, but to let Étienne go for even one moment would mean losing him. She whispered encouragement in his ear, begged him to hold on just a little longer, but her appeals were in vain. His groans became less frequent and then ceased altogether. *"Non, non, mon chéri, ne me quitte pas,"* Sophie pleaded, to no avail. Étienne's blood had all left him; his heart had nothing left to pump. His eyes, once so luminous and full of life, had been in an instant irrevocably dimmed. A distraught Sophie opted to hold on to his lifeless body rather than procure the orange box, but after several minutes of hopeless bobbing, an oceanic whitetip shark—not a huge one, but at ten feet imposing nonetheless—rendered her selfless act moot. Attracted no doubt by the thrashing and the blood, the pale phantom form slipped in from below and stole her Étienne away. She felt the intimation of a tug—testing, flinching, almost infantile—followed by a massive jerk that tore him out of her arms. There was a splash and a crimson surge of bubbles and he was gone. The now hysterical Sophie was at this point truly alone, the water around her was undeniably aflame, the cockpit fragment in which she sheltered was sinking nightmarishly into the sea, and a dinner bell had officially been sounded, noticed by every shark for miles around.

Two paths, white and shimmering as a summer day in her native Toulouse, appeared before her. Amid Sophie's immense terror, depthless loss, and visceral sadness, a clear choice took shape. Suddenly her life was a fork in the road, a binary system both horrific and beautiful in its simplicity. One path was as follows: She could close her eyes, cease her struggle, and let her body go limp. Slowly, placid as a dream, she would sink

into the dark water, enjoying a final moment of numb serenity before the ghost left her and the sharks did their work. A quick and relatively painless surrender, followed by a reunion with her husband in the beckoning deep.

Or she could swim like hell and get that *putain de merde* orange box.

Sophie Ducel chose the latter. With the walls of the narrow cockpit closing down upon her, she lunged for the box, which was underwater but still visible from the surface. She worked one buckle loose but felt her treasure sinking, moving steadily downward. She took a quick swallow of air and went down with it, her fingers struggling valiantly with the last canvas strap, her aching cheeks blistered with air. They were going down, everything, she knew that, and if she didn't get it soon . . .

And then it came. The buckle gave and the box sprang loose. With the very last of the plane descending in slow, disastrous, *Hindenburg*-like motion around her, she pursued the opposite vector, kicking and thrashing her body toward the life-giving sky and away from the cheated black hole that waited below.

She broke through the surface in a flesh-toned geyser and drank in the light. Smoke and steam abounded, but anything was better than the alternative. The orange box popped open rather easily, spilling out a nylon duffel bag, itself containing a package both rubberized and densely packed. An imperative black arrow pointed to a cord attached to a handle, not unlike the starter on a lawn mower, and Sophie subjected it to a vigorous tug. Something snapped, a python hiss of gas was released, and the orange vinyl bundle came buoyantly to life, transforming into a compact and functional life raft. Sophie clambered over its side while it was only half-inflated—a few

curious sharks had begun nuzzling her knees—and sprawled across its bottom, gasping for oxygen. The little vessel continued to take shape around her, growing sturdier by the second, until the gaseous hiss eventually stopped, leaving Sophie to bob alone in silence and smoke.

The sky above her was a jarring cobalt; the wind tasted of petrol and doom. Sophie shivered from shock, and she wept profusely. She wailed and wondered, both to herself and out loud, how a honeymoon to French Polynesia had degenerated into this. For the time being, she cared little about rescue. She was indifferent to the possibility of escape. She thought only of Étienne, with whom she had made love that very morning, following a breakfast of fresh papaya and *pain perdu,* directly beneath her, being chewed up by sharks and swallowed by darkness. And after some hours of delirious weeping, she, just like Barry in his bower, fell asleep.

Sophie drifted all night in her little raft. She was still drifting when she awoke in the morning, to a parched throat, sore muscles, a mild sunburn, and the sickening realization of the predicament she was in. She drifted right through the afternoon, beneath a sky that yielded no trace of rescue but plenty of rain, and right on into a second night, until the drifting stopped with an abrupt and gritty halt. Nudged back to reality, Sophie raised her head. Baffled, she looked around her, at low, hoary dunes and palms that quivered and silvered in the moonlight. She climbed over the side of the raft, vomited bile, moaned once more toward the god(s) she, too, assumed had forsaken her, and collapsed forward onto the sand.

And so it came to pass that two utterly disparate lives happened to overlap: a young architect from Paris's tenth arrondissement, prematurely widowed at age twenty-eight, and a relatively young banker from Manhattan's Upper East Side,

prematurely retired at age thirty-four, bound together on an uninhabited island some 2,359 miles from Hawaii, 4,622 miles from Chile, and 533 miles from the nearest living soul.

Crap, as Barry liked to say.

Putain de merde, as Sophie was known to exclaim.

5

Alone and shivering on their respective beaches, Barry and Sophie both considered themselves extremely unlucky—which, in a purely statistical sense, they were. But from a historical perspective, they were hardly alone. Becoming an island castaway in this mapped and modern twenty-first century may sound exceptional, but it was not without precedent. And while it would have likely proved little comfort, there's no shortage of individuals who could attest to that fact.

Take, for example, an Irish American most have heard of named John F. Kennedy. As a twenty-six-year-old skipper in World War II, he found himself floating in the middle of the Pacific after a Japanese destroyer rather inconsiderately sank his patrol boat. The future president and a few members of his loyal crew braved sharks and saltwater crocodiles to swim to nearby Plum Pudding Island, living off coconuts and rainwater while waiting for rescue.

And then there is Ada Blackjack, the twenty-three-year-old Inuit woman who served as both cook and seamstress on a Canadian expedition to Wrangel Island, north of Siberia, in

1921. When the rest of her party either died of scurvy or perished trying to escape in the sea, she hunkered down and survived for a solid two years on that desolate rock, hunting small game and melting ice to drink.

If it's literary renown you're after, you'll find no better example than Alexander Selkirk, a Scottish sailor marooned on the Pacific island of Más a Tierra in the early eighteenth century. He subsisted there for nearly five years on the goats and rats that plagued his uninhabited isle, whiling away the hours reading his Bible and smoking tobacco. Following his rescue, he would publish a record of his adventures—a biography that many believe inspired the novel *Robinson Crusoe,* written just a few years later. Indeed, in 1966, Más a Tierra was officially renamed Robinson Crusoe Island in honor of that noble act of plagiarism.

For longevity, you can't beat Juana Maria, the lone woman of San Nicolas Island, who was for eighteen years a castaway lost to the world; for drama, Marguerite de la Rocque, who gave birth to a bastard child during her two years on the Isle of Demons. And for pure heroism, there's always Ernest Shackleton, who rescued his men from Elephant Island after a grueling and treacherous eighteen-month ordeal. There's even some evidence that Amelia Earhart spent her penultimate days as a castaway on a lonesome Pacific atoll, although the verdict is still out on that one. Philip Ashton, Fernão Lopes, Charles Barnard, Poon Lim, Gonzalo de Vigo, Chunosuke Matsuyama—they're all right there for the skeptical and the curious alike, men and women who found themselves abandoned by civilization and left to their own devices on desolate hunks of sea-gird stone. The history books abound with such desperate plights, going back to the sailors of classical antiquity, all the way up to the Japanese tsunami victims and lost

Mexican fishermen of, yes, our mapped and modern twenty-first century.

A twenty-first century that for Barry and Sophie was only just beginning. Their joint Cessna 208 went down on the first day of April 2001, a rather severe *poisson d'avril,* to say the least. That they ended up on the same plane was merely coincidence, if one believes in such things. As passengers aboard a small semicharter flight from the relatively remote island of Tahiti, bound for an even more remote island in the Marquesas, it was pure chance that brought them together. They were both looking to visit a place at the ends of the earth that they had heard good things about, and nothing more.

For Sophie, it was to be the most romantic leg of an already exceedingly romantic vacation. She and Étienne had delayed their honeymoon because of time and financial constraints—starting an architecture firm in Paris had proved taxing on both, and the AutoCAD licenses alone had put them several grand in the hole. But the date was set for a late March departure, some three months after their wedding, and when it arrived, they were understandably elated. The first week was spent on the main island of Tahiti, at a beachside resort rife with coconut palms and equally coconutty drinks. Mornings were devoted to making love in bed beneath the gauzy veil of their mosquito netting, and afternoons to walking along the beach, discussing architecture and making plans for the future. Étienne wanted to live in Paris indefinitely, but Sophie at least entertained the notion of returning to the south one day, maybe even to the Hautes-Pyrénées, where she had spent her summers as a girl. Either way, they had several happy years to figure it out. In the meantime, they had a promising little firm in the tenth arrondissement, several new contracts for respected cultural institutions, and another full week of tropical leisure

ahead of them, to be spent on an even more idyllic island in the Marquesas that Sophie had read about in a brochure.

"*Regarde,*" she had whispered to a half-asleep Étienne while in bed together in their flat in Paris. "Jacques Brel lived there during the last years of his life. *C'est un paradis.*"

"*Oui, ma chérie,*" he had drowsily assented. "*Allons-y.*"

Barry's voyage was also a celebration of sorts, albeit one of separation rather than joining. A separation from many things, as a matter of fact. For while Sophie had been doggedly pursuing her passion in Paris, Barry had been halfheartedly bobbing along as a middling bond salesman in New York. Actually, halfhearted may be generous. Barry hated it, loathed it, despised it with a passion. Yet somehow he had become resigned to that existence, a far cry from his childhood in Cleveland and an even farther shout from his grandparents' farm in southern Illinois. But it just seemed the sort of thing one did after Princeton, even with a degree in art history, and he had been initiated unenthusiastically into the world of Excel spreadsheets and client meetings and unpleasant bar nights, while quietly dreaming of far different things.

Things like Gauguin paintings, for example. And when the tensile cord of his being finally snapped and his conscience could take no more, Barry remembered that selfsame Polynesian island whose name Sophie had uttered in bed ("Hiva Oa, Hiva Oa" . . . just saying it made his spine tingle). In a burst of resolve, he had decided to go, and with good reason: The singer Jacques Brel wasn't the only francophone who had spent the last years of his life there—the little speck in the Marquesas had served as the painter Paul Gauguin's final resting place as well. When Barry quit his job at Lehman Brothers, his boss had called him an idiot. When he told his girlfriend, she had informed him that his odds of making it as an artist were one in a million, as she packed her things and walked out the door.

But when he whispered his new path to himself, the gods said, *Well done*.

Naturally, there was some trepidation. Quitting a fairly lucrative career in his midthirties to become a painter wasn't the most fiscally prudent decision he had ever made, and giving away most of his savings to the United Way (honestly the only charity he could think of) was probably an even worse one. But if he lived frugally, he knew what remained in his bank account would sustain him for a few lean years, and the art supply store across the street from his new apartment downtown sold canvases on the cheap. Nervous but pleased with himself, and giddy with possibility, Barry felt a celebration was in order, something to commemorate a bold new adventure and provide ample inspiration for the creative period ahead.

The island of Hiva Oa was not easy to get to. But from Tahiti's smaller airport in Papeete, there was a single-engine prop plane that made the eight-hundred-mile flight to the Marquesas twice a week. Sketchbook, oil paints, and pastels in hand, Barry had stood waiting at the airstrip, half a world away from home, beside a young French couple who had booked the same flight as he. The husband introduced himself as Étienne and seemed serious but personable. As for his new wife, she was very pretty but strikingly aloof. Sophie, she had said her name was, and beyond that, she did not divulge much more. They were dressed quite appropriately in their Deauville finest: cutoff shorts, espadrilles, and matching Saint James T-shirts. Barry, on the other hand, was still wearing the same clothes he had donned for his last day at the office and felt distinctly out of place in the South Pacific. *Oh, well.* He would have plenty of time to invest in cargo shorts and tan-giving tees when he arrived in the Marquesas. And he was looking forward to it.

The sun spilled down and the palms did their thing, and

after a half hour of waiting, a rattletrap Cessna droned up, its rust-flecked wings shimmering in the heat that rose off the tarmac. From its cockpit, a groggy-looking man in a Hawaiian shirt and sunglasses beckoned them aboard.

"That's our plane?" Sophie asked worriedly, and in French.

"Oui, c'est ça," answered Étienne. "But don't worry, it will get us there."

Over the course of his life, Étienne had been correct on many counts, from his suspicion that the attractive brunette in his architecture class in Montpellier might like to join him for coffee to his conviction that it was better to set out and start a small firm of his own. But in this instance, regarding the reliability of the single-engine Cessna 208 and the integrity of its custodian, Étienne could not have been more wrong.

6

Morning number two of Barry's maroonship proved no more eventful than the one that preceded it—at least at its onset. Emerging damp and stiff from his palm shelter, he encountered the same flat, featureless sky, the same blank, unyielding sea. True, the sun was beginning to peep out from behind an ashy haze of clouds, throwing at least a tinge of gold upon the palms and turquoise upon the water. Beyond that, however, nothing had changed. A long, hot shower and a crisp change of clothes would have been most welcome, but a starchy bunch of bananas and a gulp of fresh rainwater were the only amenities the island offered. He had at least gotten some sleep, though—that was nice—and something to eat was better than nothing. Feeling reasonably energized and relatively well rested, Barry was in the process of inspecting the damage that the previous night's rain had done to his SOS signs when he noticed the raft, not to mention the half-dressed female form hanging out of it.

"Hey!" he shouted midstride, loping over the sand toward her. "Hey, are you okay?"

The female form in question flinched and did half a turn on the sand, and he saw that it was indeed the French honeymooner, although considerably worse for wear. Her eyes rolled dazedly in her head, visible through a bedraggled mat of sand-caked hair. Her Breton-striped Saint James T-shirt was gone—only a black bra remained to cover her torso—and a single soggy blue espadrille dangled from her big toe.

Barry crouched beside her (what was her name again—Silvia? Sonya?) and helped her fully out of the raft to lie flat on the sand. He pushed the hair from her eyes and gave them a closer inspection. They seemed unable to register his existence.

"Sonya, are you okay? Where's your husband? Did he make it?"

Barry recognized the cruelty inherent in the last question and immediately regretted asking it. Not that it mattered. Sonya, as he believed she was called, appeared to be in some sort of catatonic shock. She was shivering, in fact, and he removed his shirt-turban, sat her up, and draped it around her shoulders. What to do next?

Once upon a time, Barry had been a Boy Scout. And at summer camp one year in the north woods of Wisconsin had been the recipient of an earnest and well-intentioned lecture on basic first aid—very little of which Barry remembered, engrossed as he was at the time with a clandestine *Playboy* one of the other campers had snuck into the meeting. Airway, breathing, and circulation couldn't hold a candle to the magazine's glossy, trifold delights. Among those fond adolescent memories, however, he did have one recollection from the actual lesson: the necessity of warmth. Something about the body going into shock and requiring extra heat. Not that it was especially cool outside—it couldn't have been less than seventy degrees on the island. But something had to be done.

Leaving the raft where it was, Barry scooped the unresponsive Sonya(?) into his arms and did an awkward, stumbling job of carrying her back to his makeshift encampment. She was by that point shivering convulsively, and her delicate limbs seemed to be seizing up. He deposited her inside his little shelter, then set one of his frond stacks ablaze. Three rushed forays into the bush yielded a thick harvest of additional leaves, which he piled onto the growing fire. Coughing through the smoke, he lifted Sonya once again and set her down beside it.

Whew. He exhaled sharply, exhausted from the exertion, and sat in the sand. Curled beneath his shirt, his new co-castaway formed a shivering ball. He made a few attempts at conversation, none of which yielded even a hint of a response. It occurred to him that perhaps she did not speak much English, so he tried some very poor overtures in mostly forgotten middle school French, at one point even resorting to a horribly garbled rendition of "Frère Jacques." That didn't work either. Not sure what else to do, he stroked her hair—sometimes the simplest gestures are the ones that mean the most—and gradually, over the course of a breezy, surf-swept afternoon and a flamboyant, sorbet-shaded sunset, she stopped shaking.

Barry stayed up the whole night, tending to the smoldering fire, keeping his eyes out for any sign of rescue—of which there was none. No jet contrails glazed in the moonlight, not a single megaphone blast from a distant pontoon. The French girl, meanwhile, stared blankly into the embers for hours, unmoving and unresponsive. Eventually—Barry wasn't sure exactly when, but he noticed it not long after the moon set and the winds died down—she fell asleep, announcing her slumber with a faint, almost mouselike snore. Barry took a strange, paternal pleasure in this; it seemed to him a good sign, an indication that the horror was perhaps fading and that natural human rhythms were again taking hold. He stirred at the

embers and looked at the stars. Blazing, searing stars, the likes of which he had never seen before in his life. He recalled the night skies above his grandparents' farm in Illinois; the way the Milky Way made a shimmering ribbon above the frozen prairie had been more than enough to stir a boy's wonder and put an ache in his soul. But the star-fire that burned down upon him on the island, an ocean away from the incandescent smear of civilization, was something else entirely. Back in one of his college art history classes, he had once read an account from Renaissance Europe, when the nights were wondrously dark, of starlight bright enough to cast shadows, even read by. He wondered if this glimpse of the universe, afforded to him in the direst of human circumstances, was as close to those pristine, preelectric nights as he would ever get. Probably, he thought to himself, and for a moment he felt the heady sensation of traveling through time, despite being firmly planted in a rather inconvenient place.

At some point in the night, rain clouds rolled in, immense, lolling things that blotted out the heavens. The shower was brief, nothing like the previous evening's, but it was enough to kill what remained of the campfire in a sharp chorus of hisses. The rain passed, but Barry didn't bother to relight it. Dawn was coming; a blush was beginning to drown out the stars. Even Venus was on the verge of cutting her blinkers. When the first splash of sunlight spilled over the palms behind him and threw a scatter of bright scales across the water, Barry decided to call it a night. He took out his contacts, checked on the girl, who was still snoring softly, and crawled into his little shelter, where he fell promptly asleep and had an uncannily lucid dream in which he was in Rome helping Michelangelo paint the Sistine Chapel—by starlight, incidentally, which in the half logic of the dreamworld made absolute sense.

7

A kick to the shin woke Barry up. Not a hard one, but a kick with definite insistence. He shot up in a disoriented haze, still woozy from sleep and essentially blind without his contact lenses. At the entrance of his shelter, he detected the nondescript blur of a human form.

"First of all," a decidedly foreign female voice announced, "my name is not Sonya. It's Sophie. I remembered your name, and you can at least get mine right."

Barry scrambled to get in his contacts, taking a few tentative blinks to adjust to the light.

"Second of all, your French is terrible. And third of all, I need your help with the raft. I think we should move it over here."

Sophie (yes, that was her name!) was standing resolutely before him, torso cocked slightly so as to see into his frond tent. She was wearing his dress shirt, sleeves rolled up and knotted at the waist, and her short-cropped brown hair was cleaned and slicked back. Her eyes were rheumy and red, he suspected

from crying, but also clear and focused—no sign of her stupor remained.

Barry crawled out of the shelter and rose to his feet, brushing the sand from his legs and arms as he did so. "How are you feeling? Is everything okay?"

Sophie expelled an exasperated, Gallic puff of air. *Pfff.* "That's a stupid question, isn't it?"

"Did anyone else . . ." Barry trailed off, not sure how to ask the question. "Did you see anybody else after the crash?"

Sophie shook her head and bit her lip. *"Non,"* she said in French, wincing visibly. *"Il n'y avait personne."*

"God, I'm sorry."

"Well, I'm sorry for you, too. We're both in the same position at the moment, in case you haven't noticed."

It was clear she didn't want to discuss whatever had happened to her husband.

Barry made an attempt at clearing his throat. "Are you thirsty? Hungry? There's water and bananas deeper in the island."

"I know. I found them. Unlike you, I didn't spend the whole day sleeping."

No, you only spent the whole previous day practically comatose, Barry thought to himself, but he didn't dare say it. "Well, have you seen any boats or planes? Someone must be looking for us."

She shook her head again. "No, I don't think so."

"Shit." Barry shoved his hands in his sand-gritty pockets. How many days had it been? Two and a half? Three? Surely the pilot radioed back some sign of distress. Naturally alarms must have been raised when the plane failed to arrive. Unquestionably there were rescue craft out trolling the seas, checking coordinates on maps, and monitoring little electric pings on

some form of GPS device. After all, it was the twenty-first goddamn century.

"Come on, let's go get the raft." Sophie tightened the shirt knot and smoothed her hair back behind her ears. "There are some supplies in it, too."

"Supplies?"

"Like a little survival kit. It's attached to the inside."

Barry perked up. A survival kit? After having to make do with disposable Bics and unripe bananas, a shot at some viable gear offered considerable promise. Who knew what treasures such a kit might contain? Clean changes of unisex clothing? Gallons of freshwater? Freeze-dried gourmet dinners? Astronaut ice cream? Wasting no time, Barry and Sophie hurried to the other side of the island to fetch it—he, in great excitement, humming "Frère Jacques," and she, in great annoyance, kindly asking him to never sing that stupid song again, *putain de merde.*

8

There is, of course, one pressing question that deserves to be answered: Why wasn't anyone searching for survivors? The answer is that they were. Barry was correct—alarms had been sounded when their plane failed to arrive, and rescue craft were indeed out trolling the seas. Unfortunately, they were looking in the wrong place. This was the direct consequence of an unfortunate addiction on the part of their pilot and of the fact that their smallish Cessna had been downed by a colossal bolt of lightning—one that deep-fried every radio circuit on board.

As for the pilot—a fifty-year-old Filipino divorcé of Spanish Principalía ancestry by the name of Marco "Ding Dong" Mercado—both his skills and his privileged social status were sharply negated on more than one occasion by his great thirst for a Manila rum known as Tanduay. In fact, it was a bottle of Tanduay White that had cost him his captain's title five years before at Philippine Airlines, a bottle of Tanduay Dark that had severed his ties with a down-market Malaysian airline two years after that, and an entire case of Tanduay Añejo, consumed over the course of a single weekend, that had convinced his

wife to leave him forever, just one year prior to his fatal crash. Which was how he came to service a scruffy, no-name airport in Tahiti, shuttling tourists twice a week to the Marquesas. The eight-hundred-mile flight was a breeze, and given the intervals between each leg, he generally had the freedom to enjoy as much Tanduay as he liked, so long as he could slog through his hangover, throw on a pair of mirrored sunglasses to hide his bloodshot eyes, and make his way woozily down to the hangar.

Naturally, such a boozy existence gave rise to a fair amount of unadvisable liberties. Airport regulations demanded that Marco leave a detailed manifest before each trip, but he seldom complied. Control tower etiquette mandated that he keep in regular contact throughout the course of the flight, but he almost never did. Indeed, Marco wasn't even above dozing off behind the stick when his hangovers called for it. The compass beeped if he went off course, and the altimeter buzzed when he got too low—what could possibly go wrong?

Well, as it turned out, much to the detriment of those on board that fateful morning, quite a bit could go wrong. Marco's hangover from the night before was otherworldly. It had been his and his ex-wife's anniversary, and he had spent it alone at a dingy bar in Papeete, downing shot after shot of clear, unaged Tanduay, doing precisely that which had convinced her to leave him in the first place. And when his clock radio prodded him awake at eight o'clock the next morning, he was still reekingly, staggeringly drunk. But it wasn't the first time he had walked the half mile to the airstrip loaded, nor did he think—although he was sorely mistaken—that it would be his last. Shielded behind his mirrored aviators, he trudged into the hangar, waving at the mechanics as he yanked his keys off the upturned gutter nail from which they were hung. Marco glanced quickly at a clipboarded manifest, reading off the names

of his passengers: two French and one American. *Perfecto.* He choked back five ibuprofen tablets from his locker, downed them with a swig of Tanduay from a half-pint he kept there for just such an occasion, and climbed into the cockpit of his trusty Cessna 208. The mechanic gave him a thumbs-up, and Marco, donning his earphones and adjusting his mouthpiece, gave him a healthy dose of thumb in return. Time to pick up the passengers, who, if able to distinguish between the Tanduay and the gas fumes that filled the airplane, said nothing.

The first half of the four-hour flight had gone seamlessly as planned. The American stared out the window in amazed bewilderment, the French couple was all smiles and hand squeezes, and the skies were clear and . . .

Well, not *that* clear. Snoring awake from one of his infamous micronaps, Marco took note of something ahead: A bank of clouds, dark and foreboding, loomed before them. It wasn't unusual at that time of year to encounter a stormy patch, and Marco's usual strategy was simply to fly around it. It could add twenty or thirty minutes to the trip, but it was better than turning back and wasting the entire day, as traffic control generally suggested. Which was precisely why he seldom informed them of his little detours.

By the time Marco executed his slow, droning roll, raindrops were already flecking the windshield, squirming their way across the glass. He considered turning on his radio and asking for some information on the storm's size, but with his head a-throb and guts a-churn, he was in no mood to have some pissy traffic controller demand he turn the craft around. No, Marco would continue on his way, skirting the storm's dark margins, waiting patiently for the skies to clear.

Only they didn't. Because the small patch of storm clouds Marco was intent upon circumventing was nothing of the sort—a fact he did not know, because he had been too hung-

over to bother checking the morning's weather report. Its black curtain hung for miles, hiving from within with flares of orange-and-purple lightning. And more pressing than that, after spending two hours trying to flank it, his weak-winged little craft was running dangerously low on fuel. Gulping back down his Adam's apple and wiping with a shaky arm the sweat from his brow, Marco realized that he had no choice. He did not have enough gas either to fly around it or to turn back. His only chance was to fly straight through it.

At which point Marco should have radioed back to Tahiti with his position and begged feverishly for help or at the very least advice—a precautionary measure he refused to take. After having lost two decent pilot gigs and a wife to the good folks at Tanduay, he was in no hurry to lose anything else. No, he could make it, he told himself in Chavacano, the Castilian-inflected dialect of his native Zamboanga back in the Philippines. A few bumpy minutes would pass, and then they would burst triumphantly on through to clear, sunny skies. It simply had to be so.

And the truly amazing part—Marco "Ding Dong" Mercado's plan went almost exactly as planned. He shouted back to his three passengers that there would be some turbulence ahead and that they ought to fasten their seat belts. He bit his lip and righted the stick. He muttered a quick prayer to the benevolent Pilar, patron saint of Zamboanga, whose beatific face graced a paper card he had taped to the dashboard, and he plunged the little craft headfirst into the storm.

Oh, it was bumpy all right. A series of nauseating dips and teeth-grating climbs, shaking that nearly wrenched the shoulders. Some of the overhead luggage spilled out of the compartments; a bag of contact lens supplies skittered down the aisle. The French girl hid her head in her husband's shoulder, and the American in the strange office clothes turned a legitimate

shade of maritime green. *"Por favor, Pilar,"* Marco muttered aloud in his desperate Chavacano. "Grant me this one favor, and I will give up drinking for good—I'll be a better person, I'll even try to get my wife back. I'll never touch the bottle again." And it appeared that the forgiving Pilar actually listened; up ahead, a break appeared in the clouds. The fierce bumps shrank to gentle nudges. A great wash of apricot sunlight illuminated the path that had been laid out before them. *"Ay, gracias, Pilar.* Thank you, thank you, thank you." In fact, so grateful was Marco, he decided right then and there to honor her kindness with a fresh bottle of Tanduay as soon as he got—

And then the lightning struck. Like a megawatt hand swatting an escaping fly, that great arc of electricity reached out from the storm clouds just as Marco, Étienne, Sophie, and Barry were on the verge of leaving them behind forever. They had almost cleared their pitch-black hurdle and made the lemon-drop safety of the open sky beyond—almost, but not quite. The bolt deafened all aboard for a bright white moment and left a taste like tinfoil ringing in their mouths. When the electric fog cleared, Marco, Étienne, Sophie, and Barry all came to the horrifying realization that not only was the plane's single engine aflame and its radio circuitry kaput, but they were also pitched and falling at a death-dealing angle. And to make matters worse, the bolt's electric fangs had taken a smoldering bite of the plane's left wing. No gentle glides, no stone-skip landings. Instead, the most horrific, spiraling, downward trajectory a human being can imagine, with nothing but a carbon-hard sea rising to meet them and a fading drone to serve as their dirge.

Sadly, Marco "Ding Dong" Mercado died upon impact. The sheer force of the collision between plane and sea ripped his seat from the floor and crushed his body against the dashboard. His corpse was thrown in the tumult far from the rest

of the wreckage, where it sank beneath the waves and into Pilar's benevolent embrace.

Étienne was the unfortunate recipient of the twisted steel bottom of the pilot's seat—when it pitched forward, it also scythed upward, nearly severing one of his legs and gouging out a chunk of his side.

Sophie was spared a similar fate by inches; the same jagged steel that cut through his organs only narrowly missed her throat. She suffered a mild concussion, and somehow lost her shirt, but was relatively unhurt when her mortally wounded Étienne unbuckled his belt and tumbled forward into the water. She went in after him, screaming his name.

As for Barry, he and his seat had both been sucked backward when the plane's tail exploded around him. He was treated to a series of disorienting reverse somersaults through the water before he regained some sense of up, unlatched his seat belt, and began swimming toward it.

None of this should be especially surprising given what has already been disclosed about Barry and Sophie's predicament. But it does explain why the rescue that they craved was at first slow—and then utterly absent—in coming. Marco, in his poor and Tanduay-warped judgment, had piloted them almost three hundred miles off course in his vain attempt at besting the storm.

And nobody—barring Barry, Sophie, and the benevolent Pilar, patron saint of Zamboanga—had the slightest inkling of this fact.

9

"Ouch, hold up a second."

"Merde, what is it now?"

"I stepped on a piece of shell."

Barry executed a few hops on one foot to extract the sharp little shard of conch from his heel.

"Are you ready?" Sophie asked with more than a hint of annoyance.

Barry took a few limping steps. "I think it went pretty deep."

Sophie did another one of her exasperated exhales through pursed lips. *"Putain,"* she muttered as, glazed in sweat (it was significantly warmer on this day), she undid a few buttons of the borrowed shirt. "By the way, why were you dressed like this? These are office clothes. You looked ridiculous back at the airport."

Barry sat in the sand to take a closer look at his foot. "I know, I came straight from the office."

"You left for Tahiti from your office and didn't change your clothes?"

Barry shrugged. "It was my last day of work, and I didn't feel like going back to my apartment."

"So you went directly to the airport?"

"Yeah, pretty much. I'd bought the tickets the week before, but I jumped in a cab and went straight from work."

Sophie mumbled something derogatory about Americans and bloused out the shirt with her fingers to let some of the heat escape. "Well, it's absurd, wearing a shirt like this on vacation."

"I'm not wearing it, you are. And you're welcome to give it back anytime you like."

Sophie snorted. "Of course not. You will stare at my breasts."

"What?" Barry snorted as well, and punctuated it with a laugh. "You actually think your tits are on my mind at the moment?"

Sophie shrugged, the same forcedly indifferent shrug she had mastered back at the cafés of the tenth when one of her friends confessed to an affair, or being in love with her psychiatrist, or having eaten an entire Saint Honoré all by herself. "Why not? You're a man, *non*? Unless women don't interest you."

"Yes, women interest me," Barry replied, both his foot and his pride momentarily wounded.

"There, you see? I keep the shirt. *Merci beaucoup.*"

Sophie plodded off defiantly across the sand, and Barry, having the courtesy to at least wait until she was out of earshot, muttered something derogatory about the French and ill-tempered women both. He rose to his feet, though, and hobbled after her, having realized as soon as she escaped his view that it was better to be in the company of an "uppity French bitch" than to be shirtless and hopeless and utterly alone. Plus, there was a raft, possibly stocked with freeze-dried astronaut ice cream, waiting just past the sun-drenched palms.

When the bright orange rubber of the raft came into sight, Sophie was already crouched over it, undoing the fastenings on a waterproof satchel. Barry approached and knelt beside her.

"This is it?"

"*Oui*. This is the kit."

"What's inside it?"

"I'm in the process of finding out. And the raft still works. I checked. It deflated because the plug came loose, not because it had a hole."

"Well, that's good news," Barry remarked, although he wasn't sure it actually was. Even a cursory scan of the horizon revealed an obvious lack of nearby islands to row to (and yes, there were two small plastic oars bundled beside the survival kit as well—Sophie evidently had not used them). The odds of them making it on the open ocean, much like the statistical probability of his artistic success, appeared to be one in a million.

As for the survival kit, it did not contain quite the freeze-dried bounty Barry had dreamed of, but its contents proved to be far more useful in the long-term sense. One by one, Sophie removed the items from the satchel and laid them carefully out on a space of smoothed sand. Included in the lineup was:

1 white plastic first-aid kit, containing gauze, bandages, sterilized sewing needles and thread, a plethora of alcohol wipes, antibiotic cream, and, strangely enough, cold medicine.

1 flare gun with six flare cartridges—instructions to its use were stamped on the handle.

1 emergency foil blanket folded into a silver cube. (Barry recognized it instantly from the New York City

Marathon; the runners always donned them like capes after the race for warmth.)

1 box-cutter-style utility knife with six fresh blades.

12 emergency energy bars, packed, according to the labels, with carbohydrates and essential vitamins and minerals.

4 bottles of distilled water, ready to drink.

6 heavy-duty resealable plastic bags, empty and rolled, to be used for potential water storage.

1 solar still. (This one took a moment to figure out, but Barry recognized its plastic dome from his old Boy Scout manual and explained that it could be used to get limited quantities of freshwater from the ocean.)

1 spool of medium-gauge filament fishing line.

15 fishhooks of varying sizes, complete with sinkers and lures.

1 Grundig FR-200 shortwave radio with a hand-crank generator.

1 Brunton magnetic field compass.

1 waterproof match safe containing (and yes, Sophie counted each one) forty-eight matches.

1 waterproof Maglite flashlight.

1 bundle of thin nylon rope (one hundred feet or so, by Barry's rough estimation).

1 pack of Russian cigarettes. (Barry didn't recognize the brand, but the warning label was in Cyrillic.)

2 stainless-steel drinking cups/cooking pots with folding handles.

3 lightweight blue plastic tarps.

0 packages of astronaut ice cream.

There it was. Their lot. Their chance at survival. Barry grinned and reached for one of the water bottles.

"Ow!" he exclaimed when Sophie smacked his hand.

"Put that down. Those are for an emergency."

"What the hell do you call surviving a plane crash and being stranded on a goddamn island?"

"We have freshwater for the time being, so we must drink that. Actually, we should fill the extra water bags in case we need them later."

"So I suppose no energy bars either?"

Sophie shook her head. "*Non*. We might need them later as well. The best thing now would be for you to catch us a fish."

"Why should I catch the fish?"

"Because you are American, like Huckleberry Finn, no?"

"But you are French, like Jacques Cousteau, no?"

"*Non*. You can catch the fish."

"Christ." Barry plopped down on the sand. "Can I at least have a cigarette?" He asked this sarcastically.

Sophie did her shrug. "Sure, why not."

Barry picked apart the foil of the Russian cigarettes and held open the honeycomb of exposed white butts in offering toward her.

"No, thank you, I don't smoke."

"You're French, and you don't smoke?"

"You're American, and you don't know how to fish?" She said this snarkily, with an exaggerated twang she had no doubt picked up from some cowboy movie, and that infuriated Barry.

"You want fish? Fine, I'll get you some fish. See you back at camp, *ma chérie*."

"Don't ever call me that!" Sophie was suddenly enraged. "I'm not your *chérie*." She hastily undid the buttons and whipped off the shirt, throwing it at his feet.

Barry didn't reply. Detecting at last her hidden layer of heartache, he realized, as he picked up the shirt and stamped off across the sand, that as young and pretty and seemingly imper-

vious to disaster as his island-mate might seem, the ink on her widowhood was still painfully fresh—a fact that was demonstrated quite clearly by the fading sound of her sobs as she dragged the raft alone back to camp.

10

Despite her many incorrect assumptions regarding Barry and his country of origin, Sophie had been at least in the ballpark with her comment about Huckleberry Finn. Although he was raised in Cleveland, Barry's grandparents' farm, which he had visited frequently as a boy, was to be found in Macoupin County, Illinois, just across the river and a few tractor pulls away from Hannibal, Missouri, the hometown of Mark Twain. And indeed, as a boy, Barry had engaged in many similarly folksy pursuits, one of which was catching catfish, although this occurred more often in local "cricks" than on the Muddy Mississipp'. Unlike those hook-and-line aficionados Tom Sawyer and Huckleberry Finn, Barry had learned to fish with the fine-meshed nets known locally as "seines," any similarity to the river that bisected Sophie's city of residence being pure coincidence. In fact, one of Barry's most beautiful and haunting memories (and he had never told anyone this, certainly not his co-workers at Lehman Brothers and definitely not his ex-girlfriend Ashley) was going seining with his grandfather when the moon was full, the two of them waist-deep

as they dragged their gossamer nets through the quicksilver water.

So Barry was not a total stranger to fish. Of the sort one finds in southwestern Illinois, anyway. Perched on the rocks above the island's clearest little cove, however, he was a long way from the fried catfish and freshly gigged frog legs he had relished in his youth. Shirt returbaned about his head, line in hand, he gazed down at the calm pool below and squinted for a sign of anything edible. He fixed one of the artificial lures onto a hook (it reminded him of the gummy worms his mother used to put in his Easter baskets, a poor substitute for an actual night crawler), attached the float and the sinker, and, following a weak sidearm cast, watched the whole baited affair settle in the water. It seemed like a good place to fish—a sheltered semicircle of rock that created a calm patch of water, some twenty feet across and perhaps ten feet deep. He could see the white sandy bottom, rippled and duned with the soft tracks of the current; kelpy-looking things swayed in it, and corally-looking stuff at its rim formed ledges below. Dark shapes occasionally darted in the shadows, and he hoped one or more of them might have an appetite for yellow gummy worms.

The first three hours were uneventful. He smoked another cigarette, ever mindful to take an occasional scan of the horizon; he was sure somebody would be arriving soon, and he had the flare gun tucked in his waistband to welcome their landing. But neither rescue nor dinner was quick in coming. The waves rolled in steadily around the tiny cove, trade winds picked up as morning became afternoon, and the yellow gummy worm hovered beneath the surface without a nibble to its name. *Crap.*

Something occurred to Barry. He recalled hearing his cousins talk about fishing for catfish with a trotline during one of his visits to Macoupin County and remembered that they had

suggested "stink bait" to lure them in. Old chicken livers, rotten eggs, even chunks of hot dog coated in WD-40—stuff that put some funk in the water. A funk that his little gummy worm, no matter how noble its intent, simply could not exude. It was four hours in, and although he was certain he saw fish wriggling down below, his virginal lure remained untouched. It was worth a try.

But what to use? The island didn't seem to have worms—or any significant insects, for that matter, beyond a few gnatty little flies. And to use pieces of fish, he would have to catch one first. He had noticed, though, a scatter of peculiar-looking shells wedged in the crevices of the larger rocks. He suspected them to be clams of some sort, and in this instance, Barry was correct. They were maxima clams, a smaller cousin of the giant clam and favorite foodstuff of Polynesians for centuries, although Barry had no knowledge of that fact. Ready to try anything, he pulled in his line, set it at his feet, and went peeking between the rocks for a suitable specimen. Arm deep in such a hole, he found one and with three hard tugs pried it loose. Examining it in the sun, he saw that it was actually quite beautiful, blue tinged with nacreous swirls. He almost regretted having to smash it against the rocks, but alas, this was a survival situation. Two hard whacks and the fist-sized clam split apart like a coconut; its meat was tough, but the azure-colored lips stripped away easily enough. Barry removed the gummy worm lure and worked the barbed hook through several layers of clam meat, forming a tempting bunch with some dangle on the end. "Shit," muttered Barry, "if these fish don't eat this, I definitely will," oblivious at the time to the accuracy of that statement. And he retook his perch and cast it in.

The morsel had been dancing beneath the surface for no more than ten minutes when something torpedo shaped and lithe came circling in. "Yes!" Barry exclaimed with a trium-

phant hiss. It was a fish all right—and a good-sized one at that. Definitely enough for two hungry people. *Come on, you son of a bitch!*

The paddletail snapper in question (of course Barry didn't know its species, either) pecked, prodded, and then took a bite. The line jerked to a delightful tautness, accompanied by a flurry of silvery flopping. Oh, he had it, and hand over hand, Barry began pulling dinner in, despite its zigs and zags to the contrary.

What was the best way to cook such a fish? he asked himself. Skewer it? Bury it in coals? Then again, sashimi was good—could they just eat it raw? Barry didn't find out. Not that day, anyway. He was on the verge of yanking the weary fish right out of the water when one of the boulders at the sandy seafloor—it had been sitting there utterly inert since he had arrived—came bursting to life. With a horrific surge of speed, its massive bulk heaved up from the depths, engulfed the poor snapper in a tangle of limbs, and with the weight of an anvil shot back down. The initial tug was so great, it nearly pulled Barry into the drink—a terrifying prospect given what he had just learned was lurking there. Weak-kneed with adrenaline, too shocked to curse, he pulled from the water the limp remainder of his line, discovering as he did so that the creature had not only stolen his supper, but also gotten away with one of his few precious hooks. *Then* he cursed.

When the water settled, Barry peered into the pool's depths to search for some trace of the beast, but it was gone. He suspected one of the caverns at the bottom was its lair, where it was no doubt enjoying *his* sashimi dinner. Crestfallen, Barry removed the bobber and the sinker and rewound the line around the spool, wondering what to do next. Sunset wasn't far off, and he doubted he'd be able to land a second fish. Honestly, the notion of that thing coming back up scared him to

death. The idea of returning to Sophie empty-handed was also disconcerting, so he decided to pry loose a few more of the thick, blue-tinged clams and take those back instead. He found two at the pool's edge, yanked them free of the rock, tucked them in his pants pockets, and headed back to the shelter.

Barry was not the only one who'd had an eventful afternoon. Sophie had been busy, as well, using the time alone to get their camp in order. She was, after all, a committed and serious architect, and even an island maroonment was no excuse for bad taste. And besides, keeping busy also meant keeping her mind off of Étienne, whose loss she was still not prepared to cope with. Was it denial? Probably. Well, almost certainly. But what other option did she have? She could confront what had happened when she was back in Paris. She could deal with the emotional nightmare of burying her husband's empty coffin in his family's plot at Père Lachaise once she was home again. And she could begin sweeping up and dusting off the shattered pieces of her life as soon as the rescue plane had spirited her off this *putain d'île* and away from that paunchy and bumbling *imbécile d'américain*. But in the meantime, she had things to do.

First, the shelter. It definitely needed work. Sophie took Barry's ramshackle attempt down and began anew, with a far more suitable and aesthetically pleasing plan in mind. For while Barry had spent his summers on his family's farm in Illinois, riding tractors and trolling for catfish, she had spent hers at her ancestral home in the Pyrenees, the Cirque de Gavarnie. Her grandfather, although retired at the time, had worked most of his life as a local guide and mountaineer. He would take Sophie and her younger brother on long hikes outside the village, showing them how to slice *saucisson* with their little Opinel knives, teaching them the words to bawdy peasant songs that their mother did not approve of in the least ("Le

curé de Camaret" was without question their favorite), and, as it just so happens, giving them instructions on how to make a basic emergency shelter. Granted, his shelter had been intended to protect against Pyrenean blizzards and not Polynesian downpours, but she was certain it would serve its new purpose just as well. Remembering his lesson, she cut a length of the nylon rope from the survival kit and tied it securely between two carefully selected trees; she unfolded one of the three tarps and slung it over the rope, and using four small pieces of driftwood she had whittled with the utility knife, she staked down the corners. Voilà! A makeshift tent. She took a step back to appraise her work but still was not satisfied. No, the blue of the tarp was too garish, its artificial color too discordant with their primitive surroundings. She may have been the granddaughter of a peasant guide, but she was still a French architect. So she gathered up fallen fronds from the palm forest's edge and arranged them over the tent in careful layers, creating after several passes a functional and actually quite charming thatched roof. The floor, however, was still nothing more than kicked-about sand, and that she did not care for. It was tedious work, but she managed to pull off some larger frond leaves and weave them together into a sort of tropical version of a tatami mat. She put this on top of a cushioning layer of banana leaves and was pleased with the end result. It would do for sleeping, at least until she was rescued.

Shelter complete, Sophie moved on to the hearth, circling their fire pit in rocks to establish a cooking area. As for a counter space, there weren't a ton of suitable stones, but she was able to locate one larger, flat rock that she rolled through the sand to the edge of their fire pit. She found four smaller rocks, all of similar shape and size, and used those as legs, resting the flat slab upon them to create a very small but perfectly useful table.

Done. Well, almost done. There was one thing left she'd wanted to do before preparing for dinner, although she was concerned about the amount of rope it might take. She measured the coil and decided there was enough to spare; besides, they could always take it apart if needed. Using the survival kit utility knife, she began measuring out lengths, singing under her breath a bawdy mountain song that her grandfather had taught her and her brother years before, one that her mother did not approve of in the least.

Meanwhile, no longer quite so crestfallen but certainly discouraged, Barry trudged back to camp with his meager harvest of clams. Tremendous shafts of mango-colored sunlight came sloping in from the west, and the breezes whisked sea spray up from the whitecaps, spritzing the beach in a rainbow mist. Something jarringly out of place pricked at his ears; he froze for a moment to put his finger on the source.

"Sex Machine." James Brown. No mistake about it, the wind was whipping strains of its funky rhythms from around the horn of the island. Baffled, Barry picked up his pace to a steady jog, rounded the bend that preceded the camp, and dropped his jaw to an unexpected sight: a perfect, palm-thatched shelter, a small table set for two, the shortwave radio from the survival kit doing its own tinny rendition of the God-father of Soul, and, the icing on the cake, a rope hammock hanging daintily between two palms. Sophie, considerably cleaner and more composed than when he had left her, was crouched beside it, occupied with stripping a coconut of its husk.

"Wow," Barry exclaimed. "You really fixed the place up."

"It needed some work. You left it a mess." Sophie paused to push back an errant strand of chestnut hair. "Did you catch a fish?"

"No, no fish," he answered, choosing not to mention the

beast that had stolen their dinner. "But I think I found some clams." Emptying his bloated pockets, he dumped the two blue-tinted mollusks at her feet. She inspected them closely.

"*Ça marche.* I think we can eat them."

"I think so, too. I'll put them in the coals. They should cook pretty quickly, and we can have them with bananas."

"I'd rather have them with this coconut."

"Where did you find it?"

"There are just a few coconut palms on the end of the island. I saved the coconut water inside, we can drink it with dinner."

"How did you get it down from the tree?"

Sophie picked up a hunk of volcanic rock and tossed it up and down in her palm. *"Le fastball,"* she said with a slight torque of the lips that verged on a smile.

Barry did smile and celebrated their small burst of good fortune with another Russian cigarette. Three quick flicks of the Bic and it was lit, filling their wild beachhead with at least a half-civilized smell.

"Why do you think the survival kit had cigarettes, anyway?"

Sophie shrugged. "To bribe local fishermen, I presume."

Barry chuckled. "Like that would even work."

"It worked with you, didn't it?"

She had a point. Barry picked up the clams and arranged them in the coals. The palm fronds burned quick and hot and were certainly not ideal for creating coal beds, but the clams probably did not require all that much cooking. Once he was satisfied with their position, he tried out the hammock, settling gently into its web. "Sex Machine" had concluded, and a disc jockey announced the next song—"Lookin' Out My Back Door," by Creedence Clearwater Revival—in an Asian language he could not identify. He remembered hearing the

song quite often on the car radio in Cleveland, on cold winter mornings when his father drove him to school. Sometimes they'd both sing along, *Just got home from Illinois, locked the front door, oh boy . . .*

"This hammock is great," Barry remarked, locking his fingers behind his head, watching the waltz of the palm trees above.

"I'm glad you like it, because you're going to be sleeping in it."

"I am?"

"Of course. Tonight, anyway. Someone should stay outside with the flare gun for when the rescue planes come. They could pass by at night."

"Okay. Sure." The palm-thatched shelter did look inviting, but a breeze-rocked hammock wasn't a bad alternative. Barry closed his eyes; he could smell the clams now, *wow,* a goddamn clambake on a desert island in the middle of the South Pacific. Who'd believe it?

"This all feels like a dream, doesn't it?" Barry stated rather whimsically, pausing to tap a cap of ash from his Russian cigarette. "I mean, it's all so surreal, you know, both of us here, alone on this—" A hard, twisting pinch to his rib cage yanked him from his philosophizing. "Ow, shit!"

"This isn't a dream, *putain de merde.* So wake up and quit acting like a typical stupid American."

Sophie glowered at him, tremendously perturbed by something he had said. Christ, thought Barry, this French girl. He rubbed at the fresh bruise and reconsidered the situation he was in. It certainly would make a good story *someday,* having survived a plane crash and swum to an island and spent a week, maybe less, with a pretty young castaway—and after that flotilla of steaming ships came to whisk them away, he thought, he'd never have to see her again.

11

Bananas, coconuts, pools of fresh rainwater, clusters of accessible clams—the supplies that the island provided may have struck Barry and Sophie as a convenient accident, but their existence owed far more to the prescience of Polynesians than to the generosity of Providence. Barry and Sophie did not yet realize it, but they were hardly the first visitors to land on the island—in fact, early Polynesians had beaten them to it by hundreds of years. For while medieval Europeans were still clinging like frightened children to the wading pool wall of the Atlantic, these bold and inventive people were venturing into the deep end of an entire Pacific hemisphere, landing their immaculately carved outrigger canoes in such far-flung places as Samoa, Easter Island, New Zealand, Hawaii, Tahiti—and, eventually, even the tiny island that Barry and Sophie came to call home.

To those ancient Polynesians, a three-thousand-mile voyage over open seas was nothing, a mere interstate road trip to see the grandparents in Illinois. But as is the case with any good road trip, a few rest stops were in order, to stretch the legs, relieve the bladder, and restock supplies. And with Motel 6 and

Wendy's still a ways in the offing, these Polynesian adventurers had to get creative. In effect, they created their own rest stops, and Barry and Sophie's island had once been just such a place. No, the barren scrap of rock the Polynesians discovered was far too small for long-term habitation. But that didn't mean they couldn't plant a few banana trees, seed a few clam beds, release a few pigs and chickens, and stop there for the night when they needed a break. They even carved a pair of cisterns into the island's central rock face, with channels carefully chipped away to coax in the rain. The island served its purpose wonderfully, becoming a regular Howard Johnson's on the oceanic highway that connected a widely dispersed and highly peripatetic society for more than five hundred years.

Then, with the arrival of that first wave of colonially minded Europeans, all of that came to a grinding halt. By the time Gauguin landed in the Marquesas in the late nineteenth century, such times were largely forgotten, with a formerly seafaring people having become more or less sedentary in their habits and the uninhabited island in question erased from their cultural memory. It was last visited by Polynesians in the year 1762, when a Tahitian prince known to the history books as Tu-nui-ea-i-te-atua-i-Tarahoi Vairaatoa Taina Pomare spent a week there with his entourage on his way to visit distant cousins in Eiao, and last alighted upon by Westerners in 1767—Samuel Wallis of the HMS *Dolphin* dropped anchor there for the night while circumnavigating the globe, killing every wild pig and chicken on the island in the process. The coconuts, bananas, cisterns, and clam beds prevailed, however, dutifully awaiting the next batch of travelers in need of sanctuary—who, as we now know, happened to arrive almost two and a half centuries later in the form of one Barry Bleecker and one Sophie Ducel.

Not Providence, exactly, but providential indeed.

12

The night found the two fresh castaways in their designated positions—Barry cradled shirtless in the hammock, flare gun atop his belly, Sophie nested away in her shelter, trying to muffle her sobs. Barry considered checking in on her to see if she was all right but suspected such things would only result in another bilingual tongue-lashing. And frankly, he was a little afraid of her. Besides, he was an American, and a midwesterner at that—grief was far better suppressed than shared. So he remained in the hammock, staring quietly skyward, the moon above him a pearly chaperone to all manner of cosmic splendors, but sadly no blinking rescue planes or winking choppers. The closest thing was satellites, small reminders of civilized light, crawling their way through the tangle of constellations. Barry remembered them from the same Boy Scout camp that had taught him basic first aid and female anatomy. He'd received the astronomy merit badge following a full week spent under the night's perforated ceiling, and his instructor had actually known each satellite by name. "G-47-X12 should be coming along," and sure enough, a fleck of light would slip

through the stars. And Barry found comfort in that, in their lingering presence, and he wished he knew their names as well.

At some late hour, he finally took out his contacts and surrendered to the darkness, closing his eyes, drinking in the breeze. But thanks to the roughness of the ropes and his evolving sunburn, he was unable to sleep. Itchy and restless, he decided to take a crack at the shortwave radio instead. It was a portable Grundig, very much like one he had received for Christmas when he was just ten years old. He'd spent almost every night of that winter with the little radio whirring beside his pillow, adjusting the dials with a Swiss watchmaker's precision, navigating a vast ocean of static until the sweet whale song of some faraway station came rising from the deep. There was Radio Havana, Voice of Free China, Deutsche Welle, the BBC. Sure, it was no great shakes in hindsight, but to a ten-year-old Cleveland boy in a flyover state, such sounds were nothing short of magic, hints at what awaited beyond the bleak soot of the horizon. He would listen in secret, with the volume almost but not quite extinguished and the speaker pressed tightly to his ear.

And now he had at last ended up in exactly the sort of exotic, faraway locale that he had longed for as a boy, only to do exactly the same thing. But with considerably less luck. Perhaps because of solar winds or distant storms, viable stations were hard to come by. Like timid leviathans they refused to surface, remaining hidden below the rolling whitecaps of static. There was, however, *something* out there. Every so often, snatches of a disembodied voice, ghostly as sin, would come warbling through the crackling waves. Like a crossed telephone line, a conversation in the background thin as a whisper and too faint to hear. And each time it happened, Barry would press his ear even closer to the speaker, straining to make some sense of voices that he wasn't entirely sure were voices at all.

But he could not. There was no sense to make. The signals were too weak, too far away. Just comet trails, there and then gone again, drowned out and lost at sea. So he gave up trying to find them and settled instead for the comfort of static. Eventually, he dozed off and the charge on the radio wore down, the whistles settling out to a hum, the silver whiteness of that static fading into the blackness of silence. Then there was only the waves and the trees.

As for Sophie, she fell asleep shortly after Barry, after having spent most of the night gagging on her grief. She'd been able to keep it simmering quietly on the back burner for most of the day, but it came boiling back when she was all alone in the darkness. It was unbearably visceral, as if an essential organ, one that could not be replaced or transplanted, had been ripped with indifference right from her gut. Her Étienne was gone—no, much worse than gone. "Gone" was resting peacefully beneath French *platane* trees in a velvet-lined box. The place he had been dragged to was the pure stuff of nightmares, the raw substance of dread. And at the one moment he had truly needed her, his face awash in fear and regret, she'd been unable to help him, powerless to do anything. She wondered if she'd made the right choice out there in the ocean—if perhaps she should have joined him, surrendered instead and gone down by his side.

So great was her sadness, she even considered going to talk to the American, to beg him for comfort, to let him tell her that everything would be all right. But she could not. No, a French girl could not do such things, never disclose there might be a cant to the perfect posture, a shaky wheel in the noble carriage. It was impossible. So instead she let her sobs rock her to sleep, terrified of the nightmares to come but giving in at last to whatever horrors midnight might bring.

But the strangest thing. When she finally dozed off, there

were no dark things waiting for her there—no sucking whirl-
pools or circling sharks. Just her grandfather Jean-Pierre Ducel, the mountain guide from the Pyrenees with whom she had
spent her summers all those years before. He had died from a
heart attack back when she was in university, but in her dream
there he was, dressed in his wool knee breeches and red Gavarnie socks, sitting beside her, shaving off slices of *saucisson
sec* with his Laguiole knife. He smiled through the bushiness
of his mustache, told her to eat up, it was time to go. *Allons-y,
ma chérie,* he said. *Il faut avoir la niaque.* She finished the dried
sausage slices and they stood up together, brushing the pine
needles from the seats of their pants. Then they started marching upward, ever upward, clearing the spindled boles of pines,
cresting the top of an ancient ridge, entering upon a field of
pure white snow, mountains rising all around them, ancient
things that feared no sea. . . .

13

"No planes or ships during the night?"

Barry massaged the sleep out of his eyes, easing his feet over the hammock with a groan and a wince—his sunburn had worsened considerably overnight. "The French navy pulled up briefly, we had coffee and croissants, and they said they'd send for help."

"You're an *imbécile*," murmured Sophie, less than amused with his attempt at a joke.

"How did you sleep?"

"Fine," she lied. "And you?"

"Pretty well," he lied back. "Christ, I would kill for a tooth-brush."

"Maybe you can buy one on your way to get some water." She tossed him one of the plastic water bags—it bounced off his chest and fell to the sand.

"Maybe you can get it yourself."

"Do you want breakfast or not?"

"Breakfast? What . . ." And then he sniffed. Eggs. Some-how, she was cooking eggs. He squinted down over her shoulder

and noticed the little omelet she was prodding atop a small driftwood fire, using one of their stainless-steel drinking cups as a pan.

"Whoa! Where did you get that?"

"I found two eggs in a bird's nest by the rocks."

Barry felt a slight inkling of appreciation, perhaps even admiration, but was at a loss for how best to express it. "I'll go get some water" was all he said, putting in his contacts from the case and gathering up the water bag.

"*Bon.* And try to get some more eggs, too, while you're at it."

"I don't know about the eggs, but I can definitely bring back some more bananas."

He plodded off across the sand toward the island's interior, shaking his head. It was the infuriating insouciance with which she said it—she might as well have been asking him to grab a baguette on his way home from work. God, these ridiculous French.

Barry did have to admit, though, the interior of the island was growing on him. It was a nice respite from all that sea and sand, and although certainly different in terms of its foliage, it was not entirely unlike a midwestern forest. The undergrowth was tough on the soles of his feet, and the insects there were more of a nuisance, but it was peaceful, a silence tended to by the comforting rustle of trees rather than the disconcerting roll of the surf. In fact, it was almost pleasant. He wrested a bunch of green bananas from a shaggy tree and slung it over his sunburned shoulder, gaining in doing so the courage—audacity, even—to whistle, with the insouciance of someone grabbing a six-pack of beer at a bodega after work. God, these ridiculous Americans, he snickered to himself.

And the water was spectacular. Barry hadn't realized how

parched he was. At the two freshwater pools in the mountain's rocky base, he quenched his thirst with wild abandon, drinking it down in tremendous gulps. Once adequately hydrated, he dunked the water bag under, let it fill, and sealed the top. He gazed up past the rock ledges, at the pillar of seabirds that circled above, their cries that morning unduly harsh—maybe they were upset about the missing eggs. He didn't see any nests with eggs nearby, but he did notice a single white feather on one of the rocks, and something about it appealed to him. He picked it up and decided to take it back for Sophie. Who knows? Maybe she'd like it.

Barry returned to the beach along the same path, stepping carefully over the prickly undergrowth, whistling all the while. He emerged from the palms to the low burble of the short-wave radio—Sophie must have found another station. He saw her crouched next to it, listening intently, and the signal was strong, probably local. And it was in French.

"Hey, what's—"

"Shhh!" It was a hiss, really, almost violent in its intensity.

Barry set down the water and the bananas and stood beside her. The broadcast sounded like a news bulletin; he recognized not the words, but the calm, informative inflection of the voice.

Then, abruptly, the broadcast cut to Polynesian music. Guitars and singing. Distant drums. Sophie looked stunned. She covered her face with her hands and released a moan unlike anything Barry had heard before.

"What is it?" Barry repeated. He knelt at her side.

"They've called off the search." She turned to him, her lips quivering, eyes bleeding tears. "We are presumed dead. *Ils pensent que nous sommes morts.*"

Right then and there, the trapdoor on both their lives

clicked and fell out from under them. A brief, sinking sensation, and then the cold thump of reality. No one was looking for them. Not one boat, not one soul.

The restraint on Sophie's sorrow finally snapped. Unable to bear any more, she fell into Barry's arms, sobbing uncontrollably. He held her tightly and stared straight ahead, too stunned to cry, too shocked to move. The white feather fell to the sand, trembled there for a moment, and was blown away with the wind. The omelet was burning. And the waves, at that moment the only reliable, constant thing in either of their lives, kept up their rhythm, kept rolling in.

14

What could a part-time techno DJ from London and an aging war veteran from Japan possibly have to do with the story at hand? On first perusal of their biographies, the answer is not much at all. But with a closer look, it becomes more than one might think. For although exceedingly disparate in age group and origin, the techno DJ in question—Nigel Braddock, aka DJ Dirty Dolphin—and the Japanese war veteran of interest— Takehiko Ishigaki, former crewman of the I-25 submarine in the Imperial Japanese Navy—do have one terribly relevant thing in common: They were the only two living human beings, besides Barry and Sophie, of course, who were even aware of the island's existence.

In regard to young Nigel, he first learned of the island while a student at university, just prior to beginning his career in disc jockeying. As a teenager, one dreary afternoon among many in his parents' home on Kensington Church Street, he had become engrossed in the movie *Mutiny on the Bounty*. This was due in part to a latent crush on a young and exceedingly strapping Marlon Brando, but also to the glory of the bygone era it

portrayed. It was directly because of that spark that six years later, while struggling to pick a topic for his history dissertation at Cambridge, he chose to write on the exploits of the very Fletcher Christian so gallantly played by the American actor. Only his thesis adviser already had a student tackling that very same subject. Why don't you look into Captain Samuel Wallis? the adviser suggested, a man who also happened to be the last person to set foot on Barry and Sophie's desolate atoll. Nigel agreed, and he stumbled across a mention of the island while skimming the captain's log in the National Archives. The antiquated hand verged on illegible, but he was able to untangle from that skein of inky lines something about killing wild pigs on a nameless beach bereft of men. Intrigued, he decided to include it in his dissertation, to bolster his thesis on the viability of supply chains in England's eighteenth-century Pacific expansion. But alas, the academic community at Cambridge was destined never to learn of the island's existence. For in addition to British colonialism in the South Pacific, Nigel Braddock had developed a serious interest in the electronic music that was sweeping London in the late 1990s. How could musty old tomes compete with the seductive beats of Digweed and Oakenfold? Inspired more by his musical heroes than his historical ones, Nigel dropped out of university and began taking low-paying DJ gigs in the smaller clubs of London, neglecting, but never forgetting entirely, his earlier passion. In fact, he took his DJ moniker from the name of Captain Wallis's ship, the HMS *Dolphin*. And when the gigs in London petered out, he moved to Manchester, where he did find happiness, if not success.

In the case of Takehiko Ishigaki, he became aware of the island long before Nigel was even born. The son of a fisherman from Wakayama Prefecture, he had enlisted in the Imperial Japanese Navy at the age of eighteen, where he was

thrust into almost immediate combat aboard the soon-to-become-legendary I-25 submarine, under the adroit command of Meiji Tagami. In the submarine's stifling hold, he bore underwater witness to some of the most important battles of World War II, including one of the very few attacks on the American mainland. Most of their time, however, was spent far out at sea, conducting reconnaissance missions on lost little islands that might possibly have harbored Allied landing strips. The submarine remained submerged during the day, but it would surface at night, allowing those on watch duty to get some fresh air. On one such night, while Takehiko stood alone at its prow, enjoying the low chugging of the diesel engine and the parting of starlit waters, he caught sight of a form rising in the distance. His instincts flinched, for he feared it was a ship, but upon closer inspection, he realized it was nothing more than a very small island, alone and whispering in the dead of the night. He entertained a brief urge to leap from the I-25 and swim to its sands, bidding farewell forever to the mingled horror and boredom of that terrible war. But Takehiko's daydreams—or nightdreams, rather—were that and nothing more. He stayed on board the submarine, did his duty with honor, and was left clinging to flotsam when the vessel was destroyed by the USS *Patterson* near the New Hebrides islands in 1943, the sole survivor of a ninety-man crew. When he saw the Americans coming to pick him up, he considered committing seppuku with the knife at his belt, but in the end decided, *Fuck honor,* which sounds much nicer in Japanese, and he let them scoop him out of the waves. He was knocked around a bit belowdecks, but once he began cooperating with his interrogators, he was otherwise treated well—sailors tended to share more camaraderie with their opponents than foot soldiers, for they all knew that their true enemy was not the man at the rudder, but the cold, dark sea. He spent a very strange

two years at Camp Deming in New Mexico, where he stood out like a sore thumb among all the blond and lumbering Germans, before eventually being returned to his village in Wakayama. In the years that followed, he did his best to forget about the war, and his many dead comrades, although he lit an incense stick each year to honor their memory, and he still had the occasional dream about an island drifting rootless in the darkness, one he had almost leapt to in the night.

So why mention these two at all? To establish the fact that even if poor Marco "Ding Dong" Mercado had managed to signal back some feeble concept of his general location before the lightning fried his radio, and even *if* the outdated radar equipment at the airstrip in Tahiti had been able to keep a rough log of the plane's movements, rescue still would have proven difficult. The island was, with a couple of very inconsequential exceptions, unknown to man. And unless some rescue pilot or search boat captain was lucky enough to catch a glimmer in his rearview mirror of that little speck of land, *and* on top of that notice the brief spark of an emergency flare, he would have had no reason, or even inkling, to go there. It was not listed on navigation charts; it was too small to warrant mapping. It was, for all intents and purposes, lost to the world. It may have been Marco's poor judgment that had put Barry and Sophie on its sands, but it was through no fault of his that they remained there. Geography and time had simply conspired against them. They had left the known world behind them and joined the ranks of all those aforementioned castaways in the unknown world beyond.

As such, five fruitless days after Marco's Cessna took a nosedive into the ocean, the search was called off, sending a small armada of ships and reconnaissance planes back empty-handed to the French naval base in Tahiti. A reluctant call was placed from the U.S. consular agent in French Polynesia to Barry's

parents in Cleveland, who had been waiting anxiously by the phone since the Tahitian airline had first informed them that their son was missing. Sophie's parents, in their village outside Toulouse, received a similar phone call from the Départements et Territoires d'Outre-Mer. Although the languages were different, the content was identical—there was always room for hope, but it was very unlikely that their respective child was still with the living. In both countries, phones were dropped, sweaters were sobbed upon, and bouts of delirious grief bilingually ensued.

In the media, the story received little coverage, given the small size of the plane and its limited number of passengers. Both *The New York Times* and *Le Monde* made mention of it in passing, however, with single-column articles buried inconsequentially toward the back. INVESTMENT BANKER PRESUMED DEAD IN FRENCH POLYNESIA, read the headline of the former; LUNE DE MIEL MORTELLE POUR DEUX ARCHITECTES PARISIENS, proclaimed the bold print of the latter.

Neither was completely correct. As a bond salesman at Lehman Brothers, Barry was an investment banker in only the loosest sense of the term, and a recently retired one at that. As for Sophie, the honeymoon had proven fatal for only one Parisian architect, certainly not two. And for both survivors, their banishment from the world was consequential indeed.

15

"What are we going to do?"

Sophie spoke first, and for the first time since he'd met her, she sounded less angry than afraid.

Barry rubbed his face in an exasperated fashion, feeling the unfamiliar stubble of an incipient beard. He was tempted to say, *I don't have a goddamn clue,* but somehow knew he could not. This may have been the time for despair, but it was not the place for uncertainty.

"We'll wait. Even if they've called off the search, someone could still come by. Boats could pass, or a plane could fly overhead. We have the flare gun, and we can spell out SOS in rocks on the sand."

"What about food?"

Barry poked at the fire with a bone-white piece of driftwood, pushing the pot with the blackened remains of the eggs away from the coals. "Well, hopefully your next Denver omelet will turn out better than this one."

"Je suis sérieuse."

Barry set down the stick of driftwood, considered it for a

moment. "There are clams. I saw some fish over by the little cove. There are at least a few coconuts. And bananas. Christ, there's a ton of bananas."

Sophie nearly retched at the thought—Étienne had always been partial to the fruit; she'd made him *bananes flambées* every year for his birthday, and she'd carved them onto his muesli each morning before work. The notion of actually subsisting upon them made her nauseous with grief. But of course she would never say that to the American.

"I don't want to spend my life eating nothing but fucking bananas" was all that she told him.

"You'll probably have a pretty short life, then" was all he said in reply.

And he regretted it as soon as it was out of his mouth. But Barry felt entitled to administer a cold dose of reality, given the inordinately painful pinch of it she had dosed him with back in the hammock. After an uncomfortable silence lasting nearly a minute, he wisely changed the subject.

"What made you decide to go to the Marquesas, anyway? They're a little out of the way, aren't they?"

Sophie did her best Gallic puff. "Jacques Brel."

"The singer?"

Sophie nodded, flicking some kind of small beetle off her arm before settling back in the sand. "We originally planned to spend the entire trip in Tahiti, but I read that Jacques Brel had lived on the Marquesas, and that he was buried there. It was a short flight, we were only going to stay a few nights. It was all my idea, so I suppose in a way this is entirely my fault."

Sophie began to choke up. Barry froze, uncertain what to do. He felt an obligation to extend a hand for comfort or offer some form of condolence but was almost certain that she would slap both away. But after a long, shaky breath, she regained her composure.

"What about you?" she asked, reassuming her mildly annoyed tone.

Barry pushed a jet of ironic air through his nostrils to complement Sophie's earlier *pfff* and managed a weak smile. "Paul Gauguin. He's always been my favorite artist. He's buried on the Marquesas, too—right next to Jacques Brel, I believe."

"You flew all the way from New York to some island in the middle of the Pacific just to see the grave of Paul Gauguin?"

He had to admit, when described as such, it did sound improbable, if not flat-out ridiculous. Of course, there was more to it than that, but he didn't feel like going into it at that moment.

"Yeah, something like that."

"Rather romantic for an American, *non*? I thought you people just worked all the time, watched TV in your big houses, and ate terrible food."

"That's the whole reason I left. And speaking of terrible food, we should probably eat the eggs, even if they're burnt. It is protein."

Sophie grimaced in disgust. "*Dégueulasse.* You can eat them."

"Suit yourself." Barry lifted the little pot by the handle and used his fingers to shovel the charred remains of the omelet into his mouth. The flavor was sharp and acrid, but then again, so was his hunger. "Why don't we turn the radio back on? Some music might be nice."

"*D'accord.*"

Sophie gave the little generator handle a few cranks and clicked it on, to the same Tahitian French-language station they'd been listening to before. It was playing "Ne me quitte pas" by Jacques Brel.

"You have to be kidding me," Sophie snarled, before snapping off the radio. "*Putain de merde.*"

Barry burst out laughing—laughter tinged with darkness,

possibly even madness, but laughter nonetheless. Sophie resisted for a moment and then joined in. Honestly, by that point, her grief expended, her tears depleted, she didn't know what else to do.

The hours passed, and the sky turned a luminous peach before reddening and darkening to the tar pitch of night. Barry and Sophie sat on the beach and watched the slow surrender of the day, not saying much, both considering what this new development meant. Both thought about their friends and family, who were surely worried about them, if not totally distraught. And there was nothing they could do, not one single means by which they might telegraph their status and ease their concern. *I'm alive, I'm here. . . . Je suis ici, Maman. . . .* With luck and a little adjustment the shortwave could pick up incoming signals, but it was a painfully one-way conversation. The frustration of that fact was beyond description, the silent despair of Ebenezer Scrooge watching events unfold as a ghost, the longing of the wrongfully imprisoned to have the truth be told. The only human being either could talk to was sitting in the sand three feet away.

It was Barry who spoke first.

"We need a plan."

Sophie turned her head, which had been resting on her tucked-up knees; she was wearing his shirt again, buttoned high against the cool night air. "What do you mean?"

"Well, we don't know how long we're going to be stuck here. It could be a while. I think we should make a plan for how to live here. We should walk around the island tomorrow, take note of everything, and see what we have to work with."

"You mean like a system?"

"I guess so. I think a good start would be to figure out what food we have, and how much we can eat."

"*D'accord*. I can do that with you."

"We should climb the little mountain there, too." He gestured with his head in the direction of the six-story cairn that formed the island's spine. "We'll get a better view of what's around us."

"Do you think there might be another island near?"

"Maybe. I mean, there are lots of little islands in this part of the Pacific. And if we see one, we can get to it on the raft. It still works, right?"

Sophie sat up and nodded. "I think so."

"We'll see." Barry patted down his pockets for the pack of Russian cigarettes, finding nothing. "Do you have the smokes?"

"They're in the shelter. Do you want me to get them?"

Barry thought for a moment and shook his head. "Nah. Now's probably a good time to quit. If there is another island nearby, I'm going to have some serious paddling ahead of me." He flashed a smile at her, a sly grin flush with confidence. He wasn't sure where it was coming from, but he had summoned it from somewhere. Unlike his hardy midwestern forebears, he'd had no Great War in which to prove his manhood, no Great Depression to test his mettle. Perhaps this uninhabited island in the South Pacific was his Normandy beach, his own personal and palm-lined Dust Bowl. He had cheated death, he was still alive, and sometimes that fact alone was enough. "Now, let's go eat some *fucking* bananas."

Barry rose from the sand and brushed himself off; he offered his hand to help Sophie up, and to his surprise, she actually took it. She even said *merci*.

16

The question may not have occurred to Barry and Sophie, who certainly had more pressing issues weighing on their minds, but it does merit asking: How, exactly, did a postimpressionist painter of the late nineteenth century and a Belgian *chanteur* from the middle of the twentieth come to be buried within feet of each other on one of the most isolated islands in the world? And more important, what was it about Paul Gauguin and Jacques Brel that convinced the two of them to visit their graves in the first place? To answer both questions, a little comparative history is probably in order:

It's the year 1884, the impressionist movement is in full swing across Europe, and a young stockbroker by the name of Eugène Henri Paul Gauguin is not very happy at all. Stuck in a dead-end job, married to a Danish woman accustomed to the comforts of a decent, bourgeois life, and unable to tend to his beloved paints, he feels trapped, bound by conventions he cannot understand. His bohemian friends down in the quarter—Pissarro, Cézanne, and that Dutch oddball Van Gogh—see promise in him and urge him to devote himself

full-time to his passion. After much arguing with his comfort-
ably middle-class wife, he finally does, leaving behind the
stock market forever. In the poverty that follows, she in turn
leaves him, taking their five children right along with her. One
can almost hear her voice berating him on her way out the
door: "What the hell is the matter with you, Paul?" He sighs,
he slumps beside his first half-finished canvas, he does not
know.

Gauguin is quite certain, however, that he needs to get out
of Paris. Unable to find his artistic voice amid the ruins of his
life, he decides to leave it all behind forever and seek inspiration in a place that might prove gentler on the spirit. After
several years of struggling as a painter and bouncing around
the artist colonies of France, he packs his bags and jumps a
steamer bound for the French colonies in Polynesia. Settling
first in Tahiti, and later the Marquesas, he at last finds the inspiration that had previously eluded him, in a place and among
a people that set fire to his soul. In his new environs, his
faculties flourish, and he produces painting after wondrous
painting, helping to birth postimpressionism in the process.
On May 8, 1903, a fifty-four-year-old Paul Gauguin finally
bids the earthly firmament a final adieu and is buried in the
Cimetière Calvaire, on the Marquesan island of Hiva Oa.
He never did come to realize the profound impact his paintings
would have on the art world during his lifetime, nor could he
have possibly known that seventy-four years later, when a traveling exhibition of his work happened to alight at the small
but respectable Cleveland Museum of Art, a ten-year-old Barry
Bleecker, brought there by his mother as a present for his birthday, would stand fixated and bewitched before the sun-ripened
curves and alluring eyes of *The Spirit of the Dead Watching* and
decide, with boyish determination, what he wanted to be when
he grew up.

A painter. Just like Monsieur Paul Gauguin.

Years pass, times change, it is now 1973 in Paris, and a middle-aged *chanson* star named Jacques Brel is also not feeling very well at all. After several grueling decades of pouring his heart and soul into every performance, his will and body are both giving out. He knows he is not in good health, and his doctor only confirms what he has suspected for some time—his days on this earth are numbered. Against his doctor's advice, however, the world-famous singer decides he'd rather spend his life's dwindling remainder sailing around the world with his wife than wasting away in some hospital ward. He drops a sizable chunk of his fortune on a sixty-foot sailing yacht, tells his wife to pack her bags and bring along a bathing suit, and casts off into the great blue yonder. And as fate would have it, after puttering around the various ports of the globe, destiny blows him right into Atuona Bay, at Hiva Oa in the Marquesas. And there, amid the blue honey water and white sugar sands and wide-open smiles of the native Polynesians, he knows he has finally found the place— not where he wants to die, but, rather, where he wants to live. Just like Gauguin before him, he had been searching for a land that was gentler on his spirit, only to discover an island that set fire to his soul. He is happier there than he has ever been in his life, and five years later, when the tumor he'd been trying to outrun finally catches up to him, his body is laid to rest in the very same cemetery on Hiva Oa as the bold postimpressionist who preceded him, their graves literally only yards apart. Jacques may have had some inkling of the great influence he'd had on the musicians of his day, but he would never come to know the full extent of his legacy—particularly that four years after his death, a nine-year-old Sophie Caroline Ducel would be sitting in her grandparents' cottage deep in the Pyrenees, nestled snugly beneath the Brèche de Roland in the

peaks of Gavarnie, singing along with her *grand-père* to an old phonograph record of "Dans le port d'Amsterdam"—his favorite song—while her dear *grand-mère* shelled beans for a cassoulet, too shy to sing but not too timid to hum.

Two very different individuals indeed, ending up on the same remote island because of a common dream.

17

Barry and Sophie woke early the next morning, just before sunrise, to a sky that still held at its rim the faint ghosts of stars. Sophie rose first, crawling out from the palm shelter and stifling a yawn. Barry opened his eyes moments later, roused by the sound of her sipping water. He set the flare gun on the ground and swung his feet over the hammock's side, letting them both land squarely on the dew-damp sand. He plunked in his contacts from the case in his pocket, stood up straight, and looked right at her; they had both slept soundly through the night for the first time since their arrival.

"Bonjour," she said, handing him the water bag.

"Bonjour," Barry replied in his best approximation of conversational French.

"Ça va?" she asked.

"Oui," Barry answered, *"ça va."* He skinned a pair of leftover bananas and handed one her way with a *"Bon appétit"*—which, to his surprise, she actually accepted. She said something back to him that was beyond his proficiency, but he took a strategic bite to disguise that fact. Together they chewed their

starchy breakfast and watched the crowning of a newborn sun light up the waters, ushering in a whole new day.

After their banana breakfast and separate trips into the palms to alleviate bodily necessities, Barry and Sophie decided that the first step in their plan would be to better organize the camp. The deflated raft was rolled up in the duffel bag and stowed away in the shelter for safekeeping, alongside the various elements of the survival kit—excluding the flare gun, which they both agreed should be kept on hand at all times. Water and bananas, their quotidian staples, would always remain by the entrance for easy access at night. And following the aforementioned trips into the trees, it was also agreed that a latrine ought to be dug, situated a good, hygienically responsible distance away from the camp. Using the plastic oars from the raft as shovels, they cut a shallow but functional toilette from the sandy soil, in a clearing surrounded by palms for at least a hint of privacy. Barry carted in a shirtful of sand to be used for covering up that which was left behind and had the honor shortly thereafter of putting the new facilities to the test. He would have killed for a *National Geographic* to look at but settled instead for a swarming gnat cloud and the knotty burls of old palm trunks—not quite the glossy images he was accustomed to, but about as geographic as it gets.

The rest of the afternoon was devoted to conducting a survey of the island's food sources. Of course, neither Barry nor Sophie was aware of the scientific names or natural histories of their potential foodstuffs; in some cases, they weren't even sure that what they were looking at was edible. In a survival situation, however, primordial instincts kick in, and both began to see the world through a fresh pair of hunter-gatherer's eyes.

First and foremost, there were the ubiquitous bananas. Stubby, green, and riddled with buckshotlike seeds, they were

close enough to the familiar Chiquita to be edible but still wild enough to propagate without assistance from man—which was precisely why, unbeknownst to Barry and Sophie, the ancient mariners of the South Pacific had planted them there in the first place. They attempted a rough census of their number but quickly realized that the banana plants were bountiful beyond counting. With a shared gulp and a sigh of resignation, they both came to the realization that the green bunches that surrounded them would essentially be their daily bread.

It wasn't all bananas, however. There was also the small grove of coconut palms on the island's lee, with nuts rich in both milk and meat. A pass by the rocky cove revealed more maxima clams than Barry had initially estimated, not to mention a few strands of washed-up seaweed that did seem edible, if only they could find more of it. The boulder-studded mountain in the island's middle was speckled with nests of the sooty tern, more than a few of which cradled a very edible egg. And of course, the waters around them did hold fish. Paddletail snappers out by the reef, black jacks that traveled in slow-moving schools, and even the occasional mahi-mahi. However, the only decent fishing spot on the island was the very same cove where that exceedingly large octopod—theatrically dubbed "Balthazar" by Sophie when Barry pointed the creature out to her—lurked in the shadows, ready to pilfer whatever bit on the line.

And that was pretty much it. A few coconuts to contribute some much-needed electrolytes and lipids, the occasional clam to put a little protein in their diet, a sooty tern egg now and then to bump up the calorie count, the odd fish when Balthazar might happen to be sleeping, and other than that, bushel upon bushel of bright green bananas.

Their food survey concluded, Barry and Sophie decided on a quick water break before scaling the mountain. Swatting

gnats and fanning themselves with banana leaves, they made their way to the drinking pools at its base. They splashed water on the backs of their necks and faces, and they drank it in gulps from the cupped bowls of their hands. For comfort's sake, Sophie briefly unfastened the rear clasp of her bra strap and scratched at a welt that had formed beneath it.

"So tell me something," Barry began, politely opting to avert his eyes. "How did your English get so good?"

"I do not sink zat my English is zat good," she answered with a mocking smile and a comically thick Maurice Chevalier accent.

"It's a lot better than my French."

"I could know five words, and it would still be better than your French."

"I sing a mean 'Frère Jacques.'"

"No, trust me, you don't."

"Well, I'll sing 'Alouette' next if you don't tell me how you learned English."

"Please don't. It was the Beatles."

"What about them?"

"My parents loved the Beatles. I listened to Beatles songs all the time growing up. I memorized all the words. We all live in a yellow submarine. She loves you, yeah, yeah, yeah. Eleanor Bigby."

"It's Eleanor Rigby. And there's got to be more than Beatles songs."

She shrugged nonchalantly. "I guess there was Lisbon, too."

"In Portugal?"

"*Oui*. I studied architecture there for my Erasmus year through a program with my university in Montpellier."

"But what does that have to do with English?"

"I didn't speak Portuguese. Nobody there spoke French. English was the easiest way to communicate. All of our classes

were in English, too. Étienne was the only one in the city I spoke French with. That was actually when we started going out. I knew him from my university, but we weren't together until our study abroad year in Lisbon."

She had never specifically mentioned her husband before. Barry felt a sharp pang of regret for bringing it up and had to imagine she did, too. He waited to be certain she would not choke up again before saying what he had been meaning to for quite some time.

"I'm sorry, by the way. I can't imagine what this must be like for you. He seemed like a very good person."

"*Merci*. He was. But honestly, I really can't handle thinking about all that right now. So let's talk about something else."

"Like what?"

"Like why you flew all the way to the Marquesas straight from the office to see the grave of Paul Gauguin. I know there's something you're not telling me."

Barry blushed, suddenly self-conscious—he hadn't told anyone the full story, and in hindsight it seemed utterly asinine. "It's pretty stupid."

"Most of the things men do are. Just tell me."

He took a deep breath. "When I was a kid back in Cleveland, my mom took me to see a traveling exhibition of his work at the art museum. I loved it—something about it really made an impression on me, and I decided at that moment that I wanted to be an artist when I grew up."

"Ooh, the impressionists made an impression on you. But let me guess. You didn't become an artist."

Barry shook his head. "Nope. When I was eighteen, I sent my portfolio to Parsons, and I also applied to Princeton. I got into both, but everyone told me I should go to Princeton, so I did. And after graduation, I applied to an M.F.A. program at the School of Visual Arts, but also for a sales position on Wall

Street. I was accepted by both, but everyone told me I should get into finance, so I did." Barry cringed uncomfortably. "For twelve years."

"So what happened?"

"Nothing. Nothing happened. I had pretty much given up. I hated my life, I was miserable, but I had security and comfort, and I was too scared to leave it behind and venture off into the unknown like that."

"Something must have changed, then."

Barry nodded. "It did. Last month, another Gauguin exhibition came to the Metropolitan Museum of Art in New York. And like an idiot, I went."

Barry tactfully left out the part about the panic attack, and the hyperventilating, and the hour he spent weeping inconsolably in the museum cafeteria, while Ashley, still his girlfriend at the time, filed her nails and stared absently out the window.

Sophie smiled with eyebrows fully arched—maybe there was more to this *imbécile d'américain* than she had thought. "Let me guess. You decided there, in front of all those beautiful paintings of half-naked Polynesian women, to finally quit and become an artist. In a fit of self-righteous enthusiasm, you bought some tubes of Sennelier, some brand-new Kolinsky brushes, and you flew out to see your idol Paul Gauguin, hoping to find inspiration like he did far away from civilization, lost among the palm trees."

Barry put his face in his hands and shook his head, tingling with embarrassment. "Yep. Pretty much."

"Well, congratulations. Mission accomplished. I'm not Polynesian, but you can paint me if you like."

"Find me some oil paints and brushes, and I will."

"Deal." They exchanged ironic, amused glances, leaning back against the volcanic rocks, lost among the palm trees, at

the very least. "It is very noble of you," Sophie went on, "but you know, it's a dead medium. Nobody paints anymore."

"Well, it will be even deader if nobody tries."

"English isn't my first language, but I'm fairly confident that 'deader' is not a word. If something is dead, then it's dead."

"Then maybe someone can revive it."

"And you'll be the one to keep it alive?"

"I don't know. At the moment, I'm mostly worried about preserving my own life."

"Touché." Sophie nudged him teasingly but approvingly with her foot. "So who do you like, then, besides Gauguin? Let me guess. You had a poster of *Starry Night* in your bedroom, and Monet's floating lily pads. A little Pablo, perhaps?"

"No way, Picasso was a phony. He just copied his starving artist friends and took credit for their work. He never suffered for his art."

"And you've suffered for yours, Mr. Wall Street banker?"

She had a point. He winced at the insight. "No, I suppose I haven't."

"All right, so no Picasso. Who else, then?"

"Hopper, Balthus, Wyeth, John French Sloan, Hughie Lee-Smith," Barry answered, rattling off the names like old friends. "And there's a painting I love at the art museum in Cleveland by John Rogers Cox, but he's not well-known."

Sophie did another one of her most disapproving puffs. "I'm afraid your tastes are a little old-fashioned for me."

"Then let *me* guess. Your bedroom walls were smothered in Warhols and Basquiats. You get hot for Jeff Koons and Matthew Barney."

"More like Louise Bourgeois and Yayoi Kusama, but you're not far off. Anyway, I like photography more than paintings."

"Architects usually do. I'm sure you have a coffee table book of the Bechers sitting in your living room, too."

"We don't have coffee table books in France. *C'est juste pour les Américains.*" She voiced the last word with uncloaked disdain.

"Too bad, they're nice to look at."

"Coffee table books or Americans?"

"Both."

There was a moment of tension strung taut as a tennis racket, and then they both dispelled it with a laugh. What did it matter, anyway? Barry reciprocated her nudge and rose to his feet.

"Come on, let's climb up to the top. We're going to find another island and get the hell out of here."

"You think so?"

"Absolutely. I'll send you a coffee table book of Gauguin paintings as soon as we both get home."

"I don't have a coffee table."

"Then I'll send one of those, too."

Barry led the way, mounting the first round of boulders with two brisk lunges, lending Sophie a hand to help her do so as well. From that initial perch, they made their way with steady determination up the steep ledge of rocks. It was sweaty work, but once they had cleared the tops of the palm trees, the wind came in stronger, smelling fresher, of open sea and open sky. They stopped briefly to breathe it in, then continued on their way. Halfway up, the terns took notice, erupting with great squawks from their nests, circling above them in a wild frenzy. "Watch out for bird shit," Barry shouted over his shoulder; Sophie puffed out her cheeks and smiled back up in reply. They proceeded onward and upward, with forethought and care, testing each rock before lending it their weight. Not that the ascent was terribly difficult, but they both knew no one would help them in the event of an accident. Sophie asked Barry if he could see any other islands. No, not yet, he answered, but we're almost there. Ten feet above him, he could

make out the summit, where the mountain's steep sides flattened to a plateau—the crest of their island and the top of their world. Barry pushed himself up over it with his forearms as if climbing out of a swimming pool, Sophie did the same a moment behind him. They hobbled to their knees and stood upright; panting and squinting, they peered at the view their climbing had won them.

And in an instant, just like that, their buoyant mood went as flat as the remains of the rescue raft. It was a view full of splendor, but devoid of hope. No misty islands were waiting on the ocean's edge. No distant cliffs caught surf across the waves. Just a tight perimeter of turquoise, and beyond that, a nauseating amount of deep oceanic blue. Nothing but an infinity of open sea in every direction one could turn, interrupted only by a tide of dark thunderheads gathering in the west. Barry's confidence wilted; whatever general goodwill had been restored in Sophie shrank alongside it. She treated the entire universe to several moments of disparaging silence, clutching her own shoulders in a jacket of despair. Then, still without a word, she slid sideways over the edge and began to make her way back down.

"Where are you going?" Barry asked.

"Swimming," she answered with a cold indifference he found deeply unsettling.

"Are you sure?" He remembered her terror when he had first pulled her from the raft, away from the sea.

"*Oui.*"

"Want me to come with you?"

"*Non.*"

The words were peremptory and served with a sting. He let her go.

Ten minutes later she reappeared in miniature below, walking across the beach, stripping off her meager clothing, and

shaking out her hair. Barry watched her slip naked into the low waves, then turn on her back in an attitude of total repose and absolute surrender. At the end of his own emotional rope, he lay down on the rocks high above her and did the same. The two of them, though an island apart, stared up at the sky together for quite some time. Sophie waited to see if a shark would drag her under and put an end to her misery. One did not, although a school of diminutive fish did tickle her toes. Barry lay as close to the heavens as possible and waited to find out if lightning can strike twice. It can, but on that evening it did not oblige—the thunderheads dissipated without so much as a rumble, and the sun slipped down beneath a burnished copper sea, and then that day was over, too.

Crap, thought Barry as it suddenly occurred to him: He had only two extra pairs of contacts left.

PART TWO

18

The American art students catch a cab from the cemetery and have their breakfast at a café on boulevard Voltaire. Their ears are still ringing from their night at the discotheque, and their eyes are red rimmed from the cigarette smoke. They do their best to keep alive the excitement of it all, and for a while they succeed. Oh, my God, like, I can't believe you gave that guy in the turtleneck your number, one snickers. Whoever said the number I gave him was *mine,* another replies. Forget the club, interjects the third—I want to talk about what happened at that grave. I mean, like, do you think anyone's ever going to believe us?

By the time the dishes are cleared and the coffees finished, however, what lingers of their elation has begun to wear thin. They yawn, they rub their eyes. They ask for *l'addition,* and the spell is broken. The giddiness of their drunks has finally worn off, and they're ready to go back to their dorm rooms in the Latin Quarter. All except the girl with the bangs and the blue jeans, whose name is Mona. She decides to hang back, bidding her friends farewell as they step outside into the bright

light and church bells. Are you sure you don't want to come back with us? they ask. It's totally cool if you want to crash on our couch. She says thank you but that she should probably go back to her own place. Unlike them, she's on financial aid and has to rent a cheaper *chambre de bonne* in the tenth, on a derelict street called Château d'Eau.

She watches them get into another taxi and purr away. Then she turns her head into the sun and closes her eyes, alone at last, smiling bittersweetly. She loves this city, at times more than she can bear, but it also makes her unbearably sad. It doesn't seem to affect her other American friends in that way at all, though. They claim to "get the French" (which is a lie, nobody gets the French, not even the French) and to feel at home in Paris (also a dubious claim, no one except the homesick is truly at home there). But she has the distinct sense that their impressions are far different from hers. For them, the semester abroad from art school seems to be a pseudobohemian spring break of sorts. A brief rest stop on their path to graduation and then high-paying jobs at graphic design firms—a path she swore she never would take but now feels increasingly resigned to as well. They try to show off their shoddy French in cafés, while Mona, whose French is actually quite good, is timid about using it. They mention ancient streets casually, hinting at an unearned intimacy, while Mona, who knows them all too well, is hesitant to even evoke their names. Having just turned twenty-one, she is very young, and the city is very old, and she is excited and terrified to be part of it, to measure herself against it. So much history, so many lives . . . she shudders just thinking about it but smiles all the same. Her parents were right—it is definitely *not* like Pittsburgh.

Mona should be tired, but she isn't. Being on her own has left her inexplicably energized. Inspired by the sighting at the cemetery—after all, how often in life does something like that

happen?—she decides to go over to the Pompidou and complete the story. A bit of closure, perhaps. She is the only one in the group who has not seen his exhibition, but then again, she is the only one in the group who has not done a great many things.

She cuts through the quarter on rue Oberkampf, gets off it as quickly as she can—it's still in shambles from the previous night—and crisscrosses through alleyways, until the bold architecture of the museum rises from all the wrought iron and slate. A cathedral, she thinks, to all things promising and new. It's early enough that a line has yet to form, so she breezes right in, flashing her student ID for a well-deserved discount. A series of multilingual signs ushers her to the exhibition, which she approaches anxiously, filled with wonder. Her pace slows, her pulse quickens; this is it, what everyone's been talking about.

The entrance is guarded by a primitive-looking canoe suspended from the ceiling, with a strange array of objects hanging down from its sides—ticket stubs, family photos, cigarette packets, even a little rubber octopus—each attached to a fishing hook on a line. The sense of meaning they emit is imposing but indecipherable; the hovering mementos seem like fragments of an unsettling dream. *Askoy III* is carved into the prow, a name as mysterious as the sculpture itself. It feels out of place, a relic from a natural history museum, perhaps, the sole artifact of a vanished people. Why it is here at the entrance, she does not know. There's a story to be told, but she has a hunch it is one she will never fully understand.

The paintings inside, however, are beautiful—incredible— their haunting black and white pigments hovering somewhere in the murky border between the abstract and the real. One of her friends had compared them with Pat Steir's, but no, coloration aside, these are something else entirely. Murals, really,

they are immense in both scope and character, taking up entire walls. Up close, they seem to depict blending bands of nocturnal shade; a few steps back, they reveal solitary islands, slumbering in the night. The sprawling canvases are compelling, but not easy to digest. She stares at each one for a long time, struggling to make aesthetic sense of something that, much like a human life or the future before her, she suspects might not make any sense at all. They're just too big, too beautiful, too hard to take in all at once.

Except one. The final piece in the exhibition is different. Far from being an expansive, semi-abstract seascape, it is instead a portrait. It's smaller, more intimate, and it is the only one that's not black and white. It reminds her in its composition of a Rousseau, but in style more like a Gauguin, rich as it is with a slow burn of Polynesian color. It is of a woman, sleeping beneath a palm at the base of a mountain. She cradles tenderly in one arm a slumbering infant and in the other arm a single bunch of green bananas.

Mona begins weeping, she's not sure why, the tears stinging her eyes and making streaks of her makeup. She smears them away and leans forward to read the title of the painting, thinking it is one she would like to remember. *Château d'Eau,* states the little French plaque beside the frame, a name that she knows all too well. Below that, in bold italics, the English title reads **Castle of Water.** A mistranslation by some French intern, she can only assume, or some overworked printer's obvious mistake.

19

For most citizens of the "civilized," climate-controlled world, there are the usual means of measuring time. Clocks, calendars, cable television seasons—the things that dutifully gauge our progress through life. The sorts of tools one takes for granted until the little LCD screen is cracked, the watchband severed, the Casio casing filled with salt water. How does one measure the days *then*? For sure there is the rising of the sun, the setting of the moon, the slow churn of the stars—but their repetitiveness tends to make one day indistinguishable from the next. Barry Bleecker and Sophie Ducel learned that the hard way, and they gradually found other ways to keep track of time.

First, there were the disasters recorded. Not even taking into account the personal tragedy that had visited both of their lives, their first year on the island was full of calamity. When the BBC broke the news of the September 11 attack on the Twin Towers over the shortwave radio, Barry was stunned—his office at Lehman Brothers had been just across the street from the World Trade Center. When word came that both of the

towers had collapsed into cinders, he crumpled to the sand and stared feebly at the sea. Two weeks later, when Radio France informed Sophie that an explosion at a chemical plant in Toulouse had caused more than two thousand casualties, she was shocked—she had cousins who worked there, people she'd grown up with, and there was no way to know if they had escaped the inferno. A November hurricane raked across Cuba, December saw terrorists hiding bombs in their shoes, January brought a volcanic disaster in the Democratic Republic of the Congo, and all across the globe armies seemed to be gathering, marching in time to a cadence of doom.

And then there were the pounds lost. Barry did the best he could to supplement their meager diet with the odd fish that slipped through Balthazar's tentacles, or the occasional whelk that washed up from the sea, and Sophie did the best she could to make it all palatable, experimenting with conch fritters and coconut-sprinkled sashimi. But the vast bulk of their diet comprised half-wild bananas. And although the ancient Polynesians had been generous in their planting, rationing was still called for, as the green bunches were always in varied stages of ripeness; only a handful were generally edible at one time. There was no scale on the island, but after the first month, Barry reckoned he had lost some fifteen pounds; after three months, it seemed closer to thirty; and by month six, his weight had stabilized at somewhere around one hundred and fifty pounds—sixty pounds lighter than the soft-middled banker who had vanished at sea. As for Sophie, her weight loss was less dramatic, as she had been on the thin side to begin with, but it was noticeable nonetheless. In the first few weeks, her breasts shrank and her derriere flattened (*"J'ai la fesse triste!"* she cried), and several months in, she was confident that at least ten kilos had fallen from her figure. The end of that year saw them both wearing tattered loincloths and nothing else. Their

respective garments had long since ceased to fit, any coyness had long since vanished, and trimming down their baggy clothes to breechcloths made far more sense. Even Sophie's wedding ring, the only memento she had left of her beloved Étienne, had taken to slipping off her finger; she in turn had taken to wearing it around her neck on a filament of fishing line.

And then there were the fights—or, perhaps more accurately, eruptions, because they were nothing short of volcanic in their intensity. Colossal ventings of magma and steam, shouting matches in which the rage seemed directed as much at the pale silence of the universe around them as at the red-faced person screaming three feet away. Oh, at first they had been relatively civil with each other, making pleasant conversation around the fire and discussing their plans for when they returned home. Barry's constant joint cracking and nervous tics did irk Sophie to no end, and her own borderline OCD when it came to cleanliness certainly put his patience to the test. But for the first few weeks, things were more or less calm. That veneer of civility, however, held out only as long as their hope did. Once the reality of their situation became apparent, the fear and the anger both came roaring out.

One month in, sometime in early May, there was the infamous *Incident de caca,* as it came to be known by both parties involved. Barry, who back in New York was accustomed to midnight jaunts to the bathroom, had picked up the habit of relieving himself in the ocean when nature called—finding the latrine without his contact lenses proved inconvenient, if not impossible, and stumbling a few yards into the surf was considerably easier. At least, until a piercing scream startled him awake at some dim, predawn hour. Sophie had gotten up extra early to bathe in the ocean, only to encounter the evidence of his late-night escapades floating maliciously before her.

Before Barry could even get a contact lens in, he was being spun out of the hammock and kicked across the sand by the enraged Sophie, who in addition to administering deft blows with her feet showered upon him all manner of French insults. *"Non, mais t'es vraiment dégueulasse, putain! Tu chies dans l'eau comme un vieux cochon et tu laisses flotter ta merde! On t'as jamais appris à être civilisé et distingué! Putain! Putain!"* The bewildered Barry flew into a rage all his own, telling her in return that she was a psychopathic nut job, that she should be locked up in a goddamn insane asylum with her tits in a straitjacket, and then threw in for good measure that her hairy armpits made him want to throw up. But from that day forward, he found his way to the latrine no matter the hour, and Sophie never brought it up again.

Six weeks after that, coincidentally not too far from the Fourth of July, a regrettable event known as *Le débâcle de fusées de détresse* ensued. Darkness had fallen, embers were being stirred, and the shortwave was burbling out a news broadcast in an unknown tongue when something caught Sophie's eye: a pinprick of light making its way through the constellations. Mistaking the celestial body for an airplane, she leapt to her feet and showed its position with a series of vigorous, pointing jabs. *"Un avion! Un avion!"* she cried. Barry snickered—somewhat condescendingly—and retorted that she ought to sit back down, it was just a satellite. But Sophie, perhaps blinded by her own desperation, insisted that it was not and beckoned wildly for the flare gun, which was tucked in Barry's waistband. When he flatly refused, she made a lunge for it, and the two ended up struggling and rolling about the fire, cursing and maligning each other in the cruelest of terms. Sophie called him a *gros connard* and a *couillon d'américain mal élevé,* and Barry labeled her an uneducated moron, even going so far as to call into question a culture that cared more about cheese and full-

bodied wines than it did teaching its youth the basics of astronomy. Barry stood up and held the flare gun over his head, with Sophie on tiptoe attempting to pry it from his grip, when it accidentally went off, straight into the sky. They both fell to the ground and covered their eyes, expecting some fantastic explosion, and were subsequently disappointed to watch the red trail of sparks give way to a fizzling little pop—a weak and watery firework indeed. The satellite continued its crawl across the heavens while Sophie buried her head in her arms and began sobbing. Barry threw the flare gun at her feet and stormed off, cursing and lobbing nonsensical threats all the way, as furious and brokenhearted as she was yet at the same time at least mildly grateful that she had not shot his dick off in the tussle— not that he was getting much use out of it, anyway.

August saw the Great Driftwood Debate (really more of a screaming match, it was initiated when Barry insisted on building an unnecessary fire); a shortage of ripe bananas and the predominance of Balthazar produced the epic Famine Fight of November (a pushing contest born of pure hunger, fear, and nothing more); and December's inordinate heat resulted in the mingled insults and accusations of the Grand Drinking Water Dispute (Sophie committed the unforgivable sin of bathing in one of their two drinking water pools). And when the incessant rains of the wet season arrived just before the new year, the verbal battles only became that much more pitched. For while time had brought changes to both a bearded, bedraggled Barry and a scrawny, sunburned Sophie, one thing that had not changed one iota was their sleeping arrangement. Amid the vinegar showers and bitter winds that marked that dampest portion of the year, he remained faceup in his hammock and she curled beneath her tinfoil survival blanket in the tarp-covered shelter. By that point, Sophie resented Barry too much to invite him beneath its protective roof, and Barry despised

her too much to ask. He seethed and cursed through the endless downpours; she swore and smoldered from within the dankness of the shelter. "Fuck her," Barry would mutter as the rain pelted him through the long, dark night. *"Vas te faire foutre,"* Sophie would hiss each time the ropes creaked beneath his sleepless weight. There was no escaping it—the rains or their situation—and their frustration was slowly fermenting into unspeakable rage. Deserving or not, they hated each other, nearly as much as they hated the island, and neither could imagine it any other way. Even listening to the radio had become a major source of conflict, as the two of them would argue for hours before agreeing upon a station. In the end, they found it best to leave the thing off when they were together. No music programs, no weather reports, just spiteful silence— which was why they had no idea as to the danger that was headed their way.

20

Generally speaking, the South Pacific has never been especially prone to hurricanes—or cyclones, as they're known in that corner of the globe. But when they do come whirling through the neighborhood, they tend to be inordinately destructive. Tahiti, for example, has no official hurricane season to speak of. But that didn't deter six separate cyclones from hitting the islands in a single year between 1982 and 1983. The storms walloped French Polynesia in rapid succession, leaving entire towns and villages leveled in their wake. Similar destruction visited the South Pacific in the early 1990s as well, when another lethal spate of cyclones swept through the region. Why these periodic bursts of ferocious hurricane activity? El Niño. The most innocuous sounding of meteorologic phenomenon, an old weatherman's trick for explaining a wet forecast. But while that slipstream of warm equatorial water gives most of the Western Hemisphere nothing more than a few spring showers, it has a tendency to wreak havoc in the southern portion of Polynesia. And as it just so happened, 2002 turned out to be an El Niño year.

Now, Barry Bleecker was certainly no stranger to storms. He was on the sort of intimate terms with them unique to young men born in America's middle. He had come to know them very well in the rush of oak-knocking wind that always announced a tornado's arrival. The tone of the Emergency Broadcast System was never far behind, but Barry's nose, finely calibrated over the course of a boyhood of such storms, could smell them coming from a mile away. In fact, they haunted his dreams still. His one and only recurring nightmare was of being back on his family's farm in Macoupin County, Illinois, exposed and vulnerable in a cornfield and watching the dragon claws of a twister descend from the clouds. True, Barry had never actually seen a tornado firsthand—they always seemed to strike just a suburb away or one town over. But he had spent his childhood in their barometric shadow, and the storms that spawned them cut through his thin Presbyterian veneer and shook him down to his Baptist soul.

Which was why Barry knew something was seriously amiss long before there was any obvious sign. His nose had been twitching all morning. The disquieting stillness, the conspiracy of pressures, an electrical tang in the very molecules of the air—it was all too familiar. When the ragged edges of the sky took on an almost phosphorescent glow, it only made him that much more sure of it. Had he been in Illinois, his grandparents might have taken him to the root cellar. Had the feeling presented itself in Ohio, there was always the security of the cinder-block basement. But there was nothing beneath them on the island but sand, and precious little shelter from the whims of the sea.

"Why do you keep doing that?" Sophie finally asked in annoyance.

"Doing what?"

"Raising your head and sniffing, like some kind of dog."

Barry didn't answer for a moment. He set down the banana peel he'd been scraping out with a clamshell and took a squinting survey of the horizon. "I'm not sure. But I think something's not right."

"We've been on this shitty island for almost a year now and you just figured that out?"

"No, seriously, I mean it." He stood up just in time to catch an unusually cool breeze, sending a familiar wave of goose bumps rippling across his bare skin.

Sophie set aside her banana peels as well and conducted her own scan of the horizon.

"I don't know what you're talking about. It looks normal to me. A little overcast, but it's like this all the time during the rainy season."

"The rainy season should be almost over. This feels different."

Sophie rolled her eyes theatrically in Barry's direction. "So we're going off feelings now? Is that it?"

"Just turn on the radio. Maybe we can get something from Tahiti."

"Turn it on yourself, *imbécile*."

Normally, Barry would have responded with an insult, possibly even a cruel mimicry of her French accent, but on this day, he did not. Instead, he fetched the radio from the bag of survival gear in their shelter, gave it a minute's worth of cranks, and spent another finding the station. There was considerable interference, which was unusual. Some of it almost sounded like conversation, a low burble of background noise clotting up the airwaves. But the signal from Tahiti at last came warbling through the static, in French, of course, and Barry asked Sophie to listen. She did so, reluctantly.

"It's just some bulletin about the mayor of Papeete going fishing with a church group. And something about a quilting contest."

"Keep listening."

"*Pfff.*" She expressed her aggravation in the usual fashion but did keep her ear cocked toward the shortwave. Slowly, her eyes began to narrow.

"Anything?"

"Shhhh!" Evidently, there was.

The broadcast ended shortly thereafter, at which point Sophie clicked off the radio.

"Well?"

"*Comment dit-on 'cyclone' en anglais?*"

"Cyclone. It's the same word. Or hurricane."

"*Alors,* the man said a big one is moving to the north and west of Tahiti, but it is not supposed to hit any islands, and should not be a threat. You see? No big deal."

"Not a big deal to anyone on Tahiti, you mean."

"Yes."

"We're not on Tahiti."

"*Putain de merde,* Barry, what do you want me to do, become a *météorologue*? The man said it was fine, and you're probably worried about nothing."

"Nothing, huh?" He sat back down and returned to his old banana peels, from which they had been hoping to scrape enough starch to make up for a lost meal. "You're probably right."

And the two of them went back to work, Barry's nose twitching and skin prickling all the while, his entire body on high alert. He did his best to ignore it. The last thing he was in the mood for was another pointless fight.

As for Sophie, she may not have had much experience with storms, but she did know a thing or two about animals. Her

grandparents had used the summers that she and her brother spent in the Pyrenees to pass on as much as they could of the region's ample inheritance of folk wisdom. When a chamois goat came crashing down from the tree line and ran frantic circles in their village, her grandfather explained that it was suffering from a blinding sickness, a sign of general misfortune and a great danger to sheep. When a chorus of wolf howls rang out from the Spanish side of the Cirque de Gavarnie, her grandmother assured her that a June snow was coming, with the first miraculous flakes falling that same day. And when a dozen lammergeier vultures appeared circling over the church one Sunday after mass, both of her grandparents shuddered at the omen—and sure enough, an avalanche devoured two of the town's shepherds just before sunset.

Which was precisely why, when, several minutes later, the island's entire colony of sooty terns alighted from their rocks to circle the sky, Barry's concerns took on for Sophie a fresh sense of relevancy. Urgency, too. Maybe he wasn't entirely full of *merde* after all. The two of them climbed to their feet simultaneously, dropped their clamshells and banana peels, and gaped at the spectacle of a thousand birds blotting out the sun. The swarm did three counterclockwise revolutions high over their heads before elongating into a snake that climbed into the clouds.

And then they were gone. An island's worth of seabirds vanished in less than a minute.

"*Bordel*. Have you ever seen them do that before?"

Barry shook his head, slack-jawed and confounded by the thing he had witnessed. "I've never seen anything like that before."

Sophie grimaced and reconsidered her position. "You were right. Something is happening—this isn't normal."

The same unusually chill wind from before picked up again,

this time with a troubling insistency—the palm fronds reacted with a collective hiss, their silvery undersides exposed by the gust. Sophie shuddered visibly and hugged her arms across her chest. Barry rubbed at the haggardness of his beard, pondering the possibilities. Something was coming, and the sudden exodus of the birds was simply an augur of that fact.

"Let me see that radio. I'll be back in a bit. Try to stay by the shelter, and if anything happens, shoot the flare gun—I left it right next to the survival kit."

Sophie nodded, unusually cooperative. "Be careful."

"I will." And he kissed her on the cheek.

21

Barry's reason for grabbing the radio and heading to the rocks was twofold: first, to gain a better vantage point and determine if indeed anything was heading their way; and second, to locate a better source of shelter in case there was. He jogged through the underbrush—by this point bending rather violently to the wind—and began scrambling up the boulders at the base of the island's central peak, ever mindful of the shortwave under his arm. Generally, his climb would have been met by the screeches of the terns that inhabited its crannies, and he found their absence eerie and disarming; there was nothing but the whistling of the wind and the eighth notes of his heart.

Two-thirds of the way up, he found something. Not much of a cave per se, it was far too small and shallow to really dub it as such. But a crevice, a fissure in the rock face just big enough to harbor two crouching refugees from wind and rain. He made a mental note of its location and continued his climb, arriving at the summit just a few minutes later. He caught his breath and took an appraisal of the sea.

Barry noticed it immediately. Almost like glitter, a bleary scintillation in an unusually dark corner of the horizon. He used his index finger to adjust his contacts, thinking it might be some problem with the lenses, and squinted more closely.

No, it wasn't a problem with his contacts. It was lightning. It couldn't be anything else. Dozens upon dozens of flickering bolts. Hundreds, possibly. Granted, it was miles away, but still—even the very worst electrical storms he'd seen on the Illinois prairie paled in comparison. This was more like the grand finale of a distant fireworks show, but far from being the end, it felt like just the beginning.

He gave the radio's little generator handle a few cranks, until the Tahitian station it was tuned to jump-started back to life. But again, there was something else there as well. Background voices, traces of multiple far-off conversations, even more numerous from the top of the mountain. He fiddled with the dial until the voices faded, and the broadcast came through loud and clear. The Monkees' eponymous hit, "Hey, Hey, We're the Monkees," was playing, something that would have been good for a chuckle under different circumstances. But Barry didn't even crack a smile. He elongated the telescopic antenna and began moving it in a slow circle, taking careful note of where the signal was strongest. It reached a crescendo just at "People say we monkey around," the words shedding the static and becoming instantly sharp. Barry stopped there, the antenna poised like a weather vane to the southeast. That was surely the direction of the Tahitian station. It had to be. And if the cyclone was headed "harmlessly" to the north and west of the islands . . . well, he didn't need a trained meteorologist to tell him that was bad news. It meant it was coming right at them.

And as if to put an emphatic *accent aigu* over his realization, a lash of stinging rain came from out of nowhere, or rather

somewhere way up in the churning clouds above. It arrived in three sharp blasts and then steadied itself to a gusty drizzle.

Even quicker than he had come up, Barry scurried back down, hopscotching over the boulders and dodging through the palm grove. When he reached Sophie, she was standing in front of their thatched hut, pointing out across the ocean.

"Barry, *regarde*. The waves."

The coral reef that circled the island (and sheltered it, for that matter) a hundred meters out had become a ring of seething white foam. Acting like a seawall, it was catching the big waves before they reached the shore; their bases cut out, they were breaking over the top of it.

"Fuckin' birds were right." He grinned at Sophie, who did not appear to share his amusement. "I think the cyclone is coming this way."

"But what do we do? This could be a very dangerous situation, *non*?"

"If things get bad, there's a little cave up on the side of the rocks we can hide out in. We should be okay there. In the meantime, we can stay here in the shelter and wait."

Barry ducked inside the palm hut to get out of the wind and the rain, which by then had taken a turn for the vicious. He tucked the radio back into the waterproof duffel bag, beside their other essentials, and zipped it securely shut. Sophie followed him in, her brown eyes wide with mounting concern.

"And how do we know if things get bad?"

"Trust me, we'll—"

And just like that, they did. The first of the big waves came without warning—it breached the reef as a soundless swell that Barry and Sophie only half noticed out of the corners of their eyes. When it struck the beachhead, however, its sneak attack was revealed with the force of a bomb blast, causing the very

ground beneath their feet to shudder. The two castaways instinctively crouched, just as one does when startled by a close clap of thunder. The wave's humpback exploded into a white swirl of foam that came careening all the way to the edge of the shelter.

"Merde!" Sophie poked her head out to examine the wet line the wave had left only feet from the entrance. "Should we go, Barry?"

"I don't think we need to just yet."

At which point, a shredding gust of what was already very strong wind ripped back most of the roof above, sending palm fronds cartwheeling across the sand and making a wild dance of the blue tarp beneath.

"Barry!" Sophie shouted his name into the wind as the structure and all hell both broke loose around them.

"Come here, I've got you." Barry threw his arms around her and shielded her from the whipping cords and thrashing leaves; the wind was suddenly nettled with rain, and their skin stung from the storm-whipped sand. Several grains lodged themselves painfully in his contact lenses; he was in the middle of repositioning one when he noticed a second monster cresting the reef. This wave was even larger than the first, and he had already grabbed Sophie's hand and spun in the direction of the island's interior when it erupted across the shoreline behind them.

"Run!" was all Barry had time to shout, yanking Sophie out of the hut and toward what he hoped would be safety. A surge of seawater caught them knee-deep as they cleared the sand and entered into the palms, all of which were bowed and thrashing in the storm. For once, Sophie didn't argue, and Barry didn't question—they both simply ran, legitimately terrified by what was happening around them. One by one, trunks began snapping, each resounding like a twelve-gauge

shotgun blast. Several trees collapsed right in front of them, blocking the trail and causing Barry to change his zigzag course. They did not see but rather felt a third wave blindside their island, its entire stone core quaking from the force. And more were coming.

Barry didn't even break stride when they reached the first rain-slicked boulders of the mountain; he leapt upon them nimble as a cat and turned to help Sophie pull herself up.

"The little cave is close to the top. We'll be safe there."

"You're sure?"

"Positive."

As he had noted, it really was more of a half-sheltered out-cropping than an actual cave, but it would have to do. Together, they scrambled up the steep rock face, ever mindful of the slippery moss and pockets of bird guano, the latter of which turned to a slick paste when mixed with the rain. At several points in the climb, Sophie became stuck, but Barry was always right there at her side, ducking back down to lend her a helpful tug or a strategic boost, in a way that, although she would not have admitted it then, reminded her of her grandfather during her childhood hikes in the Pyrenees. Barry and Sophie barked their elbows and skinned their knees but were otherwise safe and sound when they got to the mouth of the crevice and tumbled soaked and panting onto its cold stone floor.

At last perched safe from the roaring winds and the smashing waves, they dared to look out at the storm that surrounded them. Barry was dumbfounded, amazed by the violent turn it had taken since his first glimpse from the summit. It was genuinely terrific. Not in the word's more pedestrian sense, but in its original Latinate meaning: *full of terror.* The sky and sea were welded at the seams into a single image of hell, with kohl-black mists, gouts of red steam, and monster waves reaping

their way across it. It was like something out of a Bosch painting, but at least they were safe up there, sheltered by the rocks
and out of harm's . . .

Crap.

Barry's stomach sank. It suddenly occurred to him.

"I've got to go back down."

"What? Are you out of your mind?"

"We left everything in the shelter. All of it."

The matches, the freshwater, the solar still, the flare gun, the
fishing gear, the utility knife, the radio, the energy bars, the
first-aid kit—not to mention the inflatable life raft—everything
they needed to ensure their survival was in a waterproof duffel bag in what remained of their shelter. If the waves hadn't
already washed it away, they surely would soon.

"Barry, it's okay, just stay here, *please*."

But he knew it wasn't okay. Far from it, in fact. That survival kit was their only hope.

"I'll be back. I promise." And with that he planted a smooch
on her cheek and bounded down over the edge, leaving a desperate Sophie screaming his name just as a beast of a wave, several orders of magnitude larger than the giants that had preceded
it, emerged from the depths off toward the horizon.

22

The term *lost everything* is one bandied about loosely in this day and age. More often than not, it's attached to an acrimonious divorce settlement or a declaration of bankruptcy. *Oh, they lost everything,* the misfortune is detailed in a scandalous whisper. But how often is it actually true? How many people out there—living people, for the dead are surely exempt in such matters—have ever truly lost everything? Certainly a treasured automobile or a cherished home or even a beloved spouse is painful to part with. But *everything*?

When Sophie first tumbled from the deflating raft in the immediate aftermath of the plane crash, she had lost a great deal. The people she loved, the life she had enjoyed, the simple pleasures of normal existence . . . all those things had been severed from her being by the sharp shank of that ill-timed bolt. But she had not truly lost *everything*. She still possessed a modicum of hope and at least one other human being, as imperfect as he was, to share it with. And it was only that small remainder of a normal life that discouraged her from doing

what she had almost done alone on the water. It wasn't much of a reason to keep on living, but it was something.

When Barry was swallowed by the wave and washed out to sea, that fragile reason was swept away with him. As soon as the surf receded to its standard dimensions and the rains calmed to a drizzle, Sophie climbed out from the little cleft in the side of the rocks and scrambled back down to terra firma, screaming out Barry's name the entire way. She ran to the ruined site of their beachside camp, where a tattered rope hammock fluttered from a corpse of a tree, and found no trace of him. She scoured the palms and did frantic laps of the island, shouting until her voice went hoarse, *Ba-rreeee, Ba-rreeee, Ba-rreeee*. But her pleadings went unanswered; there was only the sound of the wind in the shredded palms and a few weak rumblings of delinquent thunder. Sobbing and suddenly too weak to stand, Sophie leaned against the remains of what had once been her home and emitted a sound of pure agony. It was a sound few ever hear and even fewer ever utter. It was the sound of having lost *everything*—she literally had nothing left.

For two days and nights she held a desperate vigil, squatting in the sand and staring bleakly out at the sea. She neither ate nor drank, in part because she held no appetite, but also as a matter of circumstance—the cyclone had stripped the trees of virtually all their bananas, and the tidal waves had filled the twin cisterns with brackish salt water. Instead, she prayed. She prayed as only a lapsed Catholic can, cutting all sorts of deals, laying out all manners of bargains, if only that stained-glass-colored God she had long since left to the leaded windows of Saint-Étienne Cathedral might grant her this one small favor: Bring Barry back to me, *s'il vous plaît, Seigneur*, please, bring him back. The sea yielded nothing, however, but curt waves and sour winds.

On the morning of the third Barry-less day, following a

dawn as bleak and gray as a bone, Sophie decided she had waited long enough. *"Pardonnez-moi, Seigneur,"* she muttered as she rose to her feet and approached the stringy remains of Barry's hammock. The knots were caked with salt and bloated by water, but she was able to untangle a single length of rope about six feet long. While certainly no Boy Scout as Barry had once been, she was able to tie a rough but functional rendition of a noose and, standing on tiptoe, secure the other end to the worn-out notch in the palm that had supported her shelter. All that was left was to say farewell, fall to her knees, and wait for the rope to finish what the spiraling Cessna had begun. As she saw it, she was only quickening that which was now inevitable. Without bananas, without drinking water, without fish of any kind, she knew she wouldn't last more than a week. Frankly, there was no longer any reason to postpone it. It was time. Shaking, weeping, but resigned to her fate, she tightened the knot and prepared for the plunge.

"Good-bye," she wheezed out in English, for Barry.

"Au revoir," she sobbed to the world she'd once known.

23

Sophie's anguished assumption—that Barry had been swept out into the open ocean and had joined Étienne and Marco in the cold, dark deep—was indeed well-founded but only half-correct. The wave *did* hit him, and hard at that. He had just ducked out of the windblown shell of Sophie's palm shelter, the duffel bag in question slung over his shoulder, when he came face-to-face with the monstrous tsunami. The thing by that point was no longer the heaving swell that Sophie had noticed from her rocky perch; after breaching the reef that encircled their island, it had transformed into a thirty-foot torrent of surging white water. Barry had no time to run or climb, only a few short seconds to curse and brace.

The impact was indescribable, beyond imagining, as most forces of nature are. Once, as a teenager, Barry had been involved in a fairly serious head-on collision on a rain-slicked road on the outskirts of Cleveland. And even that crash, with all its Toyota Camry–crushing force, paled in comparison with the experience of being hit head-on by a thousand tons of angry ocean. And after that initial wallop, the situation was

slow to improve. For a full hellish minute, he became the proverbial rag doll in the washing machine, spun and yanked about, smashed mercilessly against rocks and trees and everything else the wave brought his way. Was he afraid? Yes, most definitely. Horrified, in fact, as he had not been since the sickening plunge of their damaged Cessna. But it was a peculiar, out-of-body fear, surreal in its intensity. *This can't be happening.* Oh, but it was. Barry knew he was at odds with incredible forces; he felt as if he were being ground between the molars of the jaws of the sea.

Then, suddenly, he was released. Like Jonah spit from the belly of the whale, Barry found himself squirted up to the surface. An unimaginable tug still bore him along, but he was no longer underwater. Sure enough, one of his contact lenses had been claimed by the tsunami, but the other remained intact, and with his rehearsed one-eyed squint, he was able to ascertain that he had been taken quite far from the island and that an apocalyptic storm was still raging all around him. Huge swells buckled in every direction, and a violent wind smacked salt spray right into his face. It was quite dark, but storm dark—a bruised shade of almost luminous black and blue, freeze-framed by the bolts of electricity that scissored relentlessly down from the clouds.

Shit. Barry gasped and spit water and turned onto his back, struggling with the dead weight of the duffel bag that was somehow still strapped to his shoulders. He hoisted it onto his belly while fighting to keep his head above water. He considered trying to get out the raft and inflate it but quickly came to terms with the impossibility of that option. Simply staying afloat was monopolizing every ounce of his energy, and the thing took ages to blow up. So up and down he went, simply riding the swells. With each rise, he caught a fleeting, haphazard glimpse of the island's rocky center from his one

good eye, only to have it vanish when he went crashing back down. And after several such glimpses, he reached the disastrous conclusion that he was being carried by the storm farther and farther away from it. The island, that little spit of sand and nub of stone that had seemed to him for so long like a prison, became in that instant the purest home he had ever known. And besides—Sophie was still on it.

Lightning crashed, the oceans roared, and there, at the mercy of waves as big as mountains, beholden to a storm the size of God, Barry closed his eyes and turned his face toward the heavens. And the strangest thing happened: For the first time he could remember, he felt an uncanny sense of peace. He wasn't afraid anymore. Not really, anyway. Well, okay, maybe a little. But not much. Confronting such an immense dose of destiny brought fresh clarity to the fact that some things were simply beyond his control. Out of his hands. No longer his concern. Honestly, the thought of leaving Sophie alone was more dreadful to him at that moment than the possibility of death. And *honestly*, how could death be any worse than this?

He did, however, have a bone to pick. The winds swallowed his words, but he spoke them skyward anyway, as only the only child of rural Protestants can:

"Goddamnit, if you're going to kill me, fine. I get it. No hard feelings. But if not, please quit jerking me around and help me to get back to that island, because there's a pain-in-the-ass French girl there who I can't leave alone."

The first time Barry had made such a request, floundering amid the burning wreckage of a plane, destiny or a deity—take your pick—had delivered to him a Ziploc bag full of contact lenses, an uninhabited island within swimming distance, and, although it took a few days to materialize and nearly a year to realize, a companion whom he truly cared about. The second time he pleaded his case, he was given:

A log.

Or a tree, more accurately. For Barry wasn't the only thing that the tidal wave had ripped up by the roots and carried far out to sea. One of the island's few coconut palms had been swept along with him. It didn't happen right away—he noticed it after some ten minutes of being convinced that the god(s) above had finally forsaken him. But once it finally arrived, it was hard to miss—it smacked him right upside the head, causing him to briefly see stars in the midst of the cyclone. The fact that it was a large, floating palm tree took a moment to register, and his initial reaction was that the half-emerged form was some sort of primordial aquatic beast (at this point, just about anything seemed possible). But after a few pokes and prods, he ascertained its true identity: a big floating log. He slung the duffel bag over it, wrapped his arms and legs around it, and clung to it tighter than a baby koala. The storm was still raging, but if he could survive it, just wait it out, then he might be able to paddle the thing back to Sophie and back to his home. In fact, to keep his mind occupied, he shut his eyes and sang the words to the John Denver song "Take Me Home, Country Roads," just as he had done nearly two decades before, while listening to the radio in his grandfather's pickup truck, the bed loaded with feed sacks and the smell of fresh-cut timothy grass rushing in through the window.

Barry wasn't able to keep an exact accounting of time. But after what felt like a few hours, the waves regained normal proportions and the rain eased up—giving him the chance at last to put in a new pair of contacts from the duffel bag and restore his full vision. The island was well out of sight by that point, but based on a few quick glimpses he'd managed to sneak at the survival kit compass, he figured he had been moving away from it in a generally northern direction. Which meant once the setting sun appeared dim and milky through

the post-typhoon haze, it was simply a question of kicking his log and keeping its glow to his right. His fingers were pruned beyond sensation, and the single water bottle he pried loose from the duffel bag hardly put a dent in his thirst, but Barry was alive. He had something to keep him from drowning, and he knew in which direction his home could be found. A few minutes' rest, he finally decided, and he would turn the log that way and begin the journey. After all, what other option did he have?

Twilight came quickly and made way for the darkness. A profound darkness that left Barry grateful for the phosphorescent markings on the dial of his compass. Not even starlight could poke its way through the clouds. He was sitting atop his log, squinting at the compass face, and trying to orient himself back toward the south when he noticed it. But the sight of it didn't register at first. It was just too improbable, entirely too surreal. He sat there, rocking to and fro on the steady roll of the waves, unable to make sense of what he saw in the distance.

No, that was impossible, he told himself. The very thing he had been begging for, pleading for, for almost a year, to suddenly appear like this? It had to be a trick—a ruse of the mind born of wishful thinking, or at the very least some effect from the new pair of contacts. Barry closed his eyes, felt the log buck ever so slightly beneath him on the cusp of a swell, and counted to ten. Then he blinked and opened them once again.

But they were still there. Three simple lights, like wandering magi, flickering on the horizon, seeking their star. Ships, freighters maybe, they could be nothing else. How far away, Barry had no way of knowing. Five miles? Ten miles? Twenty? It was impossible to say, although they certainly were a long ways off.

Stay calm. He had to, he reminded himself, which, when one is lost in the middle of the Pacific Ocean, is far easier said

than done. His heart was off to the races, and his hands were shaking to a beat all their own, but he had to keep his thoughts in order. This was no time for rash decisions or thoughtless impulses. A sudden urge to both laugh and cry and possibly scream ascended from his guts, but he fended it off with a deliberate swallow and unzipped the corner of the duffel bag instead. With an almost exquisite level of care, he pried the flare gun loose, inserted a single cartridge into its exaggerated barrel, and pointed it directly over his head. He executed a quick countdown—why, he could not say, but it felt like the right thing to do before a momentous event—and pulled the trigger. There was a hiss of sparks, a tense moment of silence, and then a brilliant pop. For a few precious seconds, the world glimmered red, before returning once again to inimitable darkness. "Please, please, please," Barry begged aloud, "please, please, please."

He waited five torturous minutes before firing again. Another brilliant, crimson moment, followed by a second wave of gut-wrenching dark. He was loading up to fire a third when something profound occurred to him. *The radio.* Was it possible? Was that where the background interference had been coming from? He uncovered the shortwave, being extra careful not to tip the log while the electronics were loose from the waterproof duffel bag. On the verge of hyperventilating, he turned the generator crank and gave the tuning dial a gentle whirl, wondering if his hunch might actually prove correct.

It did. Those same disembodied voices, ghostly as sin, were suddenly rising from the static in a cosmic symphony, only louder now and far more clear. Some were in Russian, others Chinese, and at least one in English. It was the maritime frequency band—it had to be. He'd been listening to transmissions from ships all along, broadcasting on shortwave frequencies when they were too far out at sea for their standard

transmissions. He had heard them that first night when he was alone in the hammock, he had listened to them from the top of the mountain just before the storm, and now, in the middle of the ocean, he was picking up their signals from mere miles away. He was actually *looking* at them, for Pete's sake, a cavalcade of improbable hope parading across a hopeless sea.

Barry fired all of their remaining flares into the inky heavens, allowing a few minutes between each burst for an agonizing wait and an anxious prayer. They were far off, he knew that, but maybe, just maybe . . . And in the seconds that followed, he envisioned the ships turning around, the lights growing brighter, his weakened body being hoisted up by a crew of compassionate arms from the all-swallowing sea.

But it was not to be. He had begun to turn the log northward again, in their general direction, preparing to meet them, when he noticed the first of the lights vanish from view. Then the second and, shortly after that, the third. One after the other, the ships were gobbled up by the horizon, leaving him alone and bobbing in the darkness once again, that brief flicker of hope snuffed out like a flame.

"No! No! No!" Barry was startled by the sound of his own shouts. He tore at his hair, gaping helplessly at the void where the ships had just been. An entire year he had waited for this, *wailed* for this, and then to watch them slip through his fingers like fireflies and twinkle away?

For the briefest and most desperate of moments, Barry considered going out after them. True, they had appeared to be moving away from him, at a speed far faster than he could ever hope to match, but there could be more out there. Perhaps it was a sea lane—after all, he had seen three separate ships glide across his purview. Wasn't it possible that additional ships might be on their way?

Perhaps. But while the possibility existed of finding a passing

boat in a potential shipping lane untold miles to the north, the certainty of Sophie and their island was a day or two's paddle directly to the south. And he also knew that without the survival gear, she didn't stand a chance there by herself. If he went chasing after phantom boats, not only might he perish in the attempt—after all, he had no flares left to fire—but he would almost certainly doom her as well. If he went much farther from the island, it would be too far to turn around. He had been given a log, and that would have to be salvation enough. He couldn't leave her; that just wasn't an option.

And so, with no fanfare, but with plenty of determination and no small amount of relief—that moment of indecision had been far more excruciating than all the possible outcomes that scrolled through his mind—Barry put away the radio and the flareless gun and, using his glow-in-the-dark compass, began to reposition the log in a southern direction. Back to the island, back toward Sophie. And he did so with a smile, as incredible as it seemed. If the gods were going to have a joke at his expense, Barry decided, then nothing was going to stop him from laughing right along with them. While they were busy chuckling, he just might actually make it home.

He kicked for a while but quickly came around to the inefficiency of that means of propulsion. He did, however, have the raft paddles rolled up in the duffel bag, and it occurred to him that he might as well give one a try. He pulled himself out of the water and straddled the palm log, sinking the paddle into the waves to push it along. The whole affair was unsteady, occasionally rolling to one side or the other, but it worked. *Almost* like a canoe, which got Barry thinking, but other more pressing issues demanded his attention.

He kept on paddling straight through the cloud-black night, and a cotton candy–colored sunrise saw him doing the same the next day. The sky had yet to totally clear, and an occasional

drizzle peppered the water and misted his skin, but the worst of the storm seemed to have passed. He checked the compass periodically to maintain his position, and he sang old FM hits to help stay awake. He even talked to himself to keep himself company, imaginary conversations he knew he might never have the chance to actually have. He spoke at great length with his parents, caught up with college roommates, and even had a few choice things to say to his ex-girlfriend Ashley. When the sun finally set and that first rash of stars broke out above, he couldn't help wondering what his old co-workers were doing in New York at that moment, and he laughed out loud when he imagined them stirring their single-malt Scotches and complaining about their six-figure bonuses. The notion that he, now paddling his log alone across the darkened Pacific, had once been among them was almost too absurd for him to believe.

The last traces of the cyclone had vanished by the second morning; the sky and sea regained at least some of their turquoise charms. The sun beat down upon his bare shoulders, but he was tan enough by that point to tarry the burn. In the afternoon, a speck shimmied out of the horizon; two hours later, he could make out once again the cone of rock and the shag of the palms. It was so close . . . When the log finally ground to a halt on the island's sand, he felt like weeping. Sweet Jesus, it felt good to stumble onto dry land, no matter how small or isolated its acreage might be. He couldn't wait to surprise Sophie on the other side of the island, to dump at her beautiful feet the precious duffel bag he had saved. He debated whether or not to tell her about the ships he had seen but decided that was something best saved for another time. He wasn't sure how she would react to the news, and the last thing she needed was another disappointment. And using up all the

flares—that was a whole other can of worms, one he was certainly in no hurry to open.

Barry cut straight through the palm forest and past the rocks to save time, taking notice of the damage with an exclamatory whistle. Palms were rent, debris all a-scatter. Then he was pushing aside some downed foliage and emerging by the campsite, or at least what remained of it.

"Honey, I'm home!" he croaked out from his parched throat, the smile on his face splitting open his horribly chapped lips.

And there she was . . . standing beside a palm tree, with a rope around her neck.

"Sophie, what on earth are you—"

And before he could finish she was upon him, shedding the noose and tackling him to the ground, in the most colossal hug he had ever received in his life. She sobbed for quite some time, and so did he, and at some point they were both laughing, and at some point after that, they both said they were sorry.

For everything. And Barry didn't regret for one moment turning that log back around, back toward Sophie, back toward home.

24

The salad days of Barry's return were sweet indeed, but truth be told, their island was in absolute shambles. The joy of their reunion quickly gave way to the realization that there was lots of work to be done to get things back to working order. The hammock was beyond repair, but Sophie was able to recover the tarp and refashion the shelter; harvesting the palm fronds took time, but layer by layer, over the course of several days, she rethatched their tropical home. While she kept busy with the house, Barry took on the unpleasant chore of bailing the salt water that filled their two rain cisterns. It was a grueling endeavor, dumping water bag after water bag of brine out onto the sand, but it had serious ramifications—getting the pools refilled with fresh rainwater was paramount, because without them, they had nothing to drink.

Well, almost nothing. For in the initial kit of survival supplies was the solar still. And it was fortunate indeed that Barry had been able to salvage the bag and bring it back to the island, because in the miserable weeks that followed, it was the

only thing that kept them alive. The amount of potable water it was able to distill from the sea was never more than a few cups per day. Those measly sips, however, were enough to keep Barry and Sophie going through three grinding weeks of thirst, until at last, heralded by a symphony of thunder, the clouds burst once again, filling their water pools all the way to the brim. The two of them leapt and danced in celebration, Sophie a "rock and roll" dance her father had taught her as a girl to a Beatles' record, Barry a sort of improvised Irish jig he made up on the spot.

Food, however, was also a problem. The tsunami had done severe damage to the island's banana trees. A full quarter had been ripped from the ground and washed away, and another quarter still damaged and browned by the poisonous salt. The winds had loosened nearly all of the existing bunches as well, leaving only a scatter of serviceable bananas left to be eaten. With time, a few months, perhaps, Barry believed that the trees would recover. But in the immediate future, they were at risk of starvation—they needed a plan. Eggs were not a possibility, as the colony of terns was slow in returning; clams had never been all that plentiful to begin with; and the sparse supply of remaining coconuts could do only so much. The energy bars that Barry had rescued from the sea—the ones Sophie had been farsighted enough to insist that they save—did keep them going through the first few days, but even those were finally gone.

Which left only one option. And that one option was very nearly impossible, thanks to the eight-armed leviathan that lurked in the shadows. Barry did attempt fishing again in their only fishable cove, with the hope that the cyclone had pried the monster out of his hole and sent him skittering to the open sea.

But no such luck. Sure enough, at the first nibble, Balthazar resurfaced with a sickening surge, dragging the delicious-looking fish and precious lure back down to his lair, precisely as he had so many times before.

Damnit. Barry gazed down with a contained but simmering rage at the small puffs of fish scales that periodically escaped from its cave. He returned to camp empty-handed, his belly cramped into a ball of hunger. They weren't starving just yet, but if things didn't change soon . . . well, the outlook wasn't good.

"Did you catch anything?" Sophie called out, kneeling by the fire, struggling to sort anything edible out of a fly-ridden heap of moldering bananas.

"*Pas de tout,*" Barry answered in the comically bad French he had begun to pick up, shaking his shaggy head to emphasize the point.

"Was it Balthazar again?"

"*Mais oui.*"

Sophie released her trademark puff of air. "*Merde.* I checked the trees, there are no more bananas at all. *Rien de rien.*"

"These are the last of them?" Barry looked down at the pathetic little pile of rotten fruit.

Sophie nodded. "There's nothing left to eat. Absolutely nothing. *Qu'allons-nous faire?*"

"I haven't a clue," he answered, tousling her matted hair, although in truth, in the back of his mind, he already had the first inklings of a plan. The idea had come to him almost a full week before, but its genesis went back even further than that. Because that first night when the palm shelter had been resurrected following its destruction in the typhoon, Sophie had asked Barry, now hammockless thanks to the storm, if he would like to join her beneath its watertight roof. Barry pre-

tended to give it some thought, shrugged his shoulders, and said, Sure, why not?

And so from that day forth, Barry and Sophie were roommates. Not lovers—just roommates. When the Polynesian sun dipped beneath the waves and the last of whatever paltry morsels they could scrounge was eaten, they would retire to the hut and lie side by side on their mat of palm leaves, listening to the growling of their bellies and whatever station they could find on the shortwave. Then, in the darkness of their primordial night, they would sometimes talk. About anything, really, but mostly memories of what their former lives had been. It was therapy of sorts, although they only dimly realized it. Keeping the past a part of their present had become crucial to both of them; the idea that that world was both real and attainable was the only thing that kept them from abandoning hope completely.

One such night, after the radio had run its charge, Sophie spoke.

"Did you understand the radio announcer?"

"No, it was in Spanish," Barry answered. "But I liked the tango music."

"You didn't hear what he said?"

"I heard it, I just didn't understand it."

"You Americans really don't speak any other languages, do you?"

"Not if we can help it," he replied with a teasing nudge.

"Well"—and she took a breath as if preparing for a plunge—"he announced the date when he gave the news."

"Oh?"

"It's May Day. We've been here for over a year, now."

Barry considered that thought for a bit. More than 365 days. Thirteen months, to be exact. *Shit*. He sighed in the humid

night, not even sure what to do with that number. "I figured it had been about that long, but I didn't know exactly."

"What do you think about that?"

"What do you mean?"

Sophie swallowed. "Do you think we'll ever get off of this island?"

In truth, Barry pondered that question almost every minute of every waking hour. Sleep was his only reprieve from it, dreams the only place he could ever forget—although increasingly, his dreams were being visited by three sparks of light that glimmered their way across the horizon.

"I sure as hell hope so. I'm getting charged by the day for leaving my car at the airport parking lot."

Barry didn't see it in the darkness, but Sophie smiled. At first, his little jokes had offended her Gallic sensibilities—they struck her as juvenile and irresponsible given the serious nature of their situation. But with time, she had come to see them as the outward projection of a quiet and dependable fortitude. As long as they persisted, she knew he was strong, that he hadn't given up.

"You know . . ." And Barry trailed off, not quite certain how to tell her. "I saw something during the storm, when the wave washed me out to sea."

"What do you mean?"

"I think I saw ships. You know, like, boats. Three of them."

Sophie sat bolt upright, just as he was afraid she might. "What? Are you kidding me?"

"They were a long way off, I could barely see them."

"Why didn't you use the flare gun?"

"I did. They were just too far away. They kept on going until they disappeared."

"And you're just telling me this now?"

"Yes, I'm telling you now because it just came up. I fired

all the flares I had, but they didn't stop. I suppose I could have gone out after them, but I came back here instead."

Sophie lay back down on their shared palm mat, puffing out an incredulous burst of air through her lips. "*Merde.* I can't believe it."

"What? That they didn't see me, or that I used up all the flares?"

"*Non.* I can't believe you chose me over the boats. I would have gone after the boats in a heartbeat."

She gave him a jovial elbow to the ribs, and Barry chuckled with relief. He'd been afraid she might not take the news well, but that didn't appear to be the case.

"There's something else, too," he went on.

"What? Did a Montgolfier float by as well?"

"No, there were radio transmissions. You know those strange voices we hear on the radio once in a while?"

"Sure, but we don't hear them very often."

"I know. But when we do, I think it's transmissions from the ships. When I was out there, there were tons of them. More than just the three I saw. And they were all talking to each other. They sounded close."

"So what are you saying?"

"What I'm saying . . ." And Barry hesitated, to make sure there was actually some sense to what he was trying to explain. "Is that maybe there's a sea lane out there. I mean, if we're getting radio transmissions once in a while, and I saw three separate ships just while I was in the area, maybe there's something like that. That's what I'm saying."

"But it could have just been a onetime thing."

"Could be. But then again, it could be something else. I heard those voices over the radio the first week we got here—I remember listening to them in the hammock. And suddenly, I started hearing them again the week before the storm hit. It

seems like they come in bursts, like there's some kind of rea-
soning behind it."

"Like what?"

"I don't know. Maybe it's a seasonal thing, maybe it has to
do with weather patterns, maybe it's an annual regatta race.
Beats me."

"So how far away do you think it was?"

"Forty or fifty miles from here, maybe. I'm not sure."

"*Miles?* Why can't you just learn the metric system, *putain
de merde*?"

"Well, it's not that far, either way."

"You think fifty miles, or however many kilometers that
is, over the open ocean isn't that far? I don't think I drifted
more than five kilometers after the crash to get to this island,
and that felt like far enough."

"True, but you were drifting, not paddling. I think with
both of us using oars, we could do it in a couple of days."

"What about storms? What about currents we don't expect?
What if we get blown off course, or the raft starts to deflate in
the middle of the ocean?"

"Look, I'm not saying we have to do it, I'm just saying it's
an option. Like you said, it's been a year now, and it's not like
we have crowds of people coming to look for us."

"I don't know." Sophie put her hands over her face, not so
much in anguish as in exasperation—the exasperation of trying to answer a question to which there was no single correct
response.

"Let's not worry about it now. We have enough to deal with
just trying to eat for the time being, and I'm not ready to make
another trip out there just yet—my arms are still sore from the
last one. And besides, I've been listening to the radio every
night, and I haven't heard any of those transmissions since I

got back. So maybe it was just a fluke. The ships are probably all gone now."

"Good. So let's talk about something else."

"That's fine with me."

They took a moment to listen to the waves and to the low chatter of tree frogs that they could never quite place. Sophie shifted onto her side, using the crook of her arm as a makeshift pillow. She tucked up her legs, and even though Barry wasn't aware of it, she looked right at him in the darkness. "Next week is my birthday, you know."

"Seriously?"

"Oui, oui."

"You didn't tell me that last year."

"I didn't even want to think about it at this time last year."

"So the big three zero?"

"Yes. I'm turning thirty."

"Well, we'll have to celebrate."

Sophie snorted. "Sure. Bake me a *croustade aux pommes* and I'll blow out the candles."

"No, I'm serious. What do you want for your birthday?"

"Pfff. I don't know. What did you get for your thirtieth birthday?"

Barry struggled to remember. It had been more than five years. He seemed to recall his parents giving him a novelty birthday card that chimed out a tune when you opened it, and his ex-girlfriend Ashley treating him to some rather unenthusiastic fellatio. But he wasn't sure. He did remember a few of his co-workers took him out to Smith & Wollensky for dinner.

"I went out for steak," he finally replied.

"Oh, God. *Steak frites.* That would be wonderful. My father used to grill the meat in our fireplace. My mother always fried the potatoes in duck fat. It was the best."

"I don't know, I'm somewhat partial to my dad's country-fried steak myself. He made it with cream gravy and mashed potatoes, with some corn bread and green beans with bacon on the side."

"You put *lardons* in your *haricots verts*?"

"Damn right."

"Normally, I'd say that's *dégueulasse,* but right now, I think I would eat a whole plateful."

"And then for dessert, banana pudding!"

"No! No more bananas!" Sophie squealed rather comically, and they both had a good chuckle at their staple's expense. Their laughter died down, and the waves resumed.

"But seriously, if you could have anything, what would you want?"

"Anything?"

"Yep."

The one thing she truly wanted she knew she could not have or say—Étienne pulled from the sea, a crash to never happen, a blissful return to their little architecture studio on rue des Vinaigriers. But anything else?

"If I could have anything . . ." And she paused briefly, to do perfection justice. "I think I would like one more night in Lisbon. I'd like to take a warm bath with a real bar of soap, put on a dress and a pair of nice earrings, and I'd like to go to a little café in the Alfama for a big plate of octopus salad with a glass of *vinho verde*. And after dinner, I'd like to go on a walk down by the water and look at the stars."

"That's all?"

"*Oui. C'est tout.*"

"And how do you say 'happy birthday' in French?"

"*Joyeux anniversaire*. That, or *bon anniversaire*."

"Banana-versaire?"

She giggled, as was her habit by that point, at his horribly mangled French. "Close enough, Captain America."

"I'll have to practice saying it before the big day." He leaned over and gave her a peck on the forehead. "Good night, Sophie."

"*Bonne nuit,* Barry."

He closed his eyes and pretended to sleep, but in the silence and darkness, his mind was racing. And those double r's—God, her accent was cute when she said his name.

25

The earrings were by far the easiest variable to solve in Sophie's perfect birthday equation, and making them proved a
convenient distraction from the fact that they were running
out of food. Barry had made a habit of keeping the prettier of
their clamshells and using them for the odd bowl-like task—
there was one whose nacreous swirls Sophie had always been
especially fond of. A few careful whacks with a volcanic rock
and he had himself two similarly sized mother-of-pearl fragments. Throw a pair of fishhooks with the barbs ground off
into the mix (he found two from the remaining assortment
that were too small for use in the cove), attached via a little
fishing line, and Barry had a pair of earrings on his hands that
were actually quite passable. Tiffany's probably wasn't going
to get their skirts ruffled over the competition, but they were
nice, and he was proud of them. He nervously hoped that Sophie would like them, too.

Nor did the soap portion of her wish provide too much
challenge, although there was some trial and error involved,
and he could work on the project only while Sophie was on the

other side of the island, swimming or searching in vain for bananas. One of Barry's most vivid childhood memories may have been seining for catfish with his grandfather on moonlit nights in Macoupin County, Illinois. But the other contender was the image of his grandmother and aunt making homemade soap in the farmhouse kitchen. The process consisted of two basic parts, one of rendering fat from a slaughtered hog and another of extracting lye from fresh ashes. For the latter step, both women would don, in addition to their calico housedresses, handkerchiefs tied about their faces bandit style as a means of fending off the fumes. For the handkerchief, Barry resorted to his trusty—and by this point quite tattered—Charles Tyrwhitt dress shirt. As for the lye and the hog fat, however, well, Barry had to get creative. Had he been marooned on the island during the days of Tu-nui-ea-i-te-atua-i-Tarahoi Vairaatoa Taina Pomare, he would have found no shortage of soap-worthy swine. Given the dearth of pigs some three centuries later, he had to locate another source of grease. And after much brain racking, he did just that, in the form of the humble coconut. Using again his weather-beaten shirt, he was able to mash and strain from what little coconut meat he could find a thick coconut milk. That, when rendered in one of their stainless-steel cups over the fire and left to settle, produced a layer of nearly pure coconut oil. Once the oil was scooped out, it was a relatively simple process of boiling some water and ashes in the second cup to produce lye. It took Barry a few tries to get the concentration just right, but when he felt confident that the iridescent substance swirling in the cup was alkaline enough, he added it to the coconut oil, cooked it together, and lo and behold!—when left to cool, a fresh cake of coconut soap. He smiled to himself, certain that his grandmother, who had never held a coconut in her life, would have been proud.

But the octopus salad that Sophie had savored during her treasured year studying architecture in Lisbon . . . that proved to be more problematic. Because while octopuses were not uncommon in that neck of the South Pacific, they were not all that easy to come by, either—at least, not without a snorkel mask and a spear gun, of which Barry had neither. What he did have, however, was a sickening certainty that were he to dive down in the murky shallows of his fishing cove, there would be at least one exceptionally large member of the cephalopod family waiting to greet him.

Balthazar.

The scourge of his island and the thief of his lines. The day had come. It was time for a reckoning.

Barry didn't have a clear idea of its weight or dimensions, having caught only fleeting glimpses of it during its explosive ascents to pilfer his fish. But he was aware that it was large and creepy, and he was in no way enthusiastic about the idea of diving ten feet underwater, crawling headfirst into its lair, and challenging it to a death match, no matter how hungry they were and desperate for food.

But that was exactly what he intended to do. In dispatching one giant octopus with two fists, he would be killing two birds with one stone: He would be ridding the cove of a true menace and, in doing so, have one hell of a delicious birthday gift to present to Sophie. Just imagine, he thought to himself, the look on her face. . . .

And so it came to pass that Barry Bleecker, the ex-Manhattanite and former high-yield-bond salesman at Lehman Brothers, stood on the morn of Sophie's birthday on the rocky ledge above an octopus's cave. Tanned and sinewy, shaggy and bearded, clad only in a boxer-short loincloth, he bore a far closer resemblance to the Cro-Magnons that had fascinated him in his youth than the paunchy yuppie he had been not so

very long before. And indeed, the whole business smacked of the primeval—he did feel something like a Polynesian Beowulf, preparing to rid his village of a many-legged Grendel. With his box-cutter knife in one hand and waterproof flashlight in the other, Barry felt, for the first time in his life, like a man. A terrified man on the verge of wetting his loincloth, but a man nevertheless. And as a man, like it or not, he knew what he had to do—their survival depended on it. He peered down into the pool, took three deep breaths, and dove headfirst into whatever fate had in store.

A flurry of bubbles, a few quick blinks, and—*damnit*. His contacts both popped out. Barry considered returning to the surface to regroup but realized that the odds of him working up the nerve for a second dive were low indeed. No, it was now or never, contacts or no contacts. In the cool blur of the pool's blue depths he clicked on the flashlight, directing its beam into the mouth of the cave. He crouched down and ducked his head into it, not sure if what he was seeking was even—

Yep. It was there. Even without his contacts, he could make out its dark shape. Horrifically inert, twin eyes blazing, the octopus was less than an arm's length away, its mottled skin expertly camouflaged to match its surroundings. But it was there all right. The very monster that had stolen untold fish from his line, robbed him of precious metal hooks, and deprived him and his companion of life-giving protein. The day had finally come; it was Barry or the beast. With exquisite slowness, with the greatest of care, he pulled back his knife hand, preparing his box cutter for its lethal new vocation, readying himself for the imminent violence of the strike.

A strike, as it were, that never came. Not from Barry—the octopus struck first. In a blast of black ink and a nightmare of tentacles it was upon him, knocking him backward into an

eight-pronged headlock. His attempt at a scream was as ineffectual as his attack strategy; the thing was wrapped about his body and latched firmly to his face. The pure power of the creature became sickeningly apparent as Barry floundered and gurgled in its hydra grip. *Christ,* it was strong. Even the varsity wrestling squad at Saint Ignatius had never had arms like this.

Surrender. It was his only option. Short on breath, Barry knelt down to kick up from the bottom, only to discover a most unsettling fact: He was stuck. The octopus that enveloped him was still latched somehow to the rocky coral below. He thrashed and fought against it, to no avail—he was bound to the seafloor by a terrific set of cables. And as if that weren't enough, something sharp was tearing into his face. *The son of a bitch was biting him!*

Lungs bursting, blood screaming, Barry fell to his knees and felt frantically for the utility knife, which he had dropped shortly after the initial attack. His first half-dozen pats yielded nothing but sand, until—yes! He had it. With his other hand he searched for the tentacle that still clung to the rock, and when he found it, he lashed at it with everything he had . . .

Until it snapped. He was suddenly unhinged from the rock and kicking upward, still utterly engulfed in the octopus's embrace. Then he was back above the surface, clawing its membranous flesh away from his face, sucking back air in honey-sweet gulps—then he was over the rocks and running across sand, screaming for help, a virtually naked man, smeared in blood and ink and blind without his contacts, wearing wrapped about his body an enormous octopus—then Sophie was running toward him, frightened and confused.

"Barry, what is it, what's—oh, *mon dieu!*"

And then she screamed.

"Banana-versaire, baby," Barry managed to mutter, just before collapsing to the sand and fainting like a southern belle. And it was probably for the best that he was unable to see the look on Sophie's face.

26

Barry awoke half an hour later to a throbbing pain in his left cheek, an incessant whacking, and the sound, if he was not mistaken, of singing. A few tentative pokes revealed that his face was thoroughly bandaged, stirring a few hazy recollections of Sophie tending to his wounds and helping him put in a fresh pair of contacts. A dizzying emergence from the shelter showed that the source of the whacking was Sophie beating severed tentacles against the nearby rocks, a trick for tenderizing octopus that she had learned from Corsican fishermen during a high school trip to the island. And as for the singing, she was belting out the tune to "Alouette" as she worked, but with slightly altered lyrics—she had changed the refrain to *"Pieuvrette, gentille pieuvrette,"* and the familiar *"je te plumerai la tête"* to *"je t'enleverai les bras."* Of course, Barry didn't pick up on the clever alteration, but he smiled wincingly at the girlish sweetness of her song.

"You have the voice of a meadowlark, Sophie. You should join the Vienna Boys Choir."

"For that, I think I would need a pair of testicles."

"Well, you have plenty of tentacles at your disposal." Barry prodded one of the severed, sucker-covered limbs before sitting down beside her. "How's the octopus coming?"

"Almost ready to be cooked." Sophie pushed the hair from her face with the back of her tentacle-smeared hand. "And you're crazy, by the way. You could have been killed."

"Well, we might have died of starvation if I hadn't. This should last us for at least a week. And besides"—he cleared his throat and poked her playfully—"Portuguese octopus salad isn't exactly easy to come by around here."

"It's going to be grilled Polynesian octopus salad, but still, thank you."

"Well, there's more. That's not your only present."

"It isn't?"

"Nope."

Barry finally revealed the hand he had been conveniently hiding behind his back, presenting to Sophie the clamshell earrings and cake of pure white soap.

"Wait, is that—"

And then Sophie screamed, perhaps even louder than she had when he was being attacked by the octopus, but with joyful disbelief rather than fear. *"C'est du savon? C'est vraiment du savon?"*

"Oui, oui, it's soap. I made it out of coconut oil and ash lye. And if you want, you can use the other rainwater pool for a bath. I think one drinking pool is enough."

Octopus slime and all, Sophie threw her arms around Barry and laid a smarting kiss on his bandaged cheek.

"Ouch, be careful!"

"Sorry." She grinned with contrition. "How does it feel?"

"It hurts pretty bad. How did it look?"

"*Pfff.* The octopus took a big chunk out of your cheek. The wound isn't very long, but it's deep. And you're very lucky, he just missed your eye."

"Well, shoot. To think I could have had an eye patch."

"I think the scar will give you character enough."

"God knows I need it." And he winked at her, although with the bandage covering most of his right eye, Sophie didn't notice.

"What you really need are stitches. I cleaned the cut with the alcohol wipes and antibiotic cream from the first-aid kit, but you should keep the bandage on until it closes up."

"I will. And you should go try out that soap and get ready. I think I can handle Balthazar from here."

"*D'accord. Merci, Barry. Pour tout.*"

"*De nada.*"

Sophie giggled again. "That's Spanish."

"Crap. I thought it was Portuguese."

"It's the same in Portuguese."

"See?" he replied, teasing, "Maybe us *Americanos* aren't as dumb as you think."

Sophie set down the octopus tentacles, wiped off her hands with a strip of wool rag from what once had been a pair of Brooks Brothers slacks, took the earrings and the cake of coconut soap, set off toward the rainwater pool to take her first real bath in over a year, and couldn't help thinking that maybe there was some truth to that, and perhaps more to that particular American than she could have ever imagined. Well, either way, the presents were a very nice thought.

As for the bath, it was, in Sophie's own words, *vraiment extraordinaire.* She soaked her body for a good half hour in the smaller of the two collection pools, to loosen a long year's worth of salty grime. Then she worked up a lather, thick as the foam on a cappuccino, and proceeded to scrub every inch of her body

with it. And it was just as marvelous as she expected, the sensation of all that filth sloughing off from her skin, to be replaced by an otherworldly sort of cleanliness. She completely submerged herself on several occasions, holding her breath as long as she could in that baptismal warmth, feeling the volcanic rock press roughly against her bare bottom, and letting a fluttering stream of bubbles escape gradually from her lips. When at last she climbed out, she felt pruny as a newborn and just as pure. She welsh-combed the tangles out of her damp hair and braided it up into a sleek French twist. She slipped her new clamshell earrings into her lobes and refastened her loincloth with a jaunty knot. She felt slightly more exposed than usual without her hair hanging down over her breasts as it generally did, but, well, *merde*—Barry had probably earned an unobstructed view of her *nichons* after all he had done. She let what lingered of the evening's trade winds dry off her body and allowed her lips to part into an alluring smile—in the absence of her preferred Yves Saint Laurent #13 lipstick, she would have to wear it instead. As for the wedding ring that still hung about her neck on a translucent string of filament line, she debated for a moment if she should wear it or not but decided in the end to keep it. She wasn't ready to part with it yet.

The moon had risen by the time Sophie emerged fresh from the palms, stepping gracefully from between the shivering fronds into the gleam of its sterling light. Barry, crouched over the fire, watched her approach with an elegance that bordered on the spectral. When she entered the bouncing glow of the cooking fire, he received his first real glimpse, fleeting as it was, of what their first meeting may have been like under different circumstances—a blind date at a restaurant in the East Village or a chance encounter at a little café on the Canal Saint-Martin. Gone was the irritated girl he had seen for the

very first time at the Tahitian airstrip; nowhere to be found was the heartbroken woman he had shared that Alcatraz of an island with for more than a year. Instead, he saw Sophie Ducel, the brilliant architect, great beauty, and longtime resident of the tenth arrondissement, walk into the firelight and say a confident *bonsoir* as a long-lost smile spread charmingly across her face. Granted, such an encounter in an international capital would likely not have involved so much bare nipple, but Barry was hardly one to complain. Partial nudity aside, they could have been meeting for an *allongé* at Aux Deux Amis or after-work cocktails at Tavern on the Green. It all felt that natural.

"You look . . ." And his voice trailed off in buoyant wonder.

"*Oui?*"

He was going to say something trite like "incredible" but instead stated what was to him the obvious, and even more complimentary. "Like a Gauguin painting."

"Which one?"

"Like a cross between *Vairumati* and *Two Tahitian Women.*"

"Well, there's just one of me."

"Thank the Lord for that. I don't think I could handle two of you."

"*Imbécile,*" she shot back, although for once she meant it endearingly.

"So should we eat?"

"*Pfff.* We're in the middle of a banana famine, and you need to ask?"

"Then *bon appétit.*"

Barry laid two skewers of roasted octopus sections across their stone table, and for a solid ten minutes neither of them spoke, occupied as they were with stuffing their faces full of the tender grilled meat. The fact that said meat had belonged

to their archnemesis Balthazar only made the feast that much sweeter.

"Better than Lisbon?" Barry finally asked, cheeks bulging with roasted octopus.

"Better than anything," Sophie replied through a mouth just as full. "I can't stop eating. *Je suis trop gourmande.*"

They gorged until their bellies distended, washed everything down with two tall, stainless-steel cups of coconut water, and crumpled in tandem onto the sand, lying side by side beneath a mother lode of stars. The hearth had long since burned itself out, and the only light came courtesy of their distant fire.

"Want to know one thing about it here that makes me sad?"

Sophie turned her head toward Barry, whose eyes were battened to the heavens above.

"What's that?" She had come close to answering with, *Just one thing?* but the lingering swoon of the dinner had robbed her of all snark.

"The constellations. I learned all the northern ones in Boy Scout camp when I was a kid, but in the Southern Hemisphere, I don't know a single one. It would be nice to look up and see something familiar. You know, just one thing that hadn't changed."

"You can always make new ones. You don't have to depend on the old."

"The Medium Dipper?"

"No, *totally* new ones. You just have to find them."

"Any jump out at you?"

Sophie's eyes danced across the great wash of stars. "That one, there." She jabbed at the sky with her finger. "It looks like *une grosse bite avec deux couilles tombantes.*"

"Like what?"

"A big dick with two droopy balls. Capricock."

Barry erupted with laughter, hard enough to trigger a coughing fit. It had been so long since he'd had a good laugh, he'd forgotten what it felt like—he even peed a little in his pants, or loincloth, as it were.

Sophie laughed alongside him, taking no small pleasure in the mirth she had caused. "See, maybe us French are funnier than you think."

"I never said you weren't funny."

"But you probably thought it."

"Well, if being stuck on a desert island doesn't give you a sense of humor about things, I suppose nothing will."

"Stuck on a desert island—it's like that game. Did you play it in America?"

"Which one?"

"You know, if you were stuck on a desert island, what one thing would you bring. Some people say a pocketknife, or a record player, or some beautiful supermodel. Whatever matters most."

"Yeah, sure."

"So?"

"You mean what would I bring with me?"

"*Oui.*"

"Not including a French architect with a strange sense of humor and a lifetime supply of little green bananas?"

"*Oui.* Not including that."

"Hmmm." Barry mulled it over. The irony of playing the game while actually on a desert island was rich indeed and, frankly, rather mind-boggling. But it didn't take long to find his answer. "My paints. I miss painting."

"That's the only thing? *Quel artiste.*"

"Well, fried chicken and a cold beer would be nice, too, but I can live without those. Painting, on the other hand . . . that's something else. That's part of why I hated my old job so much.

I had hardly any time to paint. And then when I did have time, my—" And Barry caught himself. "Ex-girlfriend hated it."

"Why?"

"She said she didn't like the smell of the turpentine I used to clean my brushes."

"You could have stopped using oil paints and just switched to acrylics. Nobody uses oils anymore."

"I think the real issue was that she thought it was a waste of time. No money in it, I guess. No future."

Sophie sniffed sympathetically. "Well, you never know. An easel and some watercolors could wash up any day now."

"I won't hold my breath." Barry nudged her. *"Et vous?"*

"You say *'toi,'* *'vous'* is for people you don't know well."

"You think we know each other well?"

"Starting to, I suppose. And I would bring an espresso machine. Coffee would be nice. A subscription to *Le Monde,* too, so I could have something to read and keep up with the world."

"No drafting table and AutoCAD?"

"Pfff, no, I don't think so," she answered, frowning at the thought. "Architecture was something Étienne and I did together. We were a good team, and we would build off of each other's ideas. I'm not sure I could do it without him."

"I don't know. You did a pretty good job on our little house here."

"Robinson Crusoe is a less demanding client than the *ministre de la culture.* And my little sand castles aren't quite up to par with Le Corbusier."

"Great artists have to work with the materials they have."

Sophie was quiet for a moment; Barry worried he had said something wrong.

"Everything okay?"

"Oui. And there's one part of my birthday wish still left."

"What's that?"

"I said that after my octopus salad, I'd like to take a walk down by the water."

"I think that can be arranged." Barry climbed to his feet and helped Sophie to hers, brushing the loose sand from her back. *"Après vous."*

"It's not *'vous,'* it's *'toi,' putain,* how many times do I have to tell you?" And she feigned annoyance, but in reality she was quite pleased. Far from saying something wrong, Barry had given her an idea with his last comment about great artists, and the brisk clockwork of her mind was already whirring—Barry's birthday was less than two months away.

They did a lap of the island over the course of a moonset, after which Sophie suggested a swim. Barry was reluctant at first— he didn't want to get his bandages wet, and the incident with Balthazar still gave him the willies. But then again, Sophie had experienced far worse with sharks. Sure, why not, he finally agreed.

Sophie went in first, stirring the water around her with her fingers. Barry followed close behind. The warmth of the day persisted in the shallows, and he couldn't recall the ocean ever feeling so pleasant. They waded out until it reached their chests, then turned on their backs to admire the light show above. The distance from the shore was making Barry nervous, but Sophie didn't turn back, so neither did he.

The moon was low and bright. The ripples shimmered. They took to treading water and floated side by side. From their vantage point, they could see the entirety of their island, a quiet sanctuary in a star-crossed sea. *"C'est tellement beau,"* Sophie whispered over the sloshing of the water. Barry, whose French had improved enough to at least understand that much, concurred. She looked at him, eyes glossy with moonshine, and smiled. He smiled back, his heart quickened, and she moved in, just a little bit closer . . .

And then something pale and sleek came crashing down into the water between them.

"What the fuck?"

Then it happened again to the left of them, and twice more behind, and in seconds, a hail of feathery torpedoes was raining all around. Sophie dove under the water while Barry shouted and covered his head. At least until the anonymous dive bombers came plopping up to the surface, many with fish still wriggling in their mouths. Sophie resurfaced just a few seconds behind them, pushing the wet hair from her eyes for a better view.

"It's the birds!" she cried out in pleasant surprise. "They've come back to the island!"

Indeed they had. The island's entire colony of sooty terns had returned that very eve, from wherever they had fled to avoid the destruction of the cyclone. Habitual night feeders, they exploited the nocturnal habits of fish to their own advantage—when the schools rose to the surface to feed in the moonlight, the sooty terns were happy to greet them.

Barry slapped water at a nearby tern and couldn't help laughing. Sophie splashed water at Barry and couldn't help joining in. The return of the birds felt like something fortuitous, if not portentous, their own Capistrano brought down to miniature.

"Let's head back in and let them eat in peace. They're probably starving."

"So? Two hours ago, so were we."

"Come on, it's time."

Sophie led the way with an elegant sidestroke; Barry trailed reluctantly behind, doing his very best doggy paddle. They swam until the water became too shallow, then stood up on the sand and walked the rest of the way in.

"I think I'm going to sleep," Sophie pronounced with an exaggerated yawn. *"Bonne nuit."*

"You're going to bed already?"

Sophie nodded. "I am. But thank you again. It was the best birthday I've ever had."

She kissed him on his one unbandaged cheek before ducking into their palm-thatched hut. Barry stood alone in the darkness for a sad and solitary minute, letting the breeze do the delicate work of drying his skin. Then he took a seat beside what remained of their fire and set the shortwave radio upon his knee. He clicked it on and turned the volume down low, scanning the same frequencies he had listened to before for some hint of a voice, something akin to what he had heard out at sea. But there was nothing. Had he picked up just a small snippet of a radio transmission, or even some snatch of a casual conversation between ships, he might have been able to make the case for inflating the raft and going back out there. Whatever transmissions he had detected before, however, were not repeated. In fact, even the Tahitian station had called it a night. Once again, nothing but those haunting whistles and the silver of static. Once again, sitting outside all alone beneath the stars. He clicked the radio off and leaned back against a palm tree, envisioning an alternate universe in which Sophie had never been married, a world in which sooty terns did not exist, and a place where ships did not pass in the night but actually took heed of your lonesome flares.

27

The night of Sophie's birthday may have proved a romantic failure for Barry, but the sight of the terns did get him thinking. He had witnessed the birds dive for fish before—in addition to night feeding, they would swoop down just before sunset, when the slanted light caught the glitter of scales. But seeing the birds fish en masse out by the edge of the reef had put an idea in his head. From the flopping glints in their greedy mouths, he knew there must be fish aplenty on the cusp of the lagoon. Whole schools, judging by their consistent success, clustered out there by the encircling coral. The question was how to traverse the hundred yards of seawater to cast his line. Not that there were no fish to be had in the erstwhile Balthazar's cove—there certainly were, and since Balthazar's demise, Barry had been angling at the respectable rate of one or two good-sized catches a week (usually snappers that Sophie either baked in the coals or steamed in a banana leaf). That, together with the bananas, which had finally begun to grow back, proved just enough to keep them alive. But in the cove, it was a question of waiting for the occasional timid straggler to nose

its way in. Out there by the reef, where the terns took their business, there appeared to be fish galore, ready and ripe for the picking. Barry was tired of hanging his hunger on fickle piscine whims. He wanted to go out and get them for a change, and if such a thing could be achieved, he knew the hard days of famine would be forever behind them. He had done it with Balthazar, why couldn't he go after fish as well?

The life raft was a possibility, but not a horribly convenient one. Inflating it by mouth was an exhausting hour-long chore, and keeping it inflated left it at the mercy of all sorts of sharp shells and sea urchin spines. Seeing as it was their only means of escape from the island in the event of an emergency, Barry and Sophie had both agreed that it was best stowed away, carefully folded in the duffel bag with the survival gear for the day they might truly need it.

Which left Barry with only one option: If he wanted to ply the fish-rich waters that surrounded the reef, he would have to build and captain a boat of his own. Not the easiest task for a midwesterner whose nautical experience was limited to a few feckless hours on a summer camp Sunfish more than two decades prior, but not beyond the realm of possibility, either. And the inkling of an idea had already formed in his head. Barry had not forgotten the coconut log that had saved him in the storm. Its supine bulk was on the beach where he had left it— he passed it daily on his way to the cove. And each time he saw it, he started to wonder: Could he make a canoe from it?

Indeed he could. The outer trunk of a coconut palm, if stripped of its pulpy core, could be used to make a lightweight, seaworthy craft. In fact, in the Maldives—not so very far in oceanic terms from Barry and Sophie's island—fishermen had been hewing their dhoni boats from coconut timber since time immemorial, traveling with ease from one atoll to the next.

Of course, Barry didn't know any of this. Aside from a few basement carpentry projects he had helped his father with as a boy, and apart from a trip to the South Street Seaport Museum in New York, he knew practically nothing of woodworking or shipbuilding. What he did possess, however, courtesy of a dusty display in the Cleveland Museum of Natural History, was the knowledge that ancient indigenous peoples of the Midwest had used fire to make dugout canoes. He recalled that on a fifth-grade social studies field trip, a docent with a bad permanent had explained the entire process, describing how they burned out the middle with coals to hollow the log. Who was to say that same technique Ohio's Paleo-Indians once used to fashion their water-going vessels couldn't be applied to a massive coconut log on a Polynesian beach? After giving it some thought, Barry decided no one was to say. He discussed the idea with Sophie, who was initially reluctant to give up precious driftwood from their cooking stash for such a far-fetched plan. But after some cajoling, along with the promise of potentially unlimited fish down the line, she agreed it was at least worth a shot. A week or two of raw sushi wouldn't kill them, and a future without a dependable food source beyond bananas just might.

The first step was to create a foundational boat log of just the right length. Ancient Polynesians would have used basalt adzes for such an undertaking, but Barry had neither the time nor the expertise to fashion advanced Neolithic tools (the Cleveland Museum of Natural History seemed to have guarded such knowledge more carefully). Instead, he picked two points on the log roughly ten feet apart, dug out pits in the sand beneath them, and, with the help of his trusty Bic and some kindling, got two driftwood fires going in just the right spots. It was a process, but eventually the coconut wood began to glow

and cinder, and voilà!—after an entire day of careful burning, Barry was able to roll away from the main trunk a ten-foot portion of serviceable lumber.

What to do next? It was Sophie, the experienced designer, who came to the rescue, as Barry was at a loss. After some rather heated deliberation, she convinced him that he needed to shape the basic canoe form and flatten the top before trying to burn out the core. As to how to initiate that, it was also her idea to recruit some of the pumice stones that littered the rocky center of their island and put them to good use as sanders. Employing the ever-versatile Charles Tyrwhitt dress shirt as a tote bag, they gathered half a dozen good-sized stones and went to work—and *work* it was. The two of them laboring side by side for two straight days yielded little more than a scuffed-up log and four excruciatingly sore arms. But patience is a virtue for a reason, and after a perspiration-filled week of relentless sanding and shaping, the thing was starting to look unmistakably boatlike. The outer palm rings had been ground down to nubs, the soon-to-be bow and stern were slowly gaining some form, and the top was just concave enough to hold a few embers.

Meticulously, with the utmost care, Barry and Sophie laid a wreath of dried fronds and wood shavings along the shallow trough that ran down its middle. Then, with a shared nod and held breath, they lit the line of kindling ablaze and watched the agonizing slowness with which it burned and smoked. The minutes turned to hours, the hours to the better part of a day, but it was working. *Holy shit,* was it working. The two of them began to jump up and down, as giddy as schoolchildren once it became clear that the fire was eating out the center of the log, turning it to a bone-white ash. The results definitely weren't pretty, but it was certainly a start.

"It looks like a big coffin," Sophie proclaimed after Barry had quenched with seawater the last of its smoldering embers.

"Then call me Ishmael, because this coffin's gonna float."

Sophie, however, was dubious. "It still needs work."

"I can sand it and smooth it down some more, but I think it's pretty good." Barry eyed his handiwork up and down, giving it an approving thump with the heel of his foot.

"*Je ne sais pas.* It doesn't really look stable enough for the ocean."

"Why are you always so cynical?"

"*Pfff.* I'm not being cynical, I'm being realistic. I don't think it's ready to go out yet."

"Well, there's only one way to find out." Barry wiped his sweaty hands with the dress shirt and tossed it into what he was confident enough to call a boat. "Let's push it down to the water. It's time for a test run."

Sophie shook her head disapprovingly but relented. "*Putain.* If you say so."

A short spate of heaves, a brief set of groans, and the crude canoe was committed to a gritty slide down toward the surf.

And Sophie was right. No sooner had the prow kissed the water and Barry pulled himself in than a wave—just a couple footer, not even a big one—tipped the whole kit and caboodle, sending its overeager captain spilling into the foam and its more prudent first mate into fits of laughter.

"I wouldn't try to circumnavigate the globe just yet, Monsieur Magellan."

Barry emerged from the water sputtering and coughing, but laughing nonetheless. "Just shut up and help me pull it back in, okay?"

"Aye, aye, Captain," she answered with a snappy salute, and waded in to assist in dragging the ponderous thing to shore.

Weary from the exertion and the disappointment, the two part-time boatbuilders and full-time castaways sat back on the damp edge of the sand and stared at the beached dugout, which, while flailing about in the surf only moments before, had borne far more resemblance to an unwieldy log than the lithe fishing vessel Barry had envisioned.

"Well, crap."

"It just needs more work, Barry. I told you that."

"How is more work going to keep it from tipping over every time a wave comes along?"

"Do you think your stupid *Mayflower* was built in ten days? You have to get it right. That's the first rule of design: You don't put an object into service until it's finished and you're sure that it's ready."

"Okay. Any ideas?"

Sophie shrugged. "Sure. You need to widen the middle and narrow the front and back to help keep it stable and going in one direction. And you probably should add that thing that the canoes have in the cave."

Barry cocked a confused eyebrow in her direction. "What?"

"You know, the pictures in the cave, up on the side of the *petite montagne*."

"Sophie, what in the hell are you talking about?"

"The paintings of boats inside that little cave where you took me during the cyclone. I thought you'd seen them."

"I was a little preoccupied at the time with a giant tidal wave, Sophie. So no, I don't recall any pictures of canoes."

"*Pfff.* Let's get the flashlight. I'll show you."

A determined Sophie Ducel and an extremely bemused Barry Bleecker marched back to the campsite, where they picked up the waterproof flashlight from the survival kit as well as a pair of bananas and two strips of smoked octopus jerky before heading to the tower of rock that composed the

island's core. Sophie took the lead this time, which Barry did not mind in the least, as it afforded him a pleasant view of her derriere.

They took the climb slowly, which was nice, and not even the occasional vomit attack from nested terns was enough to sour the mood. It was a hot day, humid, too, and once they crested the tops of the palms, the unobstructed breeze was delicious on their skin.

"Here, *regarde là*." Sophie had reached the mouth of the hollow and was jabbing at the darkness with the beam of her flashlight. "Look at the paintings."

Barry pulled himself onto the ledge and ducked inside beneath the low-hanging rock. Squinting, he examined the illuminated wall inside. Just as she had described, almost too well preserved to be true, were what he had to assume were Polynesian rock paintings. And they were stunning—a sweeping, stylized seascape of boats, painted in whites and blacks, their edges nearly as sharp as the day they were put there.

"Wow" was all that Barry could muster, crouching in the darkness and staring up at the mural. "Wow," he muttered again. Up until that point, it had never occurred to him that other human beings, let alone artists, had set foot on their island. The realization added a whole new dimension to its seemingly meager topography. He crept up close and touched ever so gently his fingers to the pigment, and in doing so he felt a shiver, as if caressing a ghost.

"See?" Sophie had assumed a crouch right beside him. "The big boat with all the little men on it is like a—*Comment dit-on 'catamaran'?*"

"We say catamaran. Same word."

"It's like a catamaran, with a plank resting on top of two canoe floats. But the little ones . . ." And she jiggled the beam to point them out. "They're thin and elegant, not big and

bulky. And they have that thing hanging off the side to help keep them stable on the sea."

Barry smacked his forehead. "Of course. They're outrigger canoes. I remember reading that the Polynesians used them to go between islands. I think it was in that Michener book."

"What Michener book?"

"*Hawaii*. It was historical fiction, like a thousand pages long. I read it in junior high."

Sophie frowned at the middlebrow sound of the thing. "I don't know about your paperback fake history book, but this is what we need for our canoe."

"So now it's *our* canoe?"

"If the damn thing floats and can get us out of here, you better believe that I'll be on it with you."

Barry's face turned to a sad smile in the flashlight's wan beam. "I don't know about that, Sophie."

"Don't know about what?"

"I haven't heard a radio transmission from a ship since the storm. I don't even know if there will be another one."

"Who said anything about ships? I'm talking about other islands."

Barry burst out laughing; he couldn't help it. "Other islands? Paddling a few miles out to the sea lane is one thing. But actually venturing out there blind and finding another island?"

"The people who made these paintings did it." She shifted the flashlight away from the cave wall, almost accusingly right upon Barry. "They used boats to go between islands."

Barry sighed and gently redirected her flashlight back on the paintings. "The people who made these knew what they were doing and where they were going. We're probably hundreds if not thousands of miles from the closest island, and we don't have the slightest clue. At a certain point, once you go out too far, there's no turning back. And the odds of us sur-

viving for weeks or months on the open ocean are one in a million."

Sophie *pfff*ed in frustration, although for once it wasn't so much at Barry as at the seemingly arbitrary cruelty of fate. She knew he was right. Their only hope, and a dwindling hope it was, was that someone out there might still find them or that the ships that passed near the island might someday return. The uncertainty of it all was sickening, almost poisonous in its in-tensity.

Eager to change the subject, Barry unwrapped the smoked octopus and bananas from the bindle of his old dress shirt. "Should we have lunch while we're up here?"

"Oui, pourquoi pas" was her dry reply as she reached for a banana.

"They are beautiful, though, aren't they?" Barry remarked between chews.

Sophie nodded, still too polite to talk with a mouth full of food, her eyes still fixed on the wall's armada of ancient ships.

"And I think you're right," Barry added. "If we make our canoe into an outrigger like those, the damn thing will float."

Sophie swallowed and shone the flashlight ghost story style directly up at Barry's face. "I know it will. Because I'm going to help you."

This time, Barry didn't push the flashlight away.

28

Sophie's refined canoe design began exactly as all of her designs had: with a sketch. Only rather than moleskin and a Parker pen, as she had preferred at her architecture studio on rue des Vinaigriers, she worked with damp sand and a thin stick of driftwood. Barry watched as she carved out the plan on the beach beneath them, listening and nodding when she explained the tapered ends, the carved oarlocks, and the angled mast for the lateen sail. There was plenty of nylon rope left over from the dismembered hammock to lash together the outrigger, and the extra plastic tarpaulin, if folded into a triangle and stitched together with fishing line, could readily provide some makeshift sailcloth.

Which left Barry with one relatively crucial question.

"So what are we going to make the outrigger and mast out of? There aren't any palms that thin, and we don't really have the tools to cut it down to lumber."

Sophie, back in her element after more than a year marooned, grinned with a maestro's mischievousness and licked her sun-chapped lips. "Follow me. I'll show you."

Twirling the driftwood stick in her hands like a drum majorette's baton, she led Barry into the palm grove and past the freshwater pools, to a secluded spot behind a dense pocket of banana trees—where Barry noticed for the first time a bristling stand of what appeared to be bamboo. It was in fact 'ohe, a close relative of the Asian species that their Polynesian predecessors had spread throughout the islands of the South Pacific alongside their various other canoe plants, but neither Sophie nor Barry had any knowledge of this fact. All they knew—or rather, Sophie knew—was that it appeared just light, buoyant, and sturdy enough to serve their maritime needs.

"So this is it?"

Sophie nodded, running her hand along a segmented stalk. "I noticed them when I was searching for bananas after the storm. I thought maybe I could use the bamboo to make a bed someday. At first I wasn't sure if it could support our weight, but it's actually quite strong."

"*Our* weight?"

"Just shut up and listen," she retorted, feigning annoyance but inwardly smiling.

"Okay. Go on."

"I think it could be perfect for the canoe. We can use the thinner stalks to make the—what do you call the central part, again?"

"The mast?"

"Yes. We can use them to make the mast and the two parts of the outrigger that stick out from the side. And we can use this one," she remarked, tapping the thickest of the stalks with the ball of her foot, "to make the part of the outrigger that floats in the water."

"You think that'll work?"

Sophie nodded, as confidently and nonchalantly as she once

had to skeptical engineers and surly contractors. "*Oui. Ça va marcher.* It's the perfect material for it."

Barry clapped his hands and took a deep breath. "All right, then. Let's get to work."

And together, they began choosing the choicest of the stalks and yanking them up from the earth.

29

It took almost a month. With Sophie as project manager, what had been a hurried and haphazard affair took on the flavor of a genuine architectural project. She planned and measured everything meticulously, using either charcoal on rock or a sharp stick and sand to diagram her blueprints and a length of fishing line as a makeshift tape measure. The extra work at first struck Barry as persnickety and unnecessary, but the evolving fruits of their labor slowly began to convince him otherwise. Initially, he had complained about all the sanding and trimming, but as the hull grew elegant and narrow, the gripes tapered off along with it. And while the additional time spent calculating the ideal length of the bamboo seemed misspent in the preparatory stages, when the outrigger was lashed and slid seamlessly into the waiting gunwales, he finally understood the value of her scrupulous nature. Barry had to admit, he was in awe of her abilities, and at night, after she went to bed, he would sometimes stroll to the other side of the island, to run his hand along the canoe's smooth body and admire its progress by moonlight. He was shocked by the almost womanly

curves the craft had assumed; he understood why mariners preferred christening their ships with feminine names. It took very little imagination to envision how sleekly she might cut through the water. He had asked Sophie on multiple occasions if they could take it for an early test spin, but she had steadfastly refused. You wait until it's ready, she told him, and then you do it right. So he waited.

And waited. Through the deliriously long afternoons spent fashioning the bow deck, the endless nights devoted to stitching the tarpaulin sailcloth, the multiple dawns given to the thwarts and the removable tiller. Through all of it, he waited. And on the morning of his thirty-sixth birthday (she remembered it, he did not), Sophie poked her head into their shelter and told him it was time.

Barry, still half-asleep, groaned and flopped onto his stomach. "What did you say?"

"I said *bon anniversaire*. I just put the finishing touches on the boat."

"It's my birthday?"

"The fifteenth of July, no?"

Barry nodded. Crap. "It is indeed."

"Well, get up and get ready, you're going to try it first."

"Wait, you mean it's totally finished?"

Sophie nodded, trying and failing to conceal her excitement. "Consider it your birthday present."

"Yes! Let me put in my contacts."

Suddenly eager as a Labrador puppy, Barry bounded out of the hut and loped across the sand, to the other side of the island where their craft kept its berth. Sophie jogged just a few feet behind him, excited, for a change, to see the look on *his* face.

And there it was, basking in the sunlight. The sight of it stopped him in his tracks. Sophie had erected the mast, fixed

firmly in place between the vise grip of two lashed driftwood planks. Its blue tarpaulin sail had been rigged but not hoisted, and one of the emergency raft's plastic paddles leaned teasingly against its side. Apparently, she had even given it a name: Carved into the smooth wood of its prow was *Askoy III*.

"It's perfect," Barry uttered, circling the craft and admiring its form. "It looks like something from a museum."

"Let's make sure it actually floats first before we give it a grade. But I feel good about it."

"And the name?"

Sophie blushed, something Barry had seldom seen her do before. "Jacques Brel's yacht, the one that took him to the Marquesas, was the *Askoy II*. He loved it. I thought it might be good luck to name ours the *Askoy III*."

"Works for me. But what's that inside?"

Indeed, something bunched and filamented was hiding inside the hull.

"Do you remember that tangled ball of old fishing net that we found buried in the sand?"

"Yeah. I thought you threw that back in the sea."

Sophie shook her head. "I untangled it and cut out a smaller section. I put some weights on it and laced a cord through the top. Maybe it will work for catching fish."

"See, I never even thought of that."

"Of course not, that's why you need me."

"I won't disagree with you there." Barry whittled his palms together eagerly—he was ready. "Come on, give me a hand and let's push this baby down to the water."

He was shocked at how light it was; in its loglike state, it had required a healthy portion of brawn to move it a few feet. The *Askoy III,* on the other hand, slid like a bobsled across the sand. And when it kissed the water, rather than buck and roll as it had before, it steadied itself and slipped across the surface.

"Son of a bitch, it's working! It's working!"

Even Sophie let out a very uncharacteristic "Wahoo!" when Barry sprang over the side and sank his paddle in the water. "Try taking it out to the reef," she called to him.

"I will, just let me get my bearings."

"The water is that way, the land is this way. What more do you need, *imbécile*?"

Grinning, Barry waved adieu and paddled the craft past the first small line of breakers, out toward the calmer waters of the island's shallow lagoon.

"Take your time," Sophie shouted through a bullhorn of cupped hands.

"Don't worry, I will," Barry answered, raising the sail.

And *whoosh*. He was gone.

30

It's common knowledge among seasoned mariners: Given the opportunity, the ocean will play tricks on you. Spend enough time away from land on that salty desert and any manner of peculiar mirages will appear. Mermaids, St. Elmo's fire, the lost city of Atlantis—anything is possible when too long at sea.

Barry, however, had been out on the water for only a few hours in the *Askoy III* when he received his first dose of maritime legerdemain. He leaned over the prow and sniffed again at the wind, thinking that he must have been mistaken. But no, it was there. Fried chicken. The aroma lingered just for a moment and then vanished like smoke on the next gust of air. Confident that no KFC had opened up shop nearby, he attributed the strange smell to one of those improbable mysteries of the nautical life and decided it best to head back in. Perhaps he *had* spent a little too long on the water.

But there it was again, giving him cause to salivate while pushing the *Askoy III* onto shore. This was bizarre, and after more than a year of bland, starchy bananas, Barry was beginning to resent the ocean's somewhat sick sense of humor. But

his instincts kicked in, and like a bloodhound, he found himself trailing the smell across the island with his nose in the air. It took him weaving into the dappled light of the palm grove, around the fern-kissed base of the rocks, through the shaggy glades of banana trees, and right smack-dab into the middle of their camp, where Sophie had their stone table set and ready for supper.

And there, on a banana-leaf plate, if his eyes were not mistaken, was his favorite food in the world, the one that reminded him of his grandmother's kitchen, Fourth of July celebrations, county fairs, and an untold number of sun-soaked picnics. Son of a bitch. Fried chicken.

"*Surprise.* I made what you asked for."

Barry was speechless. He gurgled and stuttered and made a sound like a frog.

"You don't like it?" Sophie asked, afraid that perhaps she had done something wrong.

Barry nodded to indicate some small measure of his enormous approval. He repressed the urge to fall weeping at her feet.

"So sit. Eat. There's enough for both of us."

Barry sat down on his rock stool, gazed openmouthed at the drumstick, breast, and thigh before him, and finally regained his powers of speech. "But how? I don't understand."

"You didn't realize I've been raising chickens this whole time? There's a secret henhouse at the top of the mountain."

"No, I'm serious. I . . . I don't understand."

"Relax, it's just one of the seabirds. I made a snare out of fishing line—my *papi* showed me how to catch birds in the Pyrenees—and fried it in some of your coconut oil."

Barry didn't know what to say.

"*Putain,* Barry, don't just sit there and stare at it, eat!"

So he did. Drumstick first, followed by the breast, he sank

his teeth into the most delicious thing he'd tasted in a long, long time. The skin crackled and dripped, the meat practically melted off the bone. And each chew, trailed by the most ecstatic of moans, took him that much closer to a place he seldom visited anymore except toward the coda of warm dreams, where the sweet tea still cooled in mason jars, and the church hymns still rose through a green haze of dragonflies, and the field corn still burst in a gold crown of tassels, stalks reaching high as an elephant's eye. Oh, Christ, it was good.

"And you didn't try your drink."

Barry raised an eye from the bones he'd been gnawing and noticed the stainless-steel mug set neatly beside his banana-leaf plate. Pausing midchew, he hooked an index finger through the handle, brought it to his lips, took a sizable gulp, and immediately started choking.

"Barry, what's wrong?"

Stunned yet again, he caught his breath and swallowed. "Sophie, that's booze!"

"Well, yes, it was a little harder to get a beer than fried chicken, but I did my best."

"What is it?"

"I left out some coconut water to ferment. It was still very weak, so I added alcohol to it."

"But where did you get alcohol?"

Sophie let slide her most mischievous grin yet. "I squeezed out some of the disinfectant alcohol wipes from the first-aid kit. Be careful, it's pretty strong."

"I'll be damned." It was the first trace of alcohol he'd had in well over a year, and its heady taste was still tingling on his lips. He shook his head, smiling and bewildered. "Look, I'm not going to drink alone. You've got to join me. I insist."

"You don't need to ask twice."

Sophie scooted over beside him and took a big, grimacing

swig from the stainless-steel mug, one that also sent her into a fit of coughing. Barry chuckled as he took the mug from her and gave her a trio of playful slaps on the back. When her coughs subsided, he took his second pull of the concoction, this time savoring the drink for the elixir that it was—it seemed to go down smoother with each gulp. Taking turns, they passed the cup back and forth, letting an ancient alchemy once again work its magic. Barry tasted bourbon smuggled from a liquor cabinet and Budweiser sipped from a paternal can. Sophie tasted *trou normand* and a bloodred Bordeaux decanted into a glass. The sunlight sweetened; the universe warmed. A desolate rock at the edge of the earth suddenly became the bright center of the universe, and music pulsed from a set of cosmic pipes. Barry heard Skynnard and eating-club laughter; Sophie heard fado and a plush burst of strings. It was all coming back—*all* of it, with the lives they had lost seeping back in like the tide. Between rich bouts of laughter, Barry told Sophie about the first time he'd ever gotten drunk and how he'd puked all over a schnitzel stand at the Painesville Oktoberfest. Through a nest of giggles, Sophie described her first encounter with Portuguese *ginjinha* and how she'd gone roller-skating in her underwear through the middle of the Alfama. Old stories received fresh coats of paint, long-lost friendships were rekindled anew. With their alcoholic tolerance seriously compromised, it didn't take long for the euphoria to peak and inhibitions to lower.

Which was precisely when Sophie remembered she still had one more gift for Barry.

"Close your eyes," she commanded. "There's something else."

"Come on, just tell me."

"Not on your life! *Ferme les yeux.*"

"They're closed!"

"No, you're peeking, *putain!*" she playfully scolded, her words taking on the first round edges of a drunken slur.

"Fine. My *yeux* are *fermer.*"

Sophie stumbled to her feet and fetched a bundle from the tent, wrapped neatly in Barry's long-suffering shirt. She placed it ceremoniously in his lap.

"Open them."

Barry blinked, examined the bundle, and spread apart the fabric. Inside were two carved wooden paintbrushes, one bigger and one smaller, and two of the old flare canisters, lids screwed on tight.

"Sophie, is this what I think it is?"

Sophie nodded. "I'm sorry there are only two colors, I could only make white paint from ground clamshells and black paint from charcoal. And I had to cut some of my own hair to make the brushes, so I'm not sure how well—"

She didn't finish. Barry was kissing her before she ever had the chance, and before she knew it, she was kissing him back.

31

No lurid details are required to guess what followed on the eve of Barry's thirty-sixth birthday. And it's safe to say, after more than a year of desperate loneliness and grinding celibacy, no tawdry passages are needed to illuminate just how erotically charged such an encounter must have been. One juicy tidbit, however, does warrant mention: Up until that fateful night, orgasms for both Barry and Sophie had been infrequent, lackluster, and unconditionally solitary affairs, involving some awkward fumbling in the undergrowth and a sullen dose of overimagination (Barry tended to envision encounters with a diverse cast of Victoria's Secret models; Sophie, a square-jawed Quebecois pop star she had pined for in her late teens named Roch Voisine). But that first night together, the climaxes both Barry and Sophie experienced—technically four seconds apart, but practically mutual—were more cathartic, powerful, and flat-out earth-shattering than either had ever known before. The pleasure they unloaded was transcendent; the emotion they released, indescribable. Sophie flooded the divot in Barry's collarbone with tears, Barry quaked with an almost epi-

leptic intensity, and then they plummeted together as one into the dark well of sleep, trembling their way toward the same bright dream. . . .

Then morning came. And with it, the type of hangover only medical-grade ethanol can produce and the sort of awkward regret only highly imprudent sex can bring. Granted, there was that warm moment of half-conscious bliss, when the sun poured its honey through the latticework of palm fronds and four sets of eyelashes first began to flutter. But the memories of the previous night were not far behind it.

"Merde, putain!" Sophie tore herself away from Barry's embrace and leapt to her feet, only to catch them in the panties that were still down around one ankle (it was her only pair and she seldom wore them, but she had slipped them on just for the occasion). Her frantic attempt at escape had the exact opposite result, as she lost her balance and fell directly back on top of the nude, half-awake, and severely hungover Barry, who could barely see thanks to the pair of dried-out contact lenses he'd neglected to take out the night before.

"Ow, what the hell are you doing?"

Sophie pushed herself off of him and executed a backward crab crawl to the other end of the shelter. *"Non, non, non, c'est pas possible.* This can't be happening."

"What can't . . . God, I think I'm going to be sick."

Barry lunged for the door at the same moment Sophie sprang to recover her tattered black panties, which had somehow traveled from her ankle to Barry's chest. Their heads knocked together with a cartoonishly wooden, bowling alley sound.

"Jesus Christ!" Barry yelled, rolling in agony, his headache now that much more splitting. And he would have continued to do so for several more minutes had his riled guts not suddenly

taken priority. On all fours and naked as a jaybird, he scurried across the palm mat and out of the shelter, heaving and gagging all the way.

"Real fucking romantic," Sophie shouted back, her own head in her arms, rocking as if to comfort herself.

The heaves passed and Barry ducked back inside, wiping his mouth and collapsing beside her.

"Are you okay?"

"Do I look okay?" Sophie's eyes smoldered with the same desperate mix of anger and fear he remembered seeing in them just after the crash.

"I know neither of us planned this, but—"

"Of course neither of us planned this, Barry! Do you know what could happen?"

"Well, I mean, I'm not that acquainted with standard dating protocol for island castaways, but technically we're both single and—"

"I could get pregnant, *connard*."

By that point, Barry had been called *connard* enough times to have figured out it translated roughly to "asshole," with rough connotations of "idiot" as well. But the implications of coupling on a desert island had not fully occurred to him. He did, however, recall from a similar scare some years before with his ex-girlfriend Ashley that the much-coveted negative result on the home pregnancy test was vaguely contingent on the menstrual cycle. And he suddenly felt that pang of terror once again.

"I'm sorry, I wasn't thinking."

Sophie swallowed hard and rubbed her face with the heels of her hands. "Both of us did it, not just you. And I think it will be okay. I just had my period last week."

Barry exhaled a long, relieved hiss of a sigh. "Look, you don't have to worry. It won't happen again."

Then, Sophie began to cry. She hid her face, but her shoulders shuddered in small, rhythmic, birdlike shakes.

"Sophie, I'm sorry, really, but I swear, it won't—"

"Tu es vraiment bête, Barry! Putain!"

"What? What?" Barry was desperately confused.

"I want it to happen again, you fucking asshole." And at this point she was sobbing. Relentlessly sobbing. "I haven't had a reason to live since the plane went down, and last night, for the first time, I felt like I did again. It was wonderful. *Putain de merde!*"

Before Sophie could say anything more, Barry had put his arms around her and was stroking her hair. She, in turn, wrapped her arms around him, and they held on tightly to each other until the tears subsided.

It was 9:43 A.M. local time, July 16, 2002. An asteroid the size of a soccer field had just narrowly missed earth. A burned love letter had caused one of the biggest wildfires in Colorado history. AK-47s were crackling across Afghanistan, the United States' soccer team had recently defeated Portugal 3 to 2, and Barry Bleecker and Sophie Ducel came to the unsettling realization that as absurd as it sounded, they were actually in love.

On a goddamn desert island, no less.

Several hours of joyous, exhausting, and nerve-racking conversation ensued as the two castaways struggled to make sense of an emotion that seemed ghastly out of place given their current predicament. Indeed, the idea that love—or at least something that felt an awful lot like it—could exist between them sounded totally preposterous. But there was no denying it. Sophie stuttered and fumbled over explanations of why it had taken her so long to realize it, and Barry stammered and struggled over why it had taken him so long to do something about it. Implications were discussed, agreements were made,

and precautions deemed necessary were promised to be taken—after all, if what had happened the night before was to be repeated, extreme care would be required by both of them. The whole beautifully clumsy affair ended with a surprisingly tender hug, a round of apologies and pledges, and, at last, an admission that they both needed a little time alone to consider what had transpired.

As for Sophie, she spent most of the afternoon seated on the sand with her knees tucked up under her chin. She watched the spires of cumulus climb to the high blue of the heavens and laces of foam crease the deep blue of the sea. Whatever she was mulling or struggling with was finally resolved with a relieved nod and a slow rising to her feet. She walked down to the water's edge and removed the wedding ring that still hung around her neck from a thin filament of fishing line. She laid the kindest of kisses upon the gold band, said the dignified and loving farewell that the crash had deprived her of, and threw it as far as she could out into the water, to get it as close as she could to her dear Étienne. At last, after more than a year, she could finally breathe.

As for Barry, he took up in that moment of rapture and confusion the very thing that had gotten him there in the first place. He gathered the two brushes and twin canisters of paint, walked rather pensively through the palm forest, and made his way up the steep bank of rocks. The terns honked at him and a tandem of overprotective parents executed a series of intimidating swoops, but Barry hardly noticed, so consumed was he by the memories of the night he and Sophie had shared and the promise that painting was soon to come.

At the mouth of the little cave, he took a seat. Angled sunlight was seeping in from the west, and he required no flashlight to see what he was doing. Carefully, he chose the portion of smooth gray basalt that would serve as his canvas, measur-

ing its proportions with the palms of his hands. He moistened the tips of his brushes between his lips, then took a deep breath and decided it was time to begin. Hands shaking ever so slightly, he let himself go, making a surprising discovery in the process. He found himself consumed with a single, vaporous image: that of the island, the way he had seen it when the storm was battering him out to sea, the way it had looked when he and Sophie went swimming in the starlight. And that was what he painted, in the bone-white shade of clamshells and the pitch-black stain of coal. Around it, full moons, silent stars, and an almost biblically dark sea. It was chiaroscuro in the purest sense of the unpronounceable word, rendered with a level of abstraction that he had not known himself to be capable of. His earlier paintings had always been hampered by a forced realism—perception at its most surface level. On this day, however, his brush was guided solely by a feeling, one that he knew his words could never do justice to. Painting like this was something new, something he'd never done before. And for a few hours, he wasn't a lowly mortal struggling to survive on a raw patch of sand—he was an artist, positioned like a prophet six stories above it, dabbing his brushes, casting his paints, jousting with angels, and waltzing with the gods.

The sunlight had diminished almost entirely when Barry emerged from his cave and went down the mountain, brushes and paints held tightly in hand. He returned through the palm grove and found Sophie seated, smiling at him in the plum-colored dusk. She said *bonsoir,* and he said it to her back, and he couldn't help noticing something different in her bearing. She asked him what he'd done with his afternoon. Painting, he told her, making no effort to disguise his joy or his pride. She smiled again and asked what he had painted. The island, he answered, and he sat down beside her.

They dined on a fresh bunch of bananas, as there was no driftwood left for a fire, and decided to turn in early—Barry planned on trying out the boat again in the morning, to see if it might serve its purpose and help him catch fish. He crawled through the hut entrance and onto the soft weave of the palm mat and was pleasantly surprised when Sophie slid in seamlessly beside him. She rested her head on his shoulder, and he caressed her hair. Do you think you'll ever paint me? she asked after a minute of pleasant silence. I will, he told her, once we get off this island. Really, you will? *Oui,* he replied. But I'm going to need more than two colors to do you justice.

And a little less lonely, in a night slightly less dark, the two of them both let the patter of raindrops sing them to sleep . . .

Until Barry realized that he'd forgotten, yet again, to take out his contacts.

PART THREE

32

There is also an exhibit of Ai Weiwei's latest sculptures, a Cindy Sherman photography retrospective, a corridor full of Jackson Pollocks, and an entire floor devoted to Marcel Duchamp—all of which are very good, none of which receive from Mona the consideration they deserve. She'd like to give those masterpieces her undivided attention, but the hem of her thoughts is still snagged on the hooked nail of his work. Those haunting black-and-white paintings of the island, frightening in both their scale and their beauty, and that strange floating mobile with all the fishhooks . . . She finally gives it a rest, though, when her distracted meandering causes her to nearly bump into Marcel's infamous urinal. A security guard scolds her, and Mona tiptoes quietly away.

Before leaving, however, she stops at the gift shop. She wonders if there might be some book or companion piece to the exhibition—something to tell her more than the canvases could on their own. She scans the shelves, but there is nothing. Not that it should surprise her. She knows that he never gives interviews and seldom makes anything resembling a public

appearance. There was that short profile she read in *The New Yorker,* but even that seemed more conjecture than actual fact. Just a slightly more eloquent telling of what everyone already pretended to know.

Oh, well. Resigned to keep pretending, too, Mona exits the Pompidou and only then, with that sudden burst of cool air and light, realizes that she has the beginnings of an unpleasant hangover. She also remembers that she is totally out of Nurofen tablets—and then, on top of that, recalls that the pharmacies in Paris are closed on Sundays. She sighs and walks into a Franprix instead, fishing out just enough euros from her pocket for an ice-cold Orangina—not quite ibuprofen, but it will have to do. The old man behind the counter makes a rather sassy comment in French, to which Mona feels confident enough to reply in kind. The old man smiles, evidently impressed. Not quite the *poulette* he mistook her for when she came in.

The day overall is pleasant enough, but walking down the street, Mona notices the rain clouds. Nothing too severe, just a small charcoal cluster poised above the city. But she feels the moisture in the air, and soon she sees the scatter of drops begin to freckle the cement. She doubts it will last long—spring rains seldom do in Paris—but she also has no wish to get soaked in the meantime. And she has no money left to buy a few minutes in a café. So instead, she cuts her walk short and hurries straight into the Rambuteau Métro stop, where, if she's not mistaken, she can take the eleven to République. She taps her Navigo pass just as a train is pulling in and nearly gets her purse caught in the closing doors. But she jerks it free and takes the first seat, settling back and rubbing her temples. She is on the verge of closing her eyes when she catches sight of the advertisement—a travel poster for vacations to French Polynesia. *La vie est toujours plus facile sur une île,* says the poster,

below a picture of a man and a woman strolling down a beach. Life is always easier on an island.

Mona stares at the poster with a sad, ironic smile and wonders if he would share that sentiment. Somehow she doubts it. After all, how did he do it? How did *they* do it? What does it take to not only survive such a thing, but then live the rest of your life with that thing inside you?

That's if the stories were true, of course—the answer to which she, like everyone else, could only pretend to know.

The train commences its electric glide toward home, and Mona at last can close her eyes . . . at least, until the conductor rattles off Hôtel de Ville and Châtelet, and she realizes she is going in the wrong direction.

Shit. She gets off at the last stop and stands alone in a sea of people, suddenly feeling exceptionally lost. She sighs and with an underhand toss pitches the empty Orangina bottle into the garbage. She misses. A custodian picks it up before she has the chance, setting it gently into the bin. She thanks him with an apologetic smile—he responds with a weary nod. *Still a tourist after all.*

33

If the first year Barry and Sophie spent together on the island could be called a study in torture, then the second might be deemed an exercise in patience. No, things were not quite as bad as they'd been during those first dark months. There was at least some food to eat, they had at least something resembling an actual home, and if nothing else, at the very least they had each other. But even with the realization of their mutual affection, maintaining health, both physical and mental, proved to be a constant challenge.

For the latter, they did have their memories. Nights were spent in quiet conversation, reminiscing about their past lives and wondering how their loved ones were getting along back home. The most seemingly insignificant thing could take on a fresh sense of abundance on the blank slate of an unknown island. Sophie once spent two full hours describing the drive from Toulouse to Gavarnie with her parents in the little beige Peugeot, the narrow bridges hung taut as a kite string and the reams of high rock pocketed with snow. Barry used the better part of a night to tell her about the first time his father

had taken him rabbit hunting in Illinois, how the whip-poor-wills had circled in a wild frenzy and he had been too frightened to pull the trigger on the .410 shotgun. A whole evening was devoted to Frank Lloyd Wright's Fallingwater house, including the cool smell of concrete and the black outline of elm leaves in the bottom of the plunge pool, and the MoMA—just the fifth floor, mind you—demanded from midnight until dawn to fully render its oil-based splendors, with Rousseau's *The Sleeping Gypsy* and Munch's *The Storm* both saved for another night entire. Side by side in the palm-thatched hut, Barry and Sophie would hold each other, and they would talk about the world as they remembered it, and those two things were what pulled them back from the brink. And on those especially harrowing nights when all else failed (their second Christmas Eve together was a good example), there was always the shortwave, as even something as simple as "Silent Night" on the BBC could quiet the sobs and keep a panic attack at bay. Barry kept his ears peeled for the murmur of ship transmissions undercutting the signals, but after several months, he resigned himself to the fact that they might not come again and gradually ceased thinking about them altogether. It was better for his sanity anyway, not to torture himself with such thoughts.

As for the physical aspects of their health, Barry and Sophie did what they could. The occasional nibble of vitamin-rich seaweed didn't leave them in the finest fettle, but coupled with the constant bananas, it did ward off any serious deficiencies. A pair of notched 'ohe bamboo "toothbrushes" carved by Sophie provided at least a modicum of dental hygiene, and the solar still with just a pinch of sea salt provided Barry with a passable saline solution for his contact lenses. Even the facial wound from the octopus had more or less healed, although the brand of its beak would be there forever. Barry studied the

thick white scar in the survival kit signal mirror and joked that he was only a peg leg and a parrot away from being a qualified pirate. Sophie, with a laugh, had to agree.

Without a doubt, however, the greatest advancement made in their general well-being came courtesy of the *Askoy III,* the outrigger canoe that Sophie had designed and that they had built together. It proved, in the end, to be an absolute lifesaver.

Were one to ask, Barry would have readily admitted that he had never been especially successful as a bond salesman at Lehman Brothers. Or even very competent, for that matter. Embarrassingly old to have not made director, he had simply never possessed the gilded élan so common to his cohort when it came to schmoozing with clients or sealing big deals. In matters of negotiation, he had been timid and guileless. And as far as making huge sums of money, he was more or less indifferent to that as well. After all, the oil paints and secondhand art books that filled his apartment were relatively cheap, and admission to the Met was donation only. Looking back on it, he was amazed that he'd lasted as long as he had. He and his boss had briefly been on the football team together at Princeton, not to mention in the same eating club, and Barry suspected that was the only reason he'd kept him around. Perhaps if the fateful Gauguin exhibition that shunted his course had come a decade sooner, things would have been different. But alas, that was not the case, and he had spent twelve lackluster years pitching financial products at a New York investment bank.

As a fisherman, however, Barry excelled. Tiller in hand, net at the ready, he felt inexplicably at home. The crisp snap of the sails catching the wind was an exalted sound; the weighty thump of a full net on the hull was practically music to his ears. The *Askoy III* felt from the get-go like an extension of himself, and he plied the waters around their island with the

same joy and grace he had known previously only when seated before his easel. Naturally, the net technique took a little practice, but not much. And within only a few days of trial and error, he was able to re-create a scene as old as time: a lean, wolfish man, sun cured and squinting, standing astride the prow of his boat and casting his net to harvest the sea.

By his doing so, what had been an elusive delicacy became instead a nourishing staple. And hunger, the agony that had consumed their existence, quickly became a thing of the past. Suddenly, there was charbroiled parrot fish with banana kebabs. Raw paddletail with bananas in coconut milk. Mahi-mahi baked in banana leaves. Tern-egg omelets stuffed with black jack and bananas. Goatfish sashimi sprinkled with banana paste and sea salt. Barry caught them, Sophie cleaned them, and they cooked them together. Bananas may have still composed the bulk of their diet, but rare was the day when there wasn't a healthy portion of *poisson du jour* to go along with them. Sophie even used a few slender slats of 'ohe bamboo to carve them some chopsticks, and were an outsider to ever actually set foot on their island at just the right moment, they would have found the two of them chatting and digging into a bowl of fresh-caught sushi as casually as if in a sake bar on St. Marks Place.

The effects of all that nutrition became immediately apparent. The exhaustion they had known since their arrival was replaced by a renewed sense of vigor. Their emaciated bodies regained proportions and muscle tone that bordered on normality. Their swollen gums and sour stomachs ceased to be the bane of their days. Barry's sunken cheeks lost their hollows, Sophie's whittled hips regained their womanly shape—they started to feel human again, less like the walking dead and more like the sentient, wholehearted beings they once had been.

And it didn't stop there. Far from it, their restored health ushered in a whole series of improvements. With the search for food no longer a constant distraction, both Barry and Sophie began to employ the miniature set of stainless-steel scissors from the first-aid kit for grooming. His beard was trimmed to a length of passable civility, and her hair ceased to drop past her behind (although despite Barry's good-natured chiding about Frenchwomen, Sophie steadfastly refused to do anything about her armpits). With less hair and more exposed body area, bathing became a regular occurrence, with the two of them soaping up in coconut lather each time it rained. And with skin that was suddenly borderline clean, their filthy loincloths—pieced together from the very last vestiges of boxers and cutoffs—were no longer acceptable and soon replaced by two crisp, laundered codpieces fashioned by Sophie from rope and a single Charles Tyrwhitt dress shirtsleeve. Over the course of just a few months, two exceptionally decrepit individuals who very readily could have been mistaken for Lower East Side junkies on the verge of death were replaced by a couple who very easily could have passed for tanned Parisian *bobos* on some peculiar form of nudist holiday.

Not that it was all rose-colored glasses, however. Life on the island may have lost its darkest tints, but it had hardly become *la vie en rose*. Still, no distant ships steamed across the horizon; no contrails made chalk lines across the blue slate of the sky. And as mentioned, when it came to those nearby maritime transmissions, there was nothing but an endless stream of radio silence. Barry and Sophie did their best to hide it, but they shared a common fear that the rescue they had been waiting for might never come. The facts were bare and unavoidable—no trace of humankind had done so much as skirt their purview on the island, let alone drop by to whisk them away. And even if that coveted ocean freighter or 747 was to glint

from afar in all that turquoise and sunlight, what would it take to get their attention? After all, Barry had fired every last one of their flares into the air when he saw the ships, and look how much good that had done. Their only realistic hope of salvation, it seemed, was that someone—some moneyed adventurer, some eccentric ornithologist, some curious cartographer—might land on their beach and discover them there. That, or the shipping lane, or whatever it was, might suddenly fill with boats again and jump back to life. The months, however, had taken on the sickening proportions of years, and the deliverance their souls screamed for simply did not appear.

Naturally, the fresh presence of the *Askoy III* did encourage talk around the campfire about the possibility of escape. Not simply waiting around for ships, as Sophie had suggested in the cave, but actually going out there and finding an inhabited island. It was a boat, after all, and although small, it could hold two people and harness the wind. But any hope or promise its mobility offered was quickly tempered with a hard dose of reality. Sailors and a few astronauts aside, the true proportions of the ocean are incomprehensible to most people; its breadth and depth are abstract at best. As denizens of the island, however, both Barry and Sophie had received a harsh lesson in its proper dimensions; they understood its elemental vastness. And in different ways and at different times, they had both opted against the idea of suicide. Without any knowledge of where they were or where they might be going, venturing blindly into its blue yonder in search of new lands seemed precisely that: suicidal. At least on their island there was food to eat, water to drink, earth beneath their feet, and a place to bear witness to their fate. In short, there was *something*. Out there in the ocean there was . . . nothing. And "nothing," in their condition, had become synonymous with death—the same black cloud that had swallowed their Cessna, the same shapeless

horror that had consumed Étienne. They may have argued at length about every single other thing over the course of their relationship, but on this point they were in reluctant agreement. For better or worse, that island was their home. If salvation was to come, it would be most likely to find them there.

And so . . . patience. Barry fished and painted, Sophie carved and designed, and together, when there was nothing but time to kill, they built overly elaborate sand castles, went for long afternoon swims, played a crude form of Stone Age *pétanque,* and even tried baseball—Barry taught her the basics with a driftwood bat and tight ball of rags, and Sophie, oddly enough, enjoyed it, laughing before each pitch when Barry told her to "put a little mustard on it." The fact that they loved each other ceased to be an improbable oddity and instead became as natural and reliable as the rains. And just like the rains—the heaven-sent water that filled their two rock cisterns—it was very much what kept them alive. Although it was never spoken, there was a mutual understanding that without the other, neither would have survived alone on the island. Their relationship was the bulb that burned on in the darkness; their love was the rigging that kept the sails intact. And they didn't need a preacher or a priest or an *until death do us part* to place benediction upon that which was abundantly clear.

34

They had just made love the first time it happened. It started like this: Sophie was resting her head on Barry's panting chest, stroking his arm, when she mentioned, all rather casually, that she wished they could have met each other like normal people. Somewhere else, someplace far away.

"Like where, for example?" Barry asked with a tired chuckle. "Lisbon? Eating octopus salad?"

"No, not Lisbon, although we would definitely go there someday."

"We would?"

"Yes. I would take you to the Alfama and we would drink *ginjinha* together and listen to fado music."

"What's *ginjinha* again?"

"It's the sweet liqueur made from sour cherries."

"And what's fado music?"

"It's the songs that the women sing when their men are out at sea. They're full of sadness and longing."

"I think the last thing I'd want to hear is a song about sadness and longing, or being lost out at sea."

"No, they're beautiful. You would love it."

"I'll take your word for it. But where would we meet, if Lisbon's out of the question?"

"Paris. We would meet there."

"Why Paris?"

"Why not? You Americans always think it's a romantic city. Why not Paris?"

"You don't think it's romantic?"

"I don't know. It is a city, like any city. It has good and bad. But that's where we would meet."

"All right, Paris it is. And how do we meet?"

"Well, you would be visiting of course. You'd come for just a few months to work on your paintings. You'd rent a little studio in the tenth that doubled as your apartment."

"Where exactly in the tenth? I'll need to arrange this with my travel agent."

"Rue du Château d'Eau. I used to walk down it on my way to work. I think that street would be good for a painter. Most people think it's ugly, but there was something I always liked about it. It had character and charm. Something unique."

"You mean a certain *je ne sais quoi*?"

"We never say that, you know. And while we're on the topic, we never say *c'est la vie,* either, so you might want to stop. You don't sound French, you just sound ridiculous."

"Okay, sorry. Continue."

"So yes, you'd live on Château d'Eau."

"Castle of Water?"

"No. Well, literally, it means 'Castle of Water,' but it also can mean a water tower."

"I think I like 'Castle of Water' better. It has a little more romance to it than 'Water Tower.'"

"Well, you can call it that if you like."

"I will. And what would I do on this Castle of Water Street?"

"You would stay in your little apartment and have breakfast at the café on the corner in the morning and work on your canvases in the afternoon. You would have a few affairs with other artist girls you meet there, but nothing would come of it. Just casual, you know?"

"Sounds very bohemian."

"Oh, yes. Very bohemian. That's why you'd live on Château d'Eau. You're like me, you would know it's *mal entretenue,* but you would find great beauty in it."

"I can see that. But when would you come into the picture?"

"Be patient, I'm getting there."

"All right, then, go on."

"*Alors.* One night you would be waiting to meet one of your little *cocottes,* at a café down the street called Chez Suzette. Only she wouldn't show up, because she'd become very ill."

"What kind of illness?"

"Oh, some form of hemorrhagic fever, something nasty."

"And I'm there all alone?"

"*Oui,* you'd be drinking a glass of beer all alone. But you'd notice a girl across the room, sharing a bottle of wine with her friends."

"Would she be pretty?"

"*Mais oui, une beauté incroyable.* She would be wearing a blue dress from a little thrift shop and red Yves Saint Laurent lipstick, and you would love her smile. You'd want to go talk to her."

"What would I say?"

"Nothing, because you'd be *trop timide.* You'd just watch her, trying to work up the nerve, but you wouldn't be able to. You'd

hope she'd look your way and invite you with her eyes, but she would not, because she'd be in love with the bartender Antoine, and she would be staring at him."

"Well, that would stink."

"Yes, it would. You'd watch when she gets up to speak with him, and you'd see her kiss him on the cheek, and you'd decide not to talk to her, because she's obviously in love with him."

"This doesn't sound like much of a meeting."

"Oh, it wouldn't be. You wouldn't meet her this night. You'd only see her for the first time. You'd finish your beer and walk out the door, and you'd go home, a little upset."

"Obviously."

"Yes. But you would be so filled with passion, you'd decide to make a painting of her from your memory. And you would stay up all night, painting with your shirt off, with the moon coming in through your window, and you wouldn't stop until dawn and then you'd look at it and decide it looked just like her."

"With my shirt off, huh? How would my muscles be?"

"They'd be okay."

"Just okay?"

"Come on, it's not what matters. It's your art."

"So I'd be a talented artist?"

"Yes, of course, although you wouldn't know it yet. You still wouldn't be sure what you are."

"Fine. So I'd have this painting."

"Yes. But after you finish it, you'd be disgusted with yourself, and upset that you wasted so much time on it, because you wouldn't think you would ever see her again. So you'd hide it in the bathroom behind the toilet, and you'd go to bed. And you would try to forget about this girl you had seen, and you wouldn't think about her anymore. And you'd go back to

your routine, you know, you'd eat your lunches at a little Turkish soup restaurant on Saint-Denis to save money, you'd smoke
cigarettes out your window and knock the ashes into a flower-
pot, you'd walk around the city to decide what to paint. But
two weeks later, you would see her again at the same café.
Only this time she would not smile at the bartender Antoine
and give him kisses on the cheek, because he broke her heart."

"How would he have done that?"

"He slept with her, of course. But afterwards, he would have
ignored her. Like a typical French guy. She would be very upset, but Chez Suzette is her friends' favorite café, and the best
in the *quartier,* so she would have to go back. And that is when
you would talk to her."

"I'd walk up to her this time?"

"No, of course not. You are an American, Americans
wouldn't do such things. What would happen is that you would
go to the toilet, but you wouldn't be able to find out how to use
the sink. It would be different than American sinks, and would
use a foot pedal to start the water. But you wouldn't understand it, and you'd have soap all over your hands and you
wouldn't be able to wash it off. So you'd walk out of the bathroom and ask the first person you see how the sink works."

"And that person would be her?"

"No, that person would be her friend. We can call her Berenice. But you'd start to talk to Berenice, and she'd think you
are rather nice, even for an American, and she would know
that her friend is unhappy about what happened with Antoine,
so she would invite you to come join them. And you would."

"And this girl would finally fall for me?"

"No, *pas de tout.* Not at first, anyway. But your little accent
when you speak your terrible French would be rather cute, and
you'd be different than the Parisian men she is used to with
their ridiculous scarves and leather jackets and their macho

bullshit, and she would decide to talk to you. You'd still be too shy to ask her to do something with you alone, so you'd invite her and her two friends to come over the next night for *une petite fête*. But you wouldn't realize that *fête* means 'party' because your French wouldn't be that good. You'd think it is more like a small gathering of friends. So when the girls come, they'd be disappointed. They would have been expecting a cool party full of handsome men and loud music, and instead it would be just you with a cheap bottle of wine.'"

"Sounds pretty bad."

"That's not even the worst part. The worst part is that you'd serve them *salade niçoise* from a can. This girl is from the south, where they take cuisine very seriously, and one simply does not do such things. After that she would decide she cannot stay any longer and that it was a mistake to come. But because of all the cheap wine you gave her, she would have to pee very badly. So she'd ask if she can use your bathroom before she leaves, and when she'd go in, she would see the painting behind the toilet. She would know instantly that it was her, and she would start to cry."

"Why?"

"Because no one had ever done such a thing for her. Not once in her life. And because she would feel badly for the way she had been treating you. And that is when she would decide that she is going to kiss you."

"So she'd go straight out and kiss me?"

"No, she would wait until her friends leave, then she would go with you to the market downstairs, and she would get the ingredients to make you a proper *salade niçoise,* not this American can nonsense. And then, after dinner when you are walking her home, she would pull you under the Saint-Denis arch and then she would kiss you at last."

"And I'd be a good kisser?"

"Yes, she'd be surprised. You're actually pretty good."

"Well, *merci.*"

"De rien."

"Sounds like it would make a beautiful story."

"Oui, ce sera une histoire très belle, mon chéri."

35

The second time it happened was two months later, when they were together on the slender deck of the *Askoy III*. Barry's fishing excursions had initially been solitary affairs, but after several trips out to the reef, he began to take note of all the sea life that skittered below in the coral. With only the one pair of contact lenses he was wearing remaining from his initial three, he was understandably reluctant to engage in any activity that might put them at risk. Sophie, however, whose vision was unerringly set at twenty-twenty, had no such compunction. When Barry mentioned the crabs and lobsters and conchs he had witnessed just a short dive from the surface, she volunteered for the job. And as such, perhaps once a week, she would accompany him out in the boat, bobbing like a pearl diver between the throws of his net to see what she might find below.

This day in particular had been especially good, as in addition to Barry's three netted snappers flopping on the canoe bottom, Sophie emerged from a dive with an enormous rock

lobster writhing in her hands. She tossed it over the side before climbing in and wringing out her hair. Once the lobster was corralled near the prow, she reclined at the opposite end to let the sun dry her skin. Barry, meanwhile, prepared the net for another throw. A distant shelf of cloud hinted at rain, but for the time being, the day was brilliant and clear.

"So what do you think would have happened after that first night?"

"Hm?" Barry's eyes were fixed on a tangle in the net, with his fingers patiently at work on the filament.

"After the first night, and the kiss in Paris. After I find the painting. What would happen next?"

Barry took a seat beside the twiddling lobster and the flopping fish and considered the question—weeks had passed since their first musings on the subject. "Do you really want to know?"

"Of course I want to know. I told you the first part. Now, it's your turn."

"Okay," Barry said, continuing with the snag in his net, "I'll tell you."

"Please do."

"Well, naturally, his visa would expire. He would have been in France on a tourist visa, which is only good for three months, so after that, he would have to go back to New York. You'd promise to write and keep in touch, but neither one of you would know what was going to happen."

"So what would happen?"

"At first, nothing. He'd move into his new little studio in the East Village, you'd keep working in Paris, and the two of you would go on with your lives. But neither one of you would be very happy, and every night you'd stare at the painting he made for you, which you'd keep over your bed. One day you'd

happen to walk down rue du Château d'Eau, where he used to live, and you'd decide to write him a letter."

"Not an e-mail or a phone call?"

"No, letters are more romantic."

"God, you Americans. Why does everything have to be so romantic?"

"Maybe we read too much Hemingway."

"*Pfff.* More like Hollywood. But go on. What does it say?"

"That you miss him. That you want to see him again."

"And what does he do?"

"He invites you to come visit him in New York."

"La Grosse Pomme?"

"Yep. The Big Apple. You would have plans already to take a little vacation to Lisbon, to see your friends from when you studied, but you'd rethink it. You've never been to New York, you've only been to America once, and you do miss him quite a bit. So, instead of Lisbon, you'd buy a ticket on Air France to New York City."

"Yes!"

"Indeed. And the whole flight, you'd be nervous, and you'd wonder if New York would be like it is in the movies, or completely different, and you'd wonder if you'll still like him, or if maybe your feelings have changed."

"Would my feelings have changed?"

"Nope. He'd meet you at the gate, and you'd rush into each other's arms."

"But I would be very jet-lagged, *non*?"

"Well, you would be, but you'd also be very excited. Like I said, it's your first time in the city. And for your first date, he'd take you to get a real New York hot dog at Gray's Papaya."

"Avec beaucoup de moutarde?"

"With lots of mustard."

"And what else?"

"To eat?"

"*Oui.* Tell me, I'm starving. I want to imagine it."

"Of course, a hamburger at Chumley's, the one with the buttered English muffin as a bun, and with bacon on top."

"More."

"Probably a giant corned-beef sandwich at Carnegie Deli, on rye bread with a side of pickles. Late-night Chinese at Wo Hop, crabs in black bean sauce and Peking duck. Maybe bagels at Murray's covered with cream cheese, and fried chicken down at the Great Jones Café."

"*Oh, la la.* What time of year would it be?"

"Winter. . . . No? Okay, spring. He'd take you to Central Park to see the blossoms, and then to the Met to show you his favorite paintings—you'd always argue about that, because you'd like the Hockneys and the Warhols and the Jasper Johnses, and he'd much prefer the Munchs and the Cézannes and the Gauguins. But you'd agree to disagree, and you'd talk about art and aesthetics over big cups of coffee at Caffe Reggio in the Village. And then, at night, he would show you downtown, and you would go to the seaport, beneath the big towering lights of the skyscrapers and the spindly masts of the old boats and the bridges twinkling with cars, and he'd kiss you, and you'd realize that you didn't want to leave him, that you weren't ready to go back to France."

"So I'd just stay?"

"No, you couldn't. You'd just have a tourist visa, too. So you'd have to go back. And saying good-bye at the airport would be terrible. But you'd both know that something had changed. And two months later, after being heartsick and miserable every single day, he'd get a surprise. You'd tell him that you found a job at an architecture firm in Brooklyn, and that you were moving to New York."

"Whoopee!"

"Damn right. And you'd move in with him in his little apartment in the East Village, and he'd teach you how to throw a baseball in Tompkins Square Park, and you'd go to get pancakes covered in maple syrup every Saturday morning, and *tartines* and croissants every Sunday."

"What would the apartment be like?"

"I don't think it would be very nice when you first moved in. After all, he'd be used to *la vie bohème* and all that, you know, bare mattresses and old rickety tables. There'd be paint spatters on the hardwood floor, and the walls would be dingy, and his bathroom would be a mess. You'd get in a big fight your first week there about cleaning it up and redecorating, but finally he'd give in, and eventually have to admit that you made the place pretty cozy."

"There would always be fresh flowers, *non*?"

"Naturally. You would keep tulips in a vase on the table, and the fire escape would be covered with honeysuckle and lavender, with a little herb garden that you would pick leaves off of for cooking."

"And the bedroom would have to be painted blue. Like the ocean."

"Of course."

"And we would have a record player?"

"Without a doubt. Lots of fado records, lots of *chanson,* all those guys you like, Jacques Brel and Yves Montand and that Charles guy."

"Charles Aznavour?"

"Yes, him, and that song you always sing when you're taking a bath, what's it called?"

" 'Emmenez-moi'?"

"Exactly, that one. You would listen to them over dinner, while you sat at your little table next to the kitchen."

"We would never have to eat bananas if we didn't want to, correct?"

"Maybe some banana bread now and then, and the occasional banana split, but never more than that."

"And we would be happy in the apartment?"

"Yes, very happy."

"Would I see things outside New York?"

"Well, obviously. In the summer, you'd go together to the Jersey Shore, and spend the weekends in a little beach town called Avalon, where you would watch the sunrise on the boardwalk and get ice-cream cones in the afternoon. He would show you how to catch crabs with a piece of string and a chicken leg on the docks."

"But we probably wouldn't eat that much seafood."

"No, you're right. You'd eat steaks, mostly. Big thick sirloins you'd grill together in the backyard, until they were charred on the outside but still red and juicy on the inside, and you'd eat them with grilled asparagus, and mashed potatoes covered in butter, and you'd drink ice-cold beers and big glasses of dark red wine."

"This is getting better by the minute. Where else would we go?"

"Of course he'd take you to his family's farm in Illinois to meet his relatives and see where he spent all those summers as a kid. He'd show you the creek back in the woodlot where he used to look for arrowheads with his dad, and the cemetery beside the Baptist church with the tombstones so old you couldn't read them, and the pond where he used to gig frogs, and you'd learn to drive a tractor with his uncle and make strawberry-rhubarb pies with his aunt and his mom and you'd go with him and his parents to Calhoun County when the peaches were ripe and you could pick them off the trees and buy them in wooden crates to take back for cobbler."

"Would his family like me?"

"Yes, they'd all love you. You'd never have your French attitude with them, only with him. And even though he wouldn't admit it, he'd kind of think it was sexy."

"What do you mean, 'French attitude'?"

"You know. The incessant pouting, the vast indifference, the insufferable nonchalance about everything."

"*Pfff.* I don't know what you're talking about."

"Hey, it's not me, it's him."

"Well, he sounds like a *connard*."

"You're right. He is."

Sophie smiled, leaned across the hull, and kissed Barry softly on the scar on his cheek.

"*Je t'aime.*"

Barry blushed a deep red beneath the burnished mahogany of his face, smiled shyly in return, and resumed his work untangling the net with his sea-gnarled hands. "I love you, too."

With a cheerful snatch of Charles Aznavour's "Emmenez-moi," Sophie dipped a leg over the side and prepared for another dive. But Barry, suddenly as alert as a bird dog, stopped her. "Weather's turning. We should probably head in."

Not long before, Sophie would have debated the point. After all, the sky was still a hale shade of robin's egg, and the sun was still brightly shining. But she'd seen how Barry's days on the water had heightened his instincts and how his nights on the island had honed his senses. So she pulled her leg in and picked up a paddle, while he undid the riggings on their tarpaulin sail. And sure enough, within minutes, as the two of them stroked their way steadily in from the reef, the turquoise waves turned steely beneath the incoming clouds, and a sudden wind sent a duo of terns reeling above them. In the rising

tide of gray, a single clap of thunder tolled, a solitary harbinger of the coming rains. It rolled across the water with a resonance that brought a shiver of goose bumps across the rowers' brown backs, and they did not breathe easy until they were pulling the canoe across the sand, once again safe at home.

36

The third time it happened was four months after that, in the pleasant shade of the coconut grove. It had taken considerable campaigning, but Sophie had at last convinced Barry to relocate their home from the sunbaked beachhead to the cool and breezy glade. Naturally, she had taken charge of the design, and with little more than a frame of 'ohe bamboo, a tarpaulin, and palm thatch, she had conceived of what might be called a midcentury modern bungalow. Barry's half-remembered Boy Scout lashings helped to keep the thing together, but the final structure, complete with porch, stone oven, and translucent blue skylight, was entirely her creation. She'd even made a wind chime using various lengths of bamboo, and at night, when the winds inevitably came, the darkness was filled with its marimba-like song.

They were still redecorating their new house when Barry asked Sophie the question; she was in the midst of positioning one of his clamshell paintings above the doorway and didn't quite hear him over the radio—severe storms in the region had

been predicted by the weather service in Tahiti, and the short-wave was tuned to the news station in Papeete.

"*Quoi?*"

Barry lowered the volume on the radio and said it again. "I wanted to know if you'd stay in New York. At the little apartment in the East Village. You know, after you and the American moved in together."

"Forever?"

"I guess. Or would you want to go somewhere else?"

Sophie tilted her head to check the levelness of her hang, then righted her posture and gave it some thought. "Well, this girl *you* met in Paris would certainly miss France, even though she loves New York. And at some point, sure, you would both definitely go back to live there."

"Where would they live?"

"You have to ask? Château d'Eau, of course."

"In a water tower?"

"No, *idiot,* Château d'Eau. The same poor little street where you fell in love, and where you made your first painting of her. You'd rent the exact same apartment above the courtyard, and you'd set up the extra room as your studio to work in while she found a job at an architecture firm in Paris."

"A good one?"

"The best, of course. Every fashionable boutique would beg her to design their store, and all of the best hotels would demand her services, although she would much prefer to do special community projects and small homes for people she liked. And you'd be doing well, too. Your paintings would start to get some attention. Your first public show would be at a gallery in Bastille. You'd do big canvases, huge abstract landscapes in black and white, like the ones you do up in your little cave, but unlike anything they had ever seen. People would

start talking, and gradually, they would start asking about purchasing them for their collections. You would begin getting letters and phone calls from art galleries, and then museums. Little ones at first, then big ones, but the money and the notoriety wouldn't mean that much to you. The satisfaction of painting and doing what you loved in life would be enough."

"Sounds a little unlikely, doesn't it?"

"Well, you asked, and I'm telling you. And you would have a pretty good life together, you and this woman. You would both love the old bistros and cafés in the tenth arrondissement, with all the drunks and the artists and the writers and the *bobos,* and with the teenagers asking for cigarettes from the tables on the *terrasse,* and the old men at the counter counting their coins for a pastis. You would also have picnics on the Canal Saint-Martin, with bread and cheese from the market at Chez Julhès, and watch *le pont tournant* open and close when the boats went by."

"I thought you said I was too romantic. This sounds like a very idealized version of Paris, if you ask me."

"Yes, I suppose, but that's how it is. And of course, you would certainly have to meet her family, too, just like she met yours."

"Let me guess—she's from the south."

"But of course. She'd take you to her house in the village outside Toulouse to meet her parents and her brother and her grandmother. You'd bring a bottle of good bourbon for the father and the brother, and fresh flowers for *Maman* and *Grand-mère,* and you'd all eat *confit de canard* by the fireplace, followed by a plate of very creamy cheese, and a big baba au rhum cake with flaming sauce. They'd have a dog named Pat that you'd try to pet even though you're allergic, and your eyes

would swell up and you'd break out in a rash and you'd be very embarrassed about it."

"How'd you know I'm allergic to dogs?"

"Lucky guess."

"I see."

"But you would all have fun together, and you'd drink and listen to old Jacques Brel records, maybe some Georges Brassens and Yves Montand, too, like you said, and when the bourbon ran out, you'd switch to Armagnac. The next morning, you would go to the Pyrenees to see her family's village, and you'd walk up into the mountains, through the Cirque de Gavarnie, and she would show you where her grandfather's ashes were scattered, beneath the Brèche de Roland, because he loved the mountains so much."

"Do you think we'd ever get married?"

"I think so. You'd probably ask her father's permission, even though it was old-fashioned, and you would most likely use one of your family's old rings to propose."

"Like the little ruby ring my great-grandfather gave to my great-grandmother before he left to fight in France in World War One?"

"Yes, exactly like that."

"And how would I propose? Would it be a surprise?"

"Yes. You would wait until after Christmas, and hide it in a *galette des rois.*"

"What's that?"

"It's a king cake. Normally you hide a little figurine inside for good luck, but you would hide the ring and make sure she got the right piece. Only she wouldn't notice it, and she'd actually almost eat your great-grandmother's ring."

"Almost eat?"

"Yes. Because she'd pull it out of her mouth, and you'd go

down on one knee and put it on her finger, and she'd say *oui, oui* before you even asked."

"Would it be a big wedding?"

"No, I don't think so. Just a small, beautiful wedding in the south, with both of your families and a few friends. You would have the ceremony under an olive tree in the garden behind her house, and afterward, when the sun was setting, you would all sit at a long table in the field next door for dinner. Her mother would prepare a ratatouille in an enormous pot, and her father would roast a big *gâteau à la broche* over a fire. To make it a little bit American, there would be a grill outside, and you would serve barbecue for the main course. Maybe some of that pie your grandmother used to bake, too."

"Strawberry-rhubarb?"

"Exactement."

"And the honeymoon?"

"A road trip across America, of course. With a long stop in La Nouvelle-Orléans. You'd stay in an old French hotel with a fancy wrought-iron gate in the Vieux Carré, and eat étouf-fée at Galatoire's, and dance all night to jazz on Frenchmen Street, and go to the swamps to look for alligators, and the guide would throw marshmallows into the water to attract them and call out to them in Cajun, *'Viens ici, viens ici.'* You would have breakfast at Café du Monde, too, but you'd sneeze and blow powdered sugar all over her, and you'd both laugh about it for the rest of the day."

"You seem to know a lot about New Orleans."

"My old firm back in Paris did the interior design for a house there. I didn't go, but I read all about it."

"I see."

"But there is still one thing to discuss."

"What's that?"

"Des enfants."

"Kids?"

"Yes. Do you think you'd like to have some?"

"I mean, sure, at some point."

"Tu es certain?"

"Yes, I think so."

"Really sure?"

"Yes."

"Really, really sure?"

"Yes! Jesus."

"Okay. Good."

"Good? How come?"

"Because—"

And just then, the weather report from Tahiti was drowned out by a voice. Not of a newscaster or meteorologist, but of someone else. Someone chatting over the radio in English about an approaching storm, chuckling about the copious Bloody Marys his crew had enjoyed with their breakfast, and giving his speed at roughly ten to twelve knots.

It was the ships. They had returned.

37

When Barry had guessed that the flurry of shipping activity that periodically appeared north of their island constituted a shipping lane, he wasn't exactly correct, although he wasn't entirely off the mark, either. What he had actually witnessed when the storm battered him all those miles out to sea was what is more commonly known as the Equatorial Counter-current. For while the trade winds generally create two large bands of western-moving current both north and south of the equator, a narrow slipstream of warm water can be found wedged between them, threading its way across the Pacific in the opposite direction. This corridor is common knowledge among mariners, and although used occasionally by Russian and Chinese freighter ships headed for the Panama Canal, it is especially sought after by recreational sailors and yachtsmen—it can be tricky to find, but once it has been located, the crew of a pleasure craft can sit back, relax, and allow the counter-current, like an airport conveyor belt, to ferry them pleasantly through Polynesia, all the way to South America. Indeed, hunting it down and riding it to the end is considered some-

thing of a sport among those who have the time and the money to do such things, and the current can boast a steady procession of vessels bobbing their way along it throughout the year.

The variation, however—the reason those radio transmissions would vanish for months, even years, on end, only to reappear for a few short weeks—had to do not with the number of boats, but rather with the oscillating nature of the Equatorial Countercurrent's position. For most of the year, the slender current of "upstream" water could be found *slightly* north of the equator, generally around three to five degrees up. Not a very long distance on a map, but still nearly a thousand miles away from Barry and Sophie's island. Occasionally, however, toward the beginning and end of the rainy season, the countercurrent would shift its position and drift southward. And on even rarer occasions still—generally on the heels of the region's larger storm systems—it could actually dip below the equator and take its armada of crisply trimmed sailboats and gleaming yachts right along with it. Which was precisely when the shortwave would begin picking up their transmissions and exactly how Barry had seen those three lights twinkling out at sea. It didn't happen often, and it didn't last long. But when it did, a much-traveled sea lane was no longer hundreds of miles away to the north, but only dozens. A mere two-day paddle on a raft or canoe.

It goes without saying that Barry didn't grasp the full minutiae of oceanic currents and recreational sailing habits. But when he adjusted the tuning dial and heard not just the one, but multiple radio conversations come crackling through on the maritime band after a year of silence, he understood the momentous nature of what was transpiring and the fleeting opportunity that had been laid at their feet. Just to the north—and he was now absolutely sure of it—a fleet of ships was waiting to pick them up and carry them home. The boats

probably wouldn't be there for more than a week or two, if previous experience was anything to go by, but if they wasted no time, they just might make it.

"Baby, we've got to go. *Now.*"

He shouted it over his shoulder as he began gathering water bags and looking under their cot for whatever old coconuts he could find. And where the hell had he left the first-aid kit? The wind outside was picking up, creating a flurry of agitated notes from the bamboo wind chimes; the storm the newscaster in Tahiti had warned about was coming their way.

"Barry, I don't think this is a good idea."

"Sophie, we don't have time to discuss this." He found the first-aid kit and dumped it into the duffel bag, alongside the solar still and what remained of his fishing gear. "We need to get as much water as we can, get the canoe ready, and get our asses out there. This is it. This is our ticket home."

"I think we should wait."

"What?" Barry spun around, the waterproof duffel bag now fully packed and slung over his shoulder. "These things only last a few days, maybe a week or so tops. What, exactly, do you think we should wait for?"

He edged his way past her and ran out onto the beach, greeted by a sky that was already bruised at its base by a thick wall of thunderheads. A few spits of rain pecked at his skin.

"Barry, come back."

"Baby, you need to grab whatever you can and come on. I told you, we don't have time for this."

"I'm not coming."

She stood at the doorway of their home, her feet planted firmly in the sand. She gripped the bamboo doorjambs as a show of her determination. She had made her decision—she would not budge.

Barry dropped the duffel bag. He gripped his face in frustration and groaned aloud. "Sophie, what is your problem?"

"Just look at the sky, Barry. You really think going out now is a good idea? It's too dangerous. We could die out there."

"We could die here, too! I know it's a risk, but what other choice do you think we have? There are at least a dozen ship signals coming through that radio—and they're coming through clear, I don't think they're that far away. All we have to do is get in that canoe and start paddling north. We can do it, I know we can. We might not get another chance like this." And he paused for emphasis. "Ever."

The first peal of thunder growled from somewhere out at sea. A second pattering of raindrops skipped across the palm-thatched roof of their house. Sophie shook her head.

"Non."

Barry struggled to maintain his composure. He closed his eyes, gritting his teeth. "Sophie, *you* were the one who was all for going out searching for islands, which is much crazier than this. May I ask why you suddenly think this is a bad idea?"

"Yes, you may," she answered, unable to hide the tremolo of fear in her voice. "Because things are different now."

"And why are they different?"

"Because I'm pregnant."

Barry's face screwed up into a look of profound confusion. He had heard the words, but they made no sense. "Wait. You mean with a baby?"

"No, with a cocker spaniel, you *idiot*."

Then it all made sense—then the meaning at last hit home. Barry stammered for an awkward moment before stumbling back toward Sophie and clutching her in his arms. They stayed that way for several minutes, with the heavy rain at last coming down and the gongs of lightning beginning to crash, until

Sophie took his hand and led him back inside, the radio still on, right where they had left it, a chorus of sea captains murmuring softly in the dark.

To say Barry reacted poorly to Sophie's revelation would be a generous understatement. He sat on the edge of the cot for quite some time, in a stupefied state not entirely unlike Sophie's when he had first found her in the raft. Not that he was upset or angry in any way—just terrified. Pure, raw, unadulterated terror, of the sort so many fathers-to-be no doubt experience upon encountering a fresh avalanche of responsibility. But his was compounded several thousand–fold by the risk inherent in their situation. A Stone Age island not much bigger than a football field did not strike him as the ideal place to birth a child, let alone raise one. The effort it took to fend off the quotidian specter of death had nearly driven both of them to the brink of madness on more than one occasion. While parents more securely moored to the modern world might worry about booster shots and playgroups and plastic Baggies full of Cheerios, they would have to contend with cyclones and shark fins and potentially lethal banana famines. Christ, *lethal* banana famines—patently absurd! a blindsided Barry thought to himself, oblivious to the storm that was howling outside, shaking the frame of their little bamboo house. He didn't even know if you could raise a child on bananas, and he certainly wasn't in any rush to find out.

"Are you sure?" he finally muttered, with eyes punch-drunk and unable to focus.

"Yes," Sophie replied.

"Really sure?"

"Yes."

"Really, really sure?"

"*Oui, putain!* I haven't had my period in two months. And

it's been regular ever since we built the boat and started to eat better. I've been getting sick in the mornings, and even my tits are twice as big, if you'd even bothered to notice."

"But we were careful. I mean, really, exceptionally careful."

"Well, I guess your little *spermatozoïdes* are like Harry Houdini. I don't know. I don't know how it happened. But it did."

"Jesus. Oh, Jesus." Barry sank off the edge of the cot, gripping fiercely at the matted unruliness of his hair. "What the hell was I thinking? I knew better. It's all my—"

"*Ta gueule,* Barry. Believe it or not, it's not always about you. We're both adults. We both knew what we were doing when we got into this, and I don't regret a single thing we've done. But if this is going to happen, we need to deal with it. Like adults. If we're going to have a child, we can't act like children. Especially not given the circumstances."

Barry stiffened and regained his composure; he knew she was right.

"You said it's been two months?"

Sophie nodded. *"Oui."*

"That means we have seven months to go?"

Sophie nodded again. *"Oui."*

"Is that why you got so upset when I wanted to eat the mother sea turtle that we found laying eggs?"

"Tu es vraiment trop stupide, Barry."

Barry sighed and, with the inhalation that followed, steeled his nerve for whatever was to come. This was it. Not the crash, not the tidal wave, not the octopus. *This* was the big one. The truest test of his manhood he would ever face. He swallowed back the fear and then answered.

"I guess we won't be going out looking for ships, then."

Sophie shook her head. "I'm willing to put my own life at

risk, but we're responsible for another life now, too. Maybe neither option is ideal, but as parents, we have to go with the one we're most sure of. Staying here on the island isn't great, but at least we're safe."

"I could go out by myself, you know. I did it before and—"

She cut him off again, with a maternal firmness that ended the debate. "No way. I almost lost you once in a storm, Barry, and I won't let that happen again. And with this baby inside me, it's too much of a risk. For our child to even have a chance here, it's going to need both of us. Once the rainy season is over, once we have the baby, then *maybe* we can start talking about other options. But for right now, we're staying right here. *This* is our home."

Barry recognized the truth in what Sophie was saying. And he did also feel no small sense of relief, just as he had when he'd made the decision to turn back to the island rather than paddle after the lights. That settled it, then. His heart calmed, the tension eased; the terror of the open seas receded before him. Their course was set. They would stay on the island.

"We'll just have to take it one day at a time," he said at last, following a shared moment of pensive silence. "Like everything else here. And there is still a chance that somebody might find us before the day comes."

"Do you think?"

"Anything's possible. We might end up on rue du Château d'Eau after all."

"Your 'Castle of Water'?" Sophie teased him, managing a smile.

"Yes. My 'Castle of Water.'" Barry paused for a moment, a thought suddenly occurring to him. "You know, that's not a bad name for the island, either."

"What do you mean?"

"If we're having a baby here, we have to give the island a

proper name. And besides, this way, we can still say we live on Château d'Eau, even if it's not quite Paris."

"*Pfff.* Okay, Barry. 'Château d'Eau' it is."

"Perfect. I'll be sure to put it on the birth certificate."

Sophie snickered at the thought. "And speaking of names, we'll need one for the baby, too, you know. I'm not going to name it after some stupid street in Paris."

"Jacques Cousteau Bleecker?"

"Be serious," she scolded him, although she was anything but annoyed.

Barry beetled his brow. Nothing immediate came to mind. "What do you think?"

"If it's a boy, we could name him Barry, after his father."

"Well, we could name him Barry, but he wouldn't be named after his father."

"Your name isn't Barry?"

"I go by Barry, but my real name is Bartholomew."

"Are you serious?"

"Yeah. I was named after my grandpa in Illinois, but I was always ashamed of it. It sounded too old-fashioned. Barry was easier."

Sophie shrugged. "I think Bartholomew is a nice name. Especially for a world-famous artist like yourself."

"Ha. Very funny."

"I thought so."

"But what if it's a girl?"

"What do you think?"

"We can't name her Marie-Antoinette?"

"*Pfff.* No way."

"Sophie? After her mother?"

"*Non.* We don't do that in France. It's weird."

"What about Caroline, then? Your middle name? That's pretty."

"I don't know. Maybe for the middle name, but not the first. Anyway, we have seven months to think about it. That gives us lots of time."

"Seven months," he repeated, trying to still his panic as he imagined the big day. Labor wards, midwives, trained doctors, Lamaze classes—all nonexistent. And even if everything did go off without a hitch, what kind of existence would it be for a child, to know nothing of the world beyond a few acres of sand and a meager subsistence on half-wild bananas? What kind of life would that be?

Needless to say, the mother- and father-to-be did not fall asleep easily that first night, with the rains drumming down upon their roof and the winds outside lashing at the coconut palms. Neither wanted to appear overly frightened, for the benefit of the other, but the implications were unavoidable, and that new class of fear was excruciatingly real.

But then again, there was always hope. Sophie's patois-speaking grandmother had squeezed eight children into the world through her broad Occitan hips, and although the mountain village of Gavarnie in the 1930s wasn't quite a desert island, it wasn't the maternity ward at St. Luke's, either. And while their unspoken fears sought to overshadow it, there was no small amount of pride and joy in one very simple and profoundly human realization: They were going to be a mom and a dad, *maman et papa*. Making photo albums and coaching T-ball may have been up in the air, but that one fact was as sure as the sunset. And it was not the wind in the palms or the rain on their roof, but this thought alone that eventually balmed their worries and sang them to sleep. Barry settled down onto the bamboo cot and curled up beside Sophie, his head atop hers, his arm gently cradling the invisible life in her belly, and he gave her a kiss on the pale crescent of skin behind her ear. Sophie smiled and wove her fingers through his.

Je t'aime, she told him. *Moi aussi,* he answered. *J'ai peur,* she said to him. I'm scared, too, he replied. And they stayed clasped together like that long into the night, the thunder receding gradually in the distance, the voices on the radio fading slowly into static.

38

Ironically, the very same week that Barry Bleecker discovered he was soon to be a father, he was also declared officially dead. Under normal circumstances (if a human being vanishing without a trace may ever be considered normal), obtaining a death certificate in absentia is a lengthy process, demanding seven years of inexplicable absence. In the case of Barry, the fact that his flight was known—or at least strongly presumed—to have gone down in the sea was indeed an expediting factor. And as such, almost two and a half years after he had vanished, the death certificate was rendered by the state of New York to his heartbroken parents. Barry had left no will behind him, and the vast majority of his savings had already been donated to the United Way, so there wasn't much for anyone to do. Mr. and Mrs. Bleecker held a memorial service at a Presbyterian church in Cleveland, at which a number of his childhood friends and elementary school teachers offered heartfelt eulogies, accompanied by a touching, although perhaps a tad cliché, rendition of "Amazing Grace" on the bagpipes, courtesy of the local fire department. His high school football coach offered

to make a closing speech but choked up halfway through and had to sit down. The service was followed by a picnic on the grounds outside of the Cleveland Museum of Art—all in attendance remembered how much it had meant to Barry—and a rough approximation of a funeral reception line. The guests trickled out one by one, while his mother untaped the plastic tablecloths from the picnic tables and gathered up the grease-stained paper plates. The entire affair ended for his parents with a somber car ride home in a rust-flecked Toyota minivan; they proceeded slowly up Cedar Hill, to the house they had shared for the better part of their adult lives, and released two long, desperate sobs, almost in concert, when they came to a stop beneath the sagging basketball hoop of their only son. Then they wiped their eyes and went inside. It was finally over.

As for Sophie Ducel's own version of a premature memorial service, it had occurred only six months after the Cessna was swallowed by the sea, the government of France being a little less stingy with its death certificates. The ceremony commemorated both her life and the life of her husband, at the very same church in Toulouse where they had been married. Both families were in attendance; Sophie's drove in from their village just outside the city, and Étienne's took first-class flights down from Paris. It was short, sincere, and followed by a meal of cassoulet at a restaurant on the edge of Le Capitole square, directly across from the big Occitan cross where Sophie had played *marelle* as a young girl. The portions were huge, and few of the guests were able to clean their plates, leaving her parents and her brother to clear away the sad sight of all that uneaten duck. The next day, feeling that the memorial had been only half complete, they decided to give it some closure with a hike in Gavarnie. The three of them parked in the town and followed the path up into the mountains, taking note of how the wind at their peaks stirred up a delicate curtain

of snow: The sunlight caught it in glorious suspension, a pall of pure and crystalline white, and it was done. They were at peace with it, as only those born of mountains ever truly can be.

Who among them—honestly, who—could have ever guessed that the "dearly departed" from that crash, at least two of them, anyway, were not returning to dust at all, but resting instead on a bamboo cot two feet above it, curled up together at the world's blue end, not subtracting from the great sum of humanity but quietly adding to it? Love, hope, renewal—such things all spring eternal, and although it was still far too small for Sophie to feel, the diminutive heartbeat in her belly bore testament to that fact.

Ba-bump. Ba-bump. Ba-bump . . .

And so on and so on goes the cardiac beat in this polka called life.

39

The first few months of the pregnancy were among the very best Barry and Sophie spent on the island together. True, the fact that a perilous and forever life-changing event loomed half a year down the line did hang over their heads, with the steady swell in Sophie's middle a fail-proof reminder. But they had each other when solace was needed, and they wanted for little in the little life they had made.

Perhaps "little" is a bit of an understatement, but their condition had improved by leaps and bounds over the course of their third castaway year. Thanks to Sophie's tireless work and impeccable architectural design, they not only had a house, but something that one could actually call a home. Inside her postmodern bungalow of 'ohe and palm thatch there was a sturdy table to sit at, a comfortable cot to lie on, and even a covered kitchen area complete with a functioning stone oven. Hanging from the wall were shelves made of palm wood, upon which sat flare canisters and clamshells carefully arranged, holding various combinations of sea salt, coconut vinegar, dried fish flakes, and squid ink—the seasonings she used when

preparing their meals. Coconut-oil lamps with fiber wicks provided illumination at night, and while it had long since ceased to cough out any maritime transmissions, the rechargeable Grundig did issue forth a steady stream of music and bulletins, in languages both familiar and shockingly arcane. And without fail, by mutual decree, set as both snack food and centerpiece in the middle of their table, always a single bunch of green bananas—the only thing on the island, excluding sand and sunlight, that was always in an abundant supply.

All of this, when partnered with Barry's newfound success on the sea, made for a life that was at the very least bearable and at times one might even daresay pleasant. If the island had one thing going for it, it was some spectacular sunsets, rendered with a palette that boggled the mind. And for the first time since they'd set feet on its sand, Barry and Sophie started to enjoy them. Far from ending there, new details and fresh observations began to add richness and beauty to their days. The graceful glide of the terns, the ordered march of forest aphids, the patter of rain upon palm fronds, and the fleeting spark of shooting stars—discernible or not, there was a meaning to these things, and both appreciation and assurance could be gleaned from that fact.

If there was a highlight from that period of calm on the island, a time when all came closest to feeling right with the world—or as right as it could be considering the circumstances—it was unquestionably their third Christmas Eve there, December 24, 2003. They feasted on a banana-stuffed sooty tern roasted in their very own stone oven, familiar carols came cresting and falling from across the globe, and gifts were exchanged beside a makeshift Christmas tree, fashioned from 'ohe bamboo and tapered layers of fronds. Barry presented Sophie with a mother-of-pearl comb, and she gave him a cape of dried grasses to keep off the rains. Then, full bellied and content in

the flickering light of oil lamps, "The Little Drummer Boy" purring quietly from the Grundig, they lay side by side on their narrow cot. They didn't speak for some time—words were superfluous—but they held each other tightly, as tightly as they dared, and a novel idea occurred to Barry, although Sophie had known it for quite some time.

Three. That magical number. For two and a half years, their world had been a binary system, a yin and a yang, a single masculine and a single feminine. But as they were gathered about their little Christmas tree that night, it dawned on Barry that they were actually three. Their party was growing; a human being, the most endangered species in their insular world, was soon to be born. As an only child, Barry had never put his ear to his mother's stomach to detect the first shudders of a heartbeat, and he had never held a newborn creature whose countenance resembled his own. He trembled at the prospect, for the first time with anticipation and joy rather than anticipation and dread.

"We're going to have a baby, Sophie."

"*Je sais, mon amour.* I know, my love."

And one day, we're going to go home.

He didn't say that last part, but in the bobbing lamplight of their tiny house—that feeble ember encircled by an ocean of dark—he thought it. He would care for them, and he would fight for them, and if need be, he would die for them. Somehow or other, no matter the cost or how insurmountable the odds, he would keep that flame burning, and he would not let the darkness win. And if they stayed the course and weathered the storm, it seemed only logical that there would be daybreak yet. A touch melodramatic, perhaps, but parenthood can bring that out in people, and Barry Bleecker was hardly exempt.

For her part, Sophie experienced very much the same rich,

complex, and at times conflicting emotions as Barry. She in turn fantasized about the baby—smelling its powdery fresh skin, listening to it mew, watching it grow—and dreaded, like an imminent guest too important to offend, the colossal responsibilities of its impending arrival. The idea of holding a child to her breast that they together had conceived was a source of indescribable joy; the possibility of listening to it wail in the black island night filled her with unnerving dread. Unlike Barry, however, she did not feel that on the day of the baby's birth, she would be anxiously greeting a total stranger. She knew her child; had known it since that first morning when a queasy, almost electric warmth first emanated from what could only have been her womb. Longer than that, even. In one of those great maternal mysteries that Barry and his ilk would never understand, the connection, if one may call it that, between her and the life within felt not like a spontaneous combination of chromosomes, but like a revelation of that which had been part of her all along. It seemed she had known her child for as long as she had known herself, a single-celled witness that had been her companion—the same way she surely had been her mother's companion and her grandmother's before that—since the very beginning of time. The totality of womanhood nested within her like an infinite conglomeration of Russian dolls. She carried not just a life, but the very story of the whole human race.

There was something else, though. One concern that she did not share at all with Barry. A small but pesky worry that traced its origins not to any romantic, sea-swept encounter beneath Polynesian stars, but rather to a drab and cheerless waiting room in the Hôpital Saint-Louis.

The Centres de Dépistage of its free STD and sexual health clinic, to be precise, where, exactly four months before the Cessna took its plunge, she had sat amid the stale periodicals

and almost palpable regret, waiting for the nurse to call her name. To say the experience was unsavory would be an understatement—it was absolutely humiliating. But with their joint bank account and her birth control pills both thoroughly depleted, she didn't have much choice. Étienne had suggested borrowing a few thousand francs from his parents until their new architecture firm was up and running, but Sophie Ducel, with the defiant pride of the French southerner, had staunchly refused. She'd been keenly aware, in that way only daughters-in-law ever are, of their quiet displeasure when the announcement had been made that their brilliant son with the "de" in his surname was marrying a swarthy cassoulet eater from the Hautes-Pyrénées. And although she had forgiven them for it, she had never forgotten it, and she'd be damned if she was going to beg those *parigots* for a single centime. Of course Étienne said that she was being ridiculous and that she was imagining things. To which she responded that she certainly had not imagined the joke his mother made about their whole apartment smelling like *Piment d'Espelette*. To which Étienne responded with an exasperated groan. Fine, they would figure out some other way to get by until the first clients came.

And when it came to completing her *examen gynécologique* and refilling her birth control pill prescription, that other way was the bleak waiting room of Saint-Louis. Sophie did her best to hide her face behind a rumpled *Paris Match* and tried to avoid eye contact with the other patients—a number of whom she recognized from the late-night street corners of Strasbourg–Saint-Denis.

"Sophie Ducel," a nurse at last called out into the waiting room. *Merde*. Sophie set down the magazine, gathered her coat, and followed the nurse down a corridor of twitching fluorescent lights, right into the doctor's office. She had prayed

not to get the stubbly internist with the liquor-laced breath, and in that regard, at least, she was lucky. The attending physician was a matronly woman clad crisply in white.

"*Bonjour,*" she greeted Sophie, her eyes never leaving the open file she held in her hands.

"*Bonjour,*" Sophie replied, taking a seat on the examination table.

"I have all of your test results here. Everything came back normal."

"That's good news."

"Yes, it is. And I have your prescription as well. It should last for six months, and if you need a refill this time, all you need to do is call."

"Thank you."

The doctor extended her hand with the slip of paper. But when Sophie reached over to take it, she sensed a hint of resistance. An afterthought, something remembered. "Just out of curiosity," the doctor added. "Are you planning on having children anytime soon?"

The question caught Sophie off guard; she folded the prescription into the pocket of her jeans and settled back on the crinkled paper of the examination table. "To be honest, I haven't given it much thought. Maybe in a few years. I don't really know."

The older woman nodded wisely, smoothed out a crease in her white doctor's coat, and took off her glasses. "Be sure to talk to an obstetrician before you do."

"Is there some kind of problem?"

She removed a printout from the file and showed it to Sophie. "Your uterus is slightly bicornuate. Do you see the shape?" She pointed out the abnormality with a ballpoint pen, haloing the grainy image in a circle of bright blue.

"Yes. But what does that mean?"

"It's fairly common, and usually it's nothing to worry about. But in some cases, it can cause complications for the baby."

"Complications?"

"Breech births, preterm delivery, even malformations. But those are all relatively rare. Just make sure you mention it."

"Okay, I will. Thank you."

"Of course. Have a good day."

The soles of Sophie's Adidas squeaked across the sterile linoleum and out the rear exit onto rue Bichat. The temperature had fallen, as had dusk; she could see her pale breath against the gray-pink sky. She turned up the collar of her winter coat and fixed her wool Saint James cap on her head, suppressing as she did an involuntary shudder. Well, what did it matter? she thought to herself. I'll have plenty of time to worry about that when the time comes.

She did not tell Étienne then because the time had not yet come, and she did not tell Barry even when it did. She thought about it—in fact, she almost mentioned it in the panic that followed their first night together, and she came close again when she told him she was carrying their child. But in both cases, she ultimately chose not to. They already had enough on their plates with simply staying alive, and besides, the doctor had made it sound inconsequential enough.

So Sophie kept that secret. Not because she didn't want Barry to know, but because she knew there was no way to manage that parcel of information. In all likelihood, there was nothing to worry about. And in the event that there was, there was absolutely nothing either of them could do.

C'est la vie, as Barry often told her, a French phrase that she found herself constantly reminding him wasn't really French at all.

40

And of course, there was still the pressing issue of choosing a name. Barry and Sophie were as at odds on the matter as parents anywhere can possibly be. He found her suggestions to be effeminately French (*Pierre-Marie? For a boy? Are you serious?*), while she dismissed his preferences as petit bourgeois (*Brandon? Sharon? Dégueulasse!*). It appeared for the first half of the pregnancy that no name would ever suffice. Several unpleasant arguments ensued, with neither parent willing to compromise or retreat. And while recent developments in their food situation should theoretically have eased the tensions of oncoming parenthood, in the end, they seemed only to complicate things further. Because while Barry's fishing net still provided the bulk of their protein, Sophie's diving was beginning to augment their diet in no small way. In addition to the dozen or so fish Barry strained out of the sea on a weekly basis, Sophie was dumping a healthy assortment of crabs, lobsters, and clams into the mix. Her contribution provided a reliable buffer against the risk of starvation and filled in nicely

on the days when the fish were nowhere to be found. Full bellied they were not, but comfortable, yes, that they were.

This all changed, however, as soon as Barry learned of the pregnancy. He couldn't give a precise reason, yet he felt strongly that bobbing among wild reefs one hundred yards from the safety of shore was not the sort of thing a woman with child ought to be doing—especially a woman with child whom he loved very much. The inevitability of fatherhood had brought out his protective side and made him far more cautious in his various nautical pursuits. Sophie *pffff*ed him aplenty and chastised him for being *over*protective, but she eventually gave in. Things had been going well as of late, naming issues aside, and she was in no mood to upturn whatever precarious equilibrium they had achieved with yet another pointless argument. *D'accord,* Barry. She sighed. I won't go out with you on the boat anymore.

And for a couple of months, that worked out just fine. Barry compensated by increasing his fishing trips, from two or three a week to one almost daily. He began to brave the perimeter of the reef, piloting the *Askoy III* past the shallows to the open sea beyond, where the sandy seafloor—white as ivory beneath the shallow turquoise of the lagoon—vanished abruptly into a black abyss. By chumming the waters with leftover offal, he was able to summon strange fish he had never seen before. Bat-winged rays, serpentine eels, gape-mouthed groupers—things that never failed to give him a shudder. Each time he entered their domain, he was reinstilled with the wisdom of staying close to the island and reminded of all the horrific uncertainty that lurked just a short ways from it. He ventured past the reef only as long as was necessary, and as soon as a fat dolphin fish or two was netted, he would paddle furiously back to the shallows.

But then Sophie got the hunger. Or perhaps craving is more accurate. Four months in, when the morning sickness had

finally faded and the bulge of her belly was really starting to show, it came. Without cause, without warning. Just an excruciating yearning beyond anything she'd ever known. She didn't feel it so much in her gut as in her bones and her molars. It wasn't for pickles and ice cream, or even cornichons and a *cornet de glace*. It was a fearsome hanker for . . . well, at first she couldn't place it. Then, like a thunderbolt, it struck her. Something leafy, chewable, and rich in iron. *Greens*. She wanted greens, which wasn't totally inexplicable given that their diet consisted almost totally of bananas, with a few *fruits de mer* thrown in for good measure.

Racked by her craving, Sophie clenched her teeth and clutched at her stomach. There were no greens on the island. Nothing full of fiber or teeming with vitamins. No *epinards,* no *chou vert,* no mâche, no frisée. *Absolument rien.*

Nothing except seaweed, that is. Beds of it, both rich and green, clustered on the forbidden side of the reef, just before the ocean floor dropped off into darkness. She had seen it from the canoe when she had gone out with Barry; she had watched its emerald dance through smoky shafts of light. She had even tasted it, when rough seas had uprooted a stalk and left it bunched on the tide line, although such occasions were exceedingly rare. And while she had no way of knowing for sure if the *limu,* as it was known to ancient Polynesians, or *Ulva fasciata,* as it is known to modern scientists, contained all the minerals and vitamins she needed, she was confident in her hunch that alleviating the craving was within her grasp.

"No way." That was Barry's response when she explained what she intended to do.

"But you know where the seaweed is. It can't be more than four or five meters underwater. It's no different than when I used to dive for the clams and lobsters."

"Yes, it's very different," he attempted to explain as unagi-

tatedly as possible, "because you're almost five months pregnant. And that seaweed grows outside the reef. I've seen what it's like out there, it's just not a good idea."

"I'm not asking your permission, Barry, I'm telling you I'm going to get it. I've had almost nothing green in two and a half years, and now, with a baby inside me, I need it. The baby needs it. So are you going to help me or not?"

Sophie eyed him with the same fierce determination he remembered from their first weeks on the island: that way of telling him, with a burning stare and iron jaw, that she was her own person and could make her own choices. It had taken him the bulk of his tenure there to realize it, but he loved her for it. It was, after all, what had kept her alive and there alongside him.

He sighed and relented, because he knew from experience that to do otherwise was utterly pointless.

"Fine. I'll take you out in the boat tomorrow."

"We can't go today?"

"Damnit, Sophie!"

"What? You haven't gone out yet today, why can't I go with you?"

By this point fully and visibly agitated, Barry chucked a shell toward the water and swore under his breath. "All right, let's go. You can help me push the canoe into the water."

Sophie jumped to Barry's side and kissed the rough prickliness of his cheek; he in turn gathered the net and tucked the utility knife into the waist string of his breechcloth.

"*Merci,* Barry."

"*De rien,* Sophie." And he was already smiling despite his sincere attempts not to.

The beach was still damp from an earlier rain, and the *Askoy III* slid effortlessly into the water. Barry helped Sophie in first, holding her hand as she climbed aboard, then waited until he

was waist-deep before pulling himself up over the gunwale. Once situated with their paddles on their respective ends, they began stroking their way across the shallows. The rippled patterns in the seafloor echoed the tides below, while a strong breeze threw scales along the water's surface. Barry sniffed at the incoming wind; he detected no storms, but the sky was disconcertingly cloudy. It was cooler than usual, too, and he was glad he wasn't the one going for a swim.

At near one hundred yards, the reef showed through, its crinkled mass visible just below the surface. Barry and Sophie both pulled up their paddles and allowed their canoe to coast gently above it, passing into the deeper realm just beyond.

Then Barry slid his paddle breadthwise into their wake, dragging the craft to a gradual halt. Below them, twelve, fifteen feet, perhaps, a ghostly orchard of seaweed swayed in the current. And just a few paddle strokes beyond that . . . darkness. Ironclad darkness, total and profound. Where the seafloor ended marked the edge of the abyss.

Sophie slipped over the side of the *Askoy III* and into the water, steadying herself against the bamboo outrigger so she could peer down at the forest of seaweed. Her stomach contracted at the sight of all that green, waiting for her just a short dive away. A deep breath, a flurry of kicks, and she was gone, vanishing in a spurt of ripples and bubbles.

Barry's eyes found her as soon as the water regained its clarity, disarmingly small and distant below. He could see her arms yanking seaweed stalks from their bed, an occasional air bubble fluttering up toward him. After a minute that felt much longer, she pushed up from the bottom in a dark puff of sand. She returned to the surface as casually as she had left it and slung a lank shock of seaweed into the boat. A relieved Barry leaned over across the gunwale to help.

"Everything go all right down there?"

"*Bien sûr.* Some of it is a little difficult to pull up, but I'm getting it."

"Are you going down again?"

"One or two more dives should be enough."

"Enough for how long?"

"I don't know. We'll have to see if the baby likes it."

She smiled up at him, her chestnut hair plastered down her bright face, and he smiled uneasily back. Another deep breath and she vanished once again into nothing but ripples. Barry took his eyes off the water momentarily to check their position—he didn't want to drift too far from the island.

That was when it happened. He felt it before he saw it. Like a cloud that casts a cold shadow when it glides past the sun, only this shadow maker slipped in from below. Barry shuddered first, glimpsed instinctively over the side of the *Askoy III* second, and then panicked—a railroad spike of fear hammered straight into his heart. It was huge and grotesquely silent; the convexity of the water only magnified its menace. A shark. A damn *big* shark. A creature of ungodly strength and unconscionable size. And it was blackening the water in the direction of Sophie.

As to whether it was going in for the kill or merely an inquisitive nibble, Barry would never know. Nor did it particularly matter. Before its intentions could be considered, or the wisdom of diving in after a fourteen-foot tiger shark taken into account, he was already plunging headfirst with his box cutter drawn, the interests of mother and child trumping all others. An explosion of cold water and he was beside it—the danger it emitted an almost palpable force. A force, as it were, that shifted in focus, veering suddenly upward and back toward him. There was no time to plan, no time to think; Barry was moving instinctually, his muscles motored by something even older than fear. It was flight or fight, and with his family on

the line, the hand holding the blade seemed to have chosen the latter. He sliced twice and missed in a blind rush of bubbles, but with the third swipe, he felt the blade snick. Something dense as a boulder and rough as sandpaper raked across his side, followed by a haymaker of a tail swipe that caught him dead in the face. The stars and nausea lasted only a moment, then he was reaching downward for Sophie's arm, so soft and giving compared with the almost geologic mass of that primordial fish.

They broke the surface coughing and spewing. Barry pushed Sophie up over the coconut-wood keel before he'd caught his first breath and tumbled in right behind her.

"*Oh, putain!*" gasped Sophie.

"Holy shit!" choked out Barry.

Their chests heaved and their hearts hammered; fear like some chemical still shot through their blood.

"*T'as vu ça?*"

"Of course I saw it! Do you think I was practicing my swan dive for fun? It was as big as a goddamn bus!"

An especially grisly form of déjà vu gripped Sophie, glimpses of dark blood and burning seas, and she in turn gripped Barry with a strength he did not know she had.

"I'm sorry, Barry."

"Sorry for what?"

"I don't know. I just am."

"You didn't do anything wrong. It's the sea. Sharks live in it."

"Thank you, though," she panted. "For scaring him away. I saw him from under the water and I was too frightened to move."

"*Pfff,*" puffed Barry, who after two and a half years had appropriated more than a few of her habits. "I didn't do much except get smacked in the face with its tail."

Barry wiggled his nose tenderly, examining his fingertips for traces of blood.

"Is it broken?"

"No, I don't think so. But you are going to have to paddle us back toward shore."

"You're hurt?"

"No, I'm fine."

"Then what's wrong?"

"I just lost my last pair of contact lenses. I can't see a thing."

41

"Can't see a thing" may have been a slight exaggeration. But *only* slight. Barry could make out the powder blue of the sky and the azure blue of the sea and the verdant smudge of the island sandwiched in between. But beyond that, anything more than an arm's reach away was little more than pigment and haze. For several months, he had been trying to postpone the inevitable by putting in that last pair of contacts only in the afternoons for fishing and painting—the two activities in which unclouded vision was more or less essential. And through careful conservation, coupled with judicious cleaning, he had hoped to extend the life of those lenses by at least a year or two. Maybe more. Only that whole plan of action had been contingent on not having to dive into the ocean after menacing sharks. Not that he regretted it—near blindness was nothing compared with the thought, too painful to even contemplate, of something happening to Sophie or their child. He would have plunged headfirst into a whole feeding frenzy of hammerheads to prevent such a thing. So no, there was no regret. Only a grim, spirit-sucking awareness that his position

on the island, only recently stable, was once again tenuous at best. With his severely compromised vision, he could not spot the schools of fish before casting his net. He could not search the tide pools for clams or scour the rocks for tern eggs. Hell, he could barely grope his way through the trees and find low-hanging bananas. Maybe not even that.

Barry did his best to camouflage that fear with a few light-hearted quips about white canes and guide dogs, but Sophie could easily detect it. The first night of no-sightedness, she cranked up the little shortwave and fiddled with the dial until a station playing some semblance of American music came through the static. She lit the special coconut-oil lamp that he had made for her from a clamshell and began work on a batch of his favorite banana fritters, to accompany their bowls of fresh seaweed salad. They ate together in the lamplight around their new kitchen table, some Motown hit rising and falling on the whims of the stratosphere. To Barry, the room was nothing more than a half-lit smudge, and Sophie's face just four feet across from him, an indecipherable blur. He chewed and stared blankly ahead, with eyes unable to find their focus.

"It's going to be all right, Barry."

"I know."

"No, you're just saying that. But I'm telling you, it will be."

Barry nodded, exhaled, and kept on chewing.

"Are you worried about food?"

He nodded again. "I guess. Among other things. You're five months pregnant, I'm basically blind, I don't know how in the hell we're going—"

"Shhhh." Sophie rose from her palm-stump stool, stood beside him, and cradled his head. "*Ne t'inquiète pas, mon amour.* We're both alive, we're both healthy, and we will figure it all out together. You can take me out on the boat and teach me to fish with the net. I'll be your eyes, and you'll be my arms.

And everything else I can take care of. It's not hard to pick bananas or knock down coconuts."

"But I can't even see your face."

"I'm right here, my love. And there's nothing to see." Sophie blew out the oil lamp, flooded their little house with rich darkness, and pressed her face against his. "And besides, you have to admit. A blind painter—it is all rather bohemian, *non*?"

At that, Barry couldn't help laughing. He felt Sophie's forehead pressed to his own, and her life-swollen belly warm against his, and he knew if nothing else, they had each other, and on more than one occasion, that alone had been more than enough.

"Do you feel it?"

"Hm?"

"The baby has the—what do you call it in English?"

He moved his hands from the lithe curve of her back to the taut curve of her stomach and felt for the first time the stirrings of their child. His face erupted in a fatherly glow. "Well, I'll be damned. It's got the hiccups."

And that was when Sophie gasped and pulled away. "*Mais oui, c'est ça!* The name!"

"What? Hiccup?"

"Persinette!"

"What's Persinette?"

"It's from the fairy tale, you know, with the tower and the girl with the long hair and the prince."

"You mean 'Rapunzel'?"

"No, in English she's called Rapunzel, in French her name is Persinette. This is just like the story. The pregnant wife craves the *persil,* then later the prince falls from the tower and goes blind."

"Okay. And?"

"That's what we'll call our daughter. Persinette."

"What if it's a boy?"

"*Pfff,* I don't know. Percival, maybe."

"Percival Bartholomew Bleecker-Ducel? That's worse than Pierre-Marie. People will think he's a goddamn Habsburg or something."

"Well, too bad."

"Persinette." Barry repeated the name, tested it out, let it linger in the air. "I could live with that. It has a nice ring to it."

"Good. Because that's what we're calling her. *C'est trop mignon.*"

Barry laughed, and in doing so consented. He knew from experience that to do otherwise was utterly pointless.

42

In the weeks that followed, there were spellbinding sunsets, incredible twilights, and jaw-dropping dawns—none of which were seen by the half-blind Barry. Color, certainly, he saw some of that, but form and depth were suddenly strangers. Had he books, he might have been better off. Being severely nearsighted, he could still make out what was held close to his nose. But there were no books to be read on their island, and anything more than a foot or two away was beyond the reach of his feeble eyes. He cursed himself for not packing a spare set of glasses in with his contacts and damned the doctor who'd advised him against Lasik. But it didn't matter. None of it. His ruined eyesight was a bitter pill he had no choice but to chew and swallow.

With Sophie's help, he was able to grope his way up the rocks to the tiny cave where he painted, and that served as a relief from some of his frustration. But he could see virtually nothing of what he actually did. Sophie reminded him that Beethoven had done some of his best composing while deaf, which provoked a grim chuckle but little relief. Still, she sat

with him while he dabbed at the rock wall in his clam-shell whites and charcoal blacks and offered advice when the haze was too thick. When he was finished, she would take his hand and lead him carefully back down the boulders, shoo-ing away angry mother terns as she pointed out the footholds time had carved in the stone.

As for sustenance, Sophie's prediction proved astute. At first, she served as Barry's eyes on the *Askoy III,* her pupils peeled for the shimmer of fish scales below. Using the same chum technique Barry had mastered in the deeper water beyond the reef, they were able to bring the schools up to the surface; she would point out the ripples with a gesture close to his face, and Barry would cast the net, giving it a moment to settle before yanking back the hand line and closing it like a bag. Together, they would haul the catch over the side and empty it all, flapping and thumping, into the canoe's smooth wood bot-tom. After just two trips out, Sophie was able to cast the net herself. By the fourth, she had learned which fish were ideal, which were bony but still edible, and which ones were best avoided altogether. And within a week, she could already ma-nipulate the sail and catch the wind when necessary, although her tacking technique left something to be desired. Not that it especially mattered; when all else failed, they could always use paddles.

Still, Barry insisted on going out with her. Within a short time, Sophie was more than capable of fishing and captaining the *Askoy III* on her own, but he wanted to be at her side. This was in part simply a result of protective, paternal urges as old as time. But it was also, though he would most likely not have admitted it, because of helplessness. Or rather, how much he hated the feeling of it. The both of them had long contributed in their own ways toward guaranteeing their mutual survival on the island, none less crucial or more dispensable than the

others. But on some level, Barry had always enjoyed his role as "the provider," as Neanderthal-ish as it might sound. With the loss of his last pair of contacts, he felt more like a childish burden, some helpless babe to be lugged about in a papoose, and he hated it. Of course, Sophie never saw it that way. He had helped her when she was at her most vulnerable, and in her eyes, she was simply doing the same in return. Barry's masculine pride, however, was not quite so mature in its understanding, and occasionally he let that insecurity get the best of him. Sophie was initially patient with Barry's bouts of moping and grumbling, but when he began to hover over her shoulder and criticize in snide tones the coconut-wood cradle she was sanding for their child, she finally had enough. *Putain,* Barry, she shot back. Find something to do! I know it's hard, but feeling sorry for yourself and taking it out on me isn't helping anyone.

His initial reaction was to answer with something harsh and spiteful, but halfway through, he realized she was right. He apologized begrudgingly, kicked again at the sand, and snagged the one thing he could still manipulate and enjoy without compromise before stomping out their cabana door: the short-wave radio.

Barry gave the little generator a few belligerent cranks and twirled the knob until a station came into focus. Great. Voice of Free China. And Barry snorted and closed his eyes and leaned in forced relaxation against the knobby burls of a palm trunk, feeling in reality anything but.

The setting sun was pleasantly warm, and the breezes coming in off the waves were pleasantly cool, and a broadcaster was giving a rundown of world events in a lilting Mandarin, or maybe Cantonese, when the notion came to Barry. *An idea.* Back in the States, China had been considered the Far East, which it unquestionably was. Here in the middle of the Pacific

Ocean, however, it would have to be almost directly due west—precisely where the sun was setting. Barry began to think and stroke the scruff of his beard accordingly. He recalled during the cyclone how he had used the radio antenna to gauge roughly in which direction Tahiti was to be found. The signal *had* been slightly stronger when it was pointed in that general direction. Could the same be true for more distant signals? Barry worked the radio's spoke of an antenna in a slow circle, provoking a symphony of crackles and whistles. But sure enough, the announcer's voice became slightly crisper when the antenna was pointed in the direction of the sun. To the west, as it were. Where China ought to be.

Mental gears once again grinding, Barry fiddled with the tuning knob a little more; it took some time, but a signal from America eventually came through, a religious station droning on about some form of twangy salvation. Barry climbed to his feet, adjusted his breechcloth, and followed the blur of sand to the other side of the island, darker and cooler in the mountain's long shadow. Again, the same—the signal strengthened ever so slightly when the antenna was pointed in the opposite direction, a touch north but mostly east.

With Barry's suspicions confirmed—that signal strength could be used as a crude homing beacon of sorts—his intentions shifted in a more local direction. The Marquesas. The island chain they had been supposed to land upon at one twenty-five P.M. almost three years earlier, before the storm sent their Cessna veering tragically off course. He never had been able to receive a shortwave signal. But now, upon more thoughtful consideration, he suspected that was almost certainly due to the fact that the islands were simply too small to have a shortwave station. A few ham radios, sure, but no real broadcasts. And as for FM, there was no way those signals could travel the distance over all that ocean—modulated frequencies

were great for the Doobie Brothers or Steely Dan at close range, but terrible for broadcasting outside of city limits. Standard AM signals, however . . . well, that was a possibility. As a boy, Barry recalled getting the occasional AM signal in Cleveland all the way from Quebec, that peculiar form of French trickling down from across the border. Could he have the same luck there in Polynesia? It was worth a shot. He'd never given the standard AM dial much attention, but perhaps something reasonably local could poke its way in.

It took him an hour, but he found it. Broadcasting not in French, as he expected, but in the native and vowel-rich Marquesan, faint as a whisper and just as mysterious. He couldn't make out anything that was said beyond the names of several islands, but that was enough: Nuku Hiva, Fatu Hiva, Hiva Oa, Moho Tani. Music to his ears. He recognized them instantly; he had encountered them time and time again in his biographies of Paul Gauguin and stared at their position on the map for days before quitting his job at the bank and packing up his paintbrushes. They were somewhere out there.

Like the water witches his grandpa had once used in Macoupin County, Illinois, Barry executed the slow and patient walk of a diviner, his dowsing rod the antenna of a weatherbeaten Grundig rather than a forked hazel twig. In his halfblind state, he stepped on sharp shells and stubbed his toes against rocks, but he hardly noticed. He was sure that he was on to something. And when the signal leapt enthusiastically at the island's southeasternmost terminus, so did he. They were there. How far away, he had no idea, but islands occupied by humans could be found in that direction. *Hot damn.*

An entire week passed before he picked up the Marquesan AM signal again. But this time he was ready, with the magnetic compass from the survival kit in hand. In painstaking increments, he adjusted the antenna, with the radio resting atop

a north-pointing marker he had scratched out in a patch of damp sand. He marked the second position off at the signal's crescendo, comparing it with the degree markers on the compass and using his fingers to scratch out the numerals. Just as he suspected. The Marquesas were a little south, but mostly east. Around 110, maybe 120 degrees.

Based on that revelation, he decided to sit and wait until later in the afternoon for the shortwave station to come in from Tahiti. He knew by heart the frequency that harbored the station; it was simply a matter of time before the signal came through. When it finally did, he applied the same technique, positioning the antenna just right and marking its position off in the sand. Mostly south, but just a touch west. Around two hundred degrees.

Because of his eyesight, Barry was forced to crouch directly over his diagram and study it with a fierce squint. But something was coming together. Those two vectors he knew could form a triangle, with one of the vertices representing their current location. Obviously, the storm had blown their flight far off course, to somewhere vaguely northwest of the Marquesas. Just how far, he did not know. Barry did recall, however, that Tahiti and the Marquesas were a bit over eight hundred miles apart—the third side of that magic triangle, one that he began to delineate with a trembling finger. Bent over on his knees now, the sand only inches from his face, he studied the new diagram. Angles, hypotenuses, Pythagoras, sine, cosine, tangent . . . the answer had to be there somewhere. The formula that would allow him to calculate the distance to the nearest island. Only Barry couldn't find it. For if he had been a poor student of Boy Scout first aid, he had been an even worse one of trigonometry.

Utterly perplexed, Barry collapsed onto his elbows and buried his face in his hands, grunting aloud in frustration. He

had no idea how to make sense of it all. Defeated for the time being, he gathered his hips beneath him and sat cross-legged before the diagram, staring down at its incomplete blur. Well, *almost* defeated. Because while his little exercise in triangulation had proven futile, it had not been totally unproductive. Using his finger once again, he drew two clusters of islands where he had guessed the Marquesas and Tahiti to be. Somewhere to the northwest—where, exactly, he could not say—two castaways were stranded on a minuscule and otherwise uninhabited beach. But he knew in which direction both island clusters could be found. The Marquesas were likely closer, given that they were within distance to receive the occasional AM signal and that they had been flying for some time when the storm hit. But the Marquesas were also composed of just a handful of islands—if one was to make the trek, the possibility existed of missing them altogether. Tahiti, on the other hand, must have been considerably farther. Maybe too far to even consider. But Tahiti, he knew from his time spent poring over travel guides, was surrounded by an archipelago of hundreds of tiny islands. The voyage in that direction would be far longer and even more perilous, but if one could traverse all that open sea, one would be far more likely to bump into something. The trade winds could be problematic, but between tacking and paddling, they were not insurmountable. And even if no land was ever sighted in either direction, simply being closer to inhabited islands meant the chances of running into a boat or a plane would increase exponentially—and being rescued at sea wasn't a bad option either. He remembered telling Sophie, the first time they had seen the old Polynesian cave paintings together, how those ancient people had known exactly what they were doing and precisely where they were going when they set out onto the open seas. Was he inching closer to that category? Admittedly, Barry was hardly a nauti-

cal expert, and he did not know *exactly* what he was doing. But the countless hours he'd logged on the *Askoy III* did count for something. And yes, he was far from being able to pinpoint their *precise* location on a map, had they even possessed one. But he did know in what general directions civilization could be found, if he were only to point the *Askoy*'s nose its way.

If. A big word. A humongous, daunting word, in fact, when your home was a five-acre island, your boat a rickety outrigger canoe, and the love of your life now seven months pregnant and soon to give birth. If there was only some way to get them all safely home. If only someone would come and rescue them, if only he knew what the hell he was supposed to do. *If.* Two letters the size of the world.

And just then, he felt Sophie's hand, small and cool on his sunbaked back.

"*Qu'est-ce que tu fais, mon amour?*"

"Nothing, baby." Barry stood to kiss her, using his foot to sweep away what under better circumstances might have been the first wings of a plan.

"You're a sand painter, too, now?" she said both adorably and teasingly.

"It's a little more plentiful around here than canvas. You hungry?"

"*Oui.* I could eat an elephant."

"Probably no pachyderms on the menu, but maybe I can whip up some baked bananas."

"With salt and coconut on top?"

"*Avec plaisir.* It's the only way I make 'em."

"*Ça marche.*"

"How's Junior doing?"

"I think she's hungry, too," Sophie replied, setting both hands gently on the bulge of her stomach. "She had the hiccups again earlier."

"So the baby's definitely a 'she' now?"

Sophie shrugged. "*Oui.* I think so."

"Well, if she looks anything like her mother, she's going to be very beautiful."

"*Pfff.* You sound like some ridiculous Hollywood movie, Barry."

"Then I'll just hope that she's healthy and has all of her fingers and toes."

"Much better. *Allons-y.*"

Barry put his arm around Sophie and let her lead him back across the sand to their house, tucked unobtrusively as it was in a coconut grove, sheltered from the wind, positioned away from the sun, the closest thing they had to a haven from words like "if."

43

The last time it happened, Barry and Sophie were seated together on the beach, only a few feet from where he had found her three years before, hanging half-conscious from an orange rubber raft. There was no reason for them to be there, beyond the fact that it was an exceedingly pleasant night. For once they were not toiling, were not fretting, and they were not planning—just sitting. Sitting together as couples have been doing since long before the advent of time. A drawn-out stretch of perfect silence was at last punctuated by a question on Sophie's mind.

"How does it all end?"

"What?"

"You know, how would it all end, with this couple living on Château d'Eau, and their daughter, and their lives."

"You mean *our* daughter, Persinette?"

"Yes. *Précisément.* How does it end?"

"I can't say exactly."

"You can't?"

"No. Nobody can. But I have some idea."

"Tell me. I want to know."

Barry shifted his weight and settled back in the starlight. "Hm. Well, okay. Of course I'd have to teach her baseball. In Paris, we wouldn't be able to watch games, or listen to them on the parked car radio while we had a beer in the hammock like my dad used to, so I would have to tell her all about it. I think I still have a few mitts back in Cleveland, we could get my parents to send them. Or we could go visit."

"What would it be like to visit Cleveland?"

"We would have to go in summer, because the winters are so cold and gray. But we would show her how to catch lightning bugs, and how to play kick the can, and how to trick her parents when the ice-cream truck came by cutting through the neighbor's backyard and getting your Rocket Pop on the next street over."

"Would we take her to your family's farm in Illinois?"

"Yes. She would sit on my lap while I drove the tractor, and gig frogs in the cow pond behind the barn for supper. We'd steal wooden shingles off the old pump house and whittle them into shingle darts, and we'd look for Indian arrowheads in the woodlot, and I'd show her the family cemetery by the little whitewashed Baptist church where her great-grandparents are buried. Oh, and Frito pies. We would definitely get Frito pies."

"What would our daughter be like?"

"She'd be a lot like you. Maybe a little less stubborn."

"*Pfff.*"

"Okay, fine. Just as stubborn. She would get freckles when she spent too much time in the sun the way you do, she would love to make things with her hands the way you do, and she'd probably have brown hair, too."

"How do you know?"

"Because we both have brown hair. You know, dominant genes, Mendel's bean plants and all that. What do you think?"

"About what?"

"About what she'd be like."

"I don't know. I don't think you can predict something like that. I would want it to be a surprise. I'd like to discover new things about her every day. The things that would make her unique."

"Yeah, you're probably right about that. It's silly to guess."

"But I would still take her to the Pyrenees. That, she has to do."

"You mean hiking in the mountains?"

"*Oui.* The same path my grandfather used to take us on. We would pack a picnic of *saucisson sec* and *fromage de Bethmale.* We would have a little dog named Astazou that would follow behind us. You would be very *allergique* to him, but you wouldn't be able to get rid of him because Persinette would love him so much."

"But would we stay in Paris? To live, I mean?"

"Well, most of the time. But when you really became a great painter, you would probably surprise me with a cute little house in Portugal. Maybe in Cascais."

"That sounds like a lot of paintings to sell."

"No, not so many. Each one would be worth a lot."

"I wouldn't get your hopes up, baby. Architects make a lot more than aspiring painters."

"Then we'd save up and buy it together. We would spend some of the summers there, and get coffee and *pastéis de nata* from Belém in the mornings, and go into Lisbon in the evenings and take the little trolley car up the steep sides of the hill, all three of us, together."

"Well, that all sounds great, but she's not ever going to want

to go to Cleveland if she's spending all that time in the south of France, and on a beautiful beach in Portugal."

"Of course she will. She'll love both. She'll love my half, and she'll love your half, too."

"How do you know?"

"I know because I do. Even though I've never been to the places you've told me about, I love them because they're part of you. I can close my eyes and see them. Cleveland in the summer is beautiful—deep, dark, sad, and green. The farm in the south of Illinois is all gold—golden sunlight, golden corn. New York at night is like a giant paper lantern, but during the day . . . Are you crying?"

"Yes."

"Shhh. It's okay, my love. But really, now might not be the best time to talk about this."

"Why's that?"

"Because my water just broke."

44

For the first few minutes of what he assumed to be impending labor, Barry was consumed by a fatherly panic. Sophie calmed him, assuring him that unlike the taxicab childbirth scenes of Hollywood movies, labor was hardly a speedy affair. We probably have hours ahead of us, she informed him, and on that score she was absolutely right.

Neither could make it back to the house very easily alone, between bad eyesight and severe contractions, so they hobbled arm in arm and helped each other home. Once there, Sophie settled onto the bamboo cot while Barry lit the oil lamps and started a fire in the stone oven, intending to boil as much sterile water as he could—he wasn't sure precisely why, although it seemed like something a midwife ought to do. He also burrowed through the deflated rubber folds of the life raft, rummaging around until he found the first-aid kit. Upon locating it—next to a pack of decidedly stale Russian cigarettes that in his anxious state he longed to smoke—he removed all of the gauze and bandages contained within, leaving the cigarettes right where they lay.

"How are you doing, baby?" he shouted over his shoulder as he checked the water.

"I'm okay. I don't think I want to be inside, though."

"You don't?"

Sophie, half-inclined on their bed, shook a sweaty brow. "*Non*. I want the baby to be born outside."

After taking the water off the stove, he helped Sophie as best he could to shuffle across the palm-frond mat and out the door.

"Where do you want to go?" he asked, his feeble eyes useless in the inky dark.

"The beach. Where our old shelter was. There's a large rock that's tilted a little. Do you remember? That's where we ate the octopus, and where we first kissed."

"Okay, you lead the way, I'll help you walk. I can't see a thing."

"*Je t'aime.*"

"*Je t'aime aussi.*"

The last part was said with fresh assurance in their voices, because it was the one and only thing that they could both be certain of.

After a painful half lap of the island, Sophie found the spot. She settled gingerly onto the flat stone, which Barry padded with a fresh bed of fronds. He made sure she was comfortable, then kissed her and stumbled his way back to the house, where he gathered up the bags of clean water, the first-aid supplies, and a freshly washed Charles Tyrwhitt cotton dress shirt minus one sleeve, so thin and brittle after three years of wear that it had become virtually translucent. His heart was racing. They had been waiting for months, and now the day had arrived.

Barry followed the sound of Sophie's voice to locate her, and he knelt beside the wondrous blur of her body—she had removed her breechcloth and was utterly round and naked in the

starlight. Her breathing had quickened, she was almost panting; he could feel the heat rising off of her in waves.

"What happens now?" he asked, sincerely ignorant of the answer.

"Now?" Sophie shrugged as best she could. "We wait."

45

The labor itself was unforgivingly long. The horizon took on a claret-colored glow, paled to a blush before erupting in light, and still the grunts and contractions rumbled on. By midmorning, the cramps had become closer together; the clenches of forthcoming life were now only minutes apart. By midday, with the sun shearing down on them with a relentless glare, the contractions had turned into a continuous spasm. Barry wiped Sophie's face and body with cold water, gave her sips from the stainless-steel cup to drink. She grimaced and panted and occasionally swore; he comforted her as best he could, telling her that he loved her and that he knew she could do it.

Then it was time. Their eyes met, and they both knew. Barry repositioned himself into a catcher's kneel between the capital M of her open legs. He steadied whatever remained of his nerves for whatever it was that was about to come. As for Sophie, she just wanted the being inside her to finally come out and end this thing once and for all. She howled straight up at the cloudless blue sky and managed one colossal push.

And there was a head. A head coated in a mucousy caul and purplish blood, but definitely a human head.

"It's coming, baby! I can see it! Keep pushing." Barry was ecstatic and terrified, proud and amazed. Parenthood was only moments away.

A second gargantuan effort, producing a procession of little shoulders, little arms, little legs. Barry pulled while Sophie pushed, and then, at last, it was over. He found himself holding a newborn child. Barry squinted and held the baby close to his face, eager as a father has ever been to see it.

In her premonition that their baby would be a girl, Sophie was correct. The infant she had given birth to was indeed that. In her assumption that she would see it grow, however, she was gravely mistaken. And, as Barry had hoped, the newborn cradled in his arms had been born with all ten fingers and toes. All that was lacking was a beating heart.

The child was beautiful but ghostless. Born without life. The daughter they had both dreamed of was a tiny, frail gray body and nothing more, trailing a ghost-white cord that could not save her. At first, Sophie begged to see their little girl. But when a trembling and reluctant Barry brought the baby up for her to hold, she reared away with a long wail of pain. Barry whispered he was sorry as Sophie finally took the lifeless infant in her arms, their child, losing the only warmth that the womb had given it in the rapid pull of the island air. Sophie pressed its limp body to hers and quietly wept. Barry held Sophie's one free hand, ran his bloody fingers through her sweat-soaked hair. He didn't know what to say. Another lost life, another departed soul. At least to this one they could give a proper burial, although the thought of a doll-sized coffin was more than either of them could bear.

Then, a sharp burst of pain, like a ripping. Sophie screamed.

"What is it?"

"Le placenta."

"What?"

"The afterbirth," she grunted out between clenched teeth.

As gently and as quickly as he could, Barry took the body of the stillborn child, cut the umbilical cord with the utility knife, and laid her to rest in the coconut-wood cradle Sophie had carved for her. For decency or dignity, perhaps both, he placed a wide banana leaf solemnly across it. Then he reassumed his position between Sophie's splayed legs, urging her on in encouraging tones.

"Push, baby. It's almost over. Just this, and then we're done."

Sophie obliged in one heaving, screaming effort. There was a spurt of dark fluid, and then the afterbirth appeared.

Only—and Barry had never seen a placenta before, so he couldn't be sure—this afterbirth appeared puzzlingly like the crown of an infant's head.

Then he saw eyes. A nose. A mouth. The emerging portraiture of a human face.

"Push, baby, push, push, push!"

"What's happening?" she shouted out, back arched and unable to see.

The word left his mouth and seemed to hover above, a zephyr of uncertain promise.

"Twins."

Sophie straining with a shrieking intensity, his own hands shaking at a violent pitch, Barry helped usher their second daughter into the world. She greeted it with a flurry of tiny kicks and a feisty little cry. It was the first human voice—besides their own, of course—that the two of them had heard in person in three long years.

"Let me hold her," Sophie pleaded, sitting upright, her face flushed with motherhood and tears. Barry severed the second

cord with a careful flick of the knife, kissed the mucus-coated baby on the top of her head, and lowered her into her mother's arms.

"You did it, Sophie. She's beautiful."

"Ma petite Persinette," Sophie whispered into her daughter's ear. *"Ma petite chérie."*

The two new parents shared a knowing glance, one of infinite caring and boundless love, and then Barry noticed that his knees, upon which he had been balancing for most of the delivery, suddenly felt sticky and wet. He looked down and his heart dropped.

Flowing between them was a river of blood.

46

In the world that Barry and Sophie had left behind with that first dip of their Cessna, postpartum hemorrhage was a relatively common and treatable condition. But on the island that had sheltered them since the plane hit the water, there was simply no way to repair that which had ruptured. Whereas a quick dose of oxytocin spiked with a dash of methylergometrine would have been promptly administered in any delivery room in New York or Paris—resolving the bleeding in just a few minutes—all Barry could do was pray and hold on tight as he made futile attempts with the first-aid kit gauze to stop the unstoppable flow of deep red blood. And as for Sophie, all she could do was weep, hold her living daughter to her breast, and beg for the life that was slipping steadily out of her. It was clear that something had gone terribly wrong and that something desperately needed to be done. But there was nothing to be done, and both of them knew it. For Sophie, the sensation of helplessness was a familiar one, nearly identical to that which she had experienced when the life of Étienne had ebbed out in her arms. For Barry, however, it was horrifically novel, and

that unique form of helplessness was . . . well, there are no words for that sort of thing. If there was mercy in any of it, it was in the fact that it was over quickly. Barry managed to tell Sophie that he loved her a final time before she lost consciousness; she was unable to respond, but she seemed to acknowledge it with a final tight squeeze of his hand. After that, there was a minute of shudders and rasping breaths, followed by a single bursting gasp of sentience—her eyes shot open, looked imploringly at Barry, begging for the salvation that was not there to give. And then her brown irises drifted upward, higher than the palms that bowed above them, higher even than the peaks of the Pyrenees in the Cirque de Gavarnie.

And then she was gone. Sophie Caroline Ducel, daughter and mother, age thirty-two, quietly ceased to be.

The need to scream welled within Barry—only his new sense of fatherhood prevented him from doing so. He didn't want the first sound on his newborn daughter's ears to be one of anguish. Instead he bit his own bicep, hard enough to bleed, teeth cutting through skin and down into muscle. He let the tears pour hot down his face, but he somehow held the sobs and despair captive, deep and congealed in the pit of his chest. Sophie's arm was still around their living daughter, suckling quietly at her still-warm breast. Barry lay beside them both, his body racked with the agony of the moment, and allowed the child to drink her fill—he did not know if there would be another meal. When she was finished, he wrapped her in the freshly cleaned remains of his threadbare dress shirt, rocked her gently to sleep in his trembling arms, and set her to rest, so he could bury her mother and her sister.

47

The love of his life buried beneath the palm tree where they first had kissed, his living daughter now sleeping in the coconut-wood cradle, Barry at last found himself alone on the beach, expelling the sobs he had stored for so long. Keening of the sort one hears only once or twice in a lifetime. The splitting heartache, the indescribable sorrow, the crushing guilt of being unable to save her—those would stay with him for quite some time. A lifetime, in fact. But the gagging, chest-rattling sobs came pouring out, until at last, depleted, he had nothing left to give, and in the void, his thoughts regained some semblance of clarity. The reality of the situation, and the responsibilities of a father, began to take hold. His vision may have bordered on legal blindness, but his options were clear.

Two paths, white and shimmering as a summer day in Macoupin County, appeared before Barry. Amid his immense terror, depthless loss, and visceral sadness, a choice took shape. Suddenly his life was a fork in the road, a binary system both horrific and beautiful in its simplicity. One path was as follows: He could close his eyes, cease his struggle, and let his

body go limp. He could stay on the island and watch with horribly compromised vision his child—their daughter—wail in pain and waste away without breast milk or formula, and then finally cease to breathe altogether. He could linger on, slowly succumbing himself to starvation or madness, until the day came when he no longer had the energy or will to rise from his sweat-stained pallet and face the growling incertitude of the day. At which point he, too, would give up the ghost.

Or he could gather up his child, stock the canoe, and paddle like a *motherfucker.*

Bartholomew Bleecker chose the latter.

The preparations took the better part of the day but passed like a strange and floating dream. It was as if he were outside of himself, watching these events unfold despite his imperfect vision. He watched as he inflated the life raft, his aching lungs bringing the craft to life. He looked on as he loaded it with bananas and bags of freshwater—except the one bag he filled with coconut milk, knowing an infant could not survive upon it, but hoping it might keep his child alive just a little bit longer. He gazed with bleary eyes as this other, more certain version of himself placed his sleeping daughter, bundled in a threadbare Charles Tyrwhitt dress shirt, beneath the small survival blanket tent he had made for her in the *Askoy III.* And he stood silent witness as this man hitched the supply-laden raft to the back of the canoe with a six-foot length of salvaged nylon rope.

All that remained was to say good-bye. Barry had no flowers to leave for Sophie and their stillborn child, buried together in the same shallow grave; he brought bananas instead, the freshest, greenest bunch he could find. He spoke to them quietly for some time, his tears leaving a cluster of wet dimples in the upturned sand. He told them how much he loved them, how much he already missed them, and he begged their

forgiveness for having to leave them. But he had made his decision—and he knew that Sophie would understand. When he was finished, he laid the kindest of kisses on the driftwood cross, wiped his eyes, and rose to his feet. But before he left, he made two promises:

That he would take care of their living daughter until his dying breath, no matter when that day came, and that one day, god(s) willing, he would come back for them both and take them home.

Ready at last, Barry stumbled and tripped his way back to the beach. It was time. He did one final scan of the radio to search for nearby transmissions, and just as he had expected, there were none to be found. There were no more ships, there were no more flares, and there was no turning back. He had to go all the way. He would make it to the islands or he would die trying. There was no other option. They were leaving for good.

Barry peered inside the canoe's foil blanket tent to check on his daughter, kissing her gently and whispering in her ear. He prayed quickly and calmly, hoping but not certain that a compassionate deity might be in earshot. And finally, although it was nothing to him at that moment but a blur, he took one last, lingering look at the island he had once cursed but now knew had saved them: the frayed hedge of palms, the silent skirt of sand, the inscrutable stone core that rose from the waters like a castle—

One in a million.

And then he pushed off.

48

What began on the chilly side has turned into a lovely spring day—the man decides to walk home from the cemetery instead of hailing a taxi. He takes slow, deliberate steps, soaking it all in, still enraptured by the city that surrounds him. The cars whirring by, the old men feeding pigeons, the sanitation fellows with their green plastic brooms—he passes through them with the amazed expression of a tourist, despite having lived here for more than a decade. The streets and their contents are still as brimming with wonder as the day he arrived, and he suspects they will stay that way for some time to come. He hopes so, anyway.

He's very nearly home when he gets caught in a rain shower, of the type seldom encountered in New York but endemic to Paris—the short stacks of cloud that drift in from the Channel, darkening the pavement with their brief, black bloom. He ducks under an awning beside the Saint-Denis arch, where he is quickly joined by others seeking refuge from the rain. There is an elderly woman draped in fine furs, a café waiter on cigarette break, three Chinese prostitutes in smart-looking pantsuits,

and a nun walking a dachshund called Dijon—all joined together in that small island of dryness. The waiter offers him a cigarette, but the man politely declines, telling him in French that he quit years ago; the nun, on the other hand, accepts his proposal, and she leans over in her habit to bum a light. The woman in the furs checks her lipstick in a compact mirror, while the three prostitutes share a joke in Mandarin, or perhaps Cantonese, the man doesn't know which. They wait patiently for the shower to pass and then disperse when it finally does, back to their own respective callings. Surely an unremarkable moment for most, but for the man, it is a parting tinged with a tender sadness—he has noticed over the years that even the briefest and most incidental interactions can, with the appreciation of time, take on far richer shades of meaning. It is a realization for which he is eternally grateful.

From there, it's just a few short blocks to rue du Château d'Eau, a few flights of stairs, and he's home. He closes the door as quietly as possible, thinking that she might still be sleeping. The muffled strains of French pop music leaking from her bedroom assure him that this is not the case. He sets his keys on the counter and takes out his phone, seeing that at some point during his walk he acquired a message. He lifts an apple to his teeth and the phone to his ear, both at the same time.

It's his art dealer in New York. He wants him to call back, so he does. About time you called, the dealer chides him playfully. Are you ready for some good news? The man swallows his bite of apple for the sake of politeness. Certainly, he says. I'm always up for good news. Well, he says, the museum wants to know if they can keep one of the pieces for the permanent collection. They're opening a new wing, and they really want a Bartholomew Bleecker. The man takes another bite of apple, realizes his faux pas, and swallows quickly. Wow. Tell them

thank you, and that I'd be honored. They can have any one they want. You sure? asks the art dealer. The man thinks about it for a moment. Except one, he says. Let me guess, the dealer replies. Yes, that's the one, says the man. But any other painting is fine. Perfect, says the dealer. And what about the canoe? I just got another call from the Explorers Club about it—they're persistent, I'll give them that. But they promised to take good care of it, and they said it can be on loan if you prefer. The man sighs bittersweetly, his mouth full of apple. His gaze passes over the yellowed newspaper clipping still tacked to the refrigerator, of that wild-eyed man with the baby in his arms, standing halfway between the graves of Jacques Brel and Paul Gauguin. I'll talk to my daughter, he finally replies. I know she mentioned taking it down to Portugal again this summer. But if she's okay with it, then so am I—although I probably should take all those fishhooks off first.

He thanks his art dealer, tells him he's stopping by New York next month on the way to the farm and that he would love to catch up. Thank you again for everything, we'll talk soon, and he pauses just a moment before hanging up the phone. He smiles and shakes his head, a smile that's bewildered and content and still pursed by that same tender sadness that visited him by the arch, that trails him as doggedly as his gratitude and his guilt . . . the wonder of it all, the unknowable mystery, to serve as fleshy custodian to such a fragile flame. More than anything, though, he just misses her—far more than oils and canvas will ever express, often more than his old heart can bear. He still dreams of her, the island as well, and in those dreams he holds her and tells her about their daughter. She's wonderful, he says to her, beautiful, just like her mother. But when he tries to tell her that she should have been the one to make it home, not him, when he starts to ask if she can ever

forgive him, she silences him with a smile. The waves roll, the palms whisper, and they continue to do so, even upon waking.

But enough of that for now. The man cocks his ear toward the bedroom; the shortwave has gone quiet, there's no more French pop music, and he suspects she knows that he's home from his walk. He pads across the carpeted hallway and raps gently at her door. There's a stutter of socked footsteps and the door swings open.

Bonjour, Papa, she says, and gives him a hug.

Bonjour, ma chérie, he says, and he kisses the warm part in her chestnut-brown hair.

What's in your jacket?

Oh, that? It's just a *tartine.*

Papa, you can leave the leftovers on the plate. You don't have to always take them with you.

Yes, I suppose you're right. Old habits die hard.

Did you go to see *Maman et Petite Sœur?* she asks.

Oui, he says. I went to say hello.

And they are well?

They are wonderful.

Can I go to see them with you next week?

Of course you can, my love. We can go whenever you'd like.

Are you painting today?

He considers it for a moment, furrowing his brow and pinching his chin through his beard. It is a Sunday, and a glorious morning to be at work in his studio, but he can do that anytime. His daughter, on the other hand, won't stay twelve forever. No, he says finally, I have something else in mind. *Quelque chose de plus américain.*

She grins mischievously. *Le baseball?* she asks.

Oui, he answers, *le baseball.*

Comme les Indiens de Cleveland? she asks.

Oui, he answers, *comme les Indiens de Cleveland.*

She claps her hands and rushes to retrieve the gloves and the ball from the closet, trundling down the stairs and urging her father to follow. *Allons-y, Papa!* she calls up to him from the front door. He starts to tell her that it's cold and she needs a jacket but remembers those first spring days from his own childhood and the futility of that request on a day such as this.

The man follows her outside, punching a pocket into the chapped leather of the glove, and steps into the street, where she is already tossing the ball into the air and catching it in her mitt. Okay, he tells her, let's see that fastball, and put a little mustard on it.

La moutarde? she asks, laughing at the absurdity of his idiom, just as her mother did not so very long ago.

Yes, he says, it means to throw it hard.

D'accord, she says, *un fastball avec beaucoup de moutarde, pour mon Papa chéri.*

She is in the midst of a comically exaggerated windup when she stops, evidently distracted by something past his shoulder. His first thought is that a car is coming, as they sometimes do on this street. But he sees upon stepping aside that someone is watching them. A girl in bangs and blue jeans. She is standing on the sidewalk, mouth agape and frozen in place—not that throwing a baseball in Paris is an everyday occurrence, but she appears utterly confounded by the sight of them.

Tu la connais, Papa? his daughter asks.

Non, ma chérie, je ne la connais pas.

Should we ask her if she wants to play?

Sure, says the man. Why not. Would you like to play catch with us? he shouts from across the street. We have an extra glove inside if you do.

The girl with the bangs and blue jeans is caught off guard by the question but responds with a hesitant nod.

Persinette Caroline scampers back into the apartment, re-appearing moments later with an oversize first baseman's mitt that she tosses the girl's way. See if it fits, she says in perfect English.

Their line grows into a triangle, and the spring air, already ringing like rubbed crystal with the songs of fruit vendors and the knelling of church bells, is enlivened even further by the whistling of fastballs and the crisp snap of leather as two and a half Americans share a game of catch in the tenth arrondisse-ment of Paris, on a little stretch of cobbles called Château d'Eau.

Acknowledgments

Contrary to what bylines might have you believe, completing a novel is never a solitary affair. And this novel, in particular, owes its existence to some extremely generous and talented people. I would like to extend a heartfelt thank-you to Jim Fitzgerald for stewarding it along from start to finish, Brendan Deneen for providing crucial guidance throughout the editorial process, Nicole Sohl for tightening it up in its final stages, and Will Anderson, especially, for believing in it from the very beginning. Without their help, it would be nothing more than words in a drawer. Last, and with the utmost gratitude and humility, I'd like to thank my wife, who deserves far more than a dedication or acknowledgment for the innumerable ways in which she has saved me. She is my compass and she is my home.